CW00517064

THE L~~IGHT IN YOU~~

ALSO BY LISA ELLIOT

Dancing It Out

The Light in You

∞

Lisa Elliot

For Georgiana

Chapter 1

The sun beamed onto the windows of Heart Yoga as Angela walked up to her studio and got the keys out of her bag. Glimpsing inside, she felt that familiar rush of excitement. When she'd taken over the lease, she'd danced around the studio in pure joy at her dream coming true. It was just an empty shell then, with old floors and tatty walls in dire need of renovation. Since then, she'd made it her own.

Once inside, she entered the code for the alarm: 73223. She took a sip of coffee from her colourful reusable cup, put her bag down by the door, and stretched her neck from side to side. Squatting down to pick up some letters, she sighed. One was from the bank, the other two from utility companies. She went through to the office past the row of tables in the small café. The space used to be a charity shop in its previous life. She had converted a room at the back, behind the café counter, into an office. It held her desk, bicycle, and numerous shelves. There was one window on the rear wall, which looked out onto the back greens of a row of tenements. Often, she could hear children playing out there. The odd dog barking. Sometimes the noise of work being done in one of the flats.

This morning, the only sound was of the wind taking shot at the buildings in intermittent gusts. Putting her coffee down on the desk, she pulled out her little stool and sat down, taking care to sit upright. The studio itself was completely silent. Thankfully, the road around the corner couldn't be heard from within the studio.

Her eyes felt heavy and stung a little as she rubbed them with her palms. Yesterday had been another fifteen-hour day, and she hadn't slept for long. Starting her own business had been significantly more work than she thought it was going to be. The past six months had been exhausting and had pushed her past limits she didn't know she even had. Something always needed to be done, and she did almost everything herself: the refurbishment, the café, the website, posting on social media, recruiting yoga teachers, the cleaning, the paperwork, the marketing, baking cakes and scones, even the plumbing. All she wanted to do was teach her classes: her favourite thing in the world to do.

Ripping the seal of the envelope from the bank, she took out the letter and opened it out. Her heart sank. After her second quarter, she had yet to meet her monthly targets. Despite already knowing this from her online account, somehow seeing it on paper made it more real. And why had they sent it, anyway, when she had already cancelled paper statements?

The first six months had not gone as expected, financially speaking. The business had turned over a lot less than what she had forecasted in her business case for the bank. If things didn't start picking up over the next six months, she might have to consider closing. The launch had gone well. She'd picked up some regulars and met so many great people. Others came to the studio every now and again. Of course, there had been a number of people who'd come to the opening and never returned, which still bothered her. Noticing tension in her shoulders and neck, she reminded herself to take a deep breath and not think way into the future.

Glancing at the coaster on the desk in front of her with "dream it, believe it, achieve it" on it, she slumped forward, letting her lower back relax and her shoulders fall forward. As she rested her head on her forearms, she tried to remember the belief she'd had at the beginning. A rough start in business was to be expected, and Angela was committed to riding it out. All she had to do was believe in her studio and in her abilities as a yoga teacher. After all, she'd seen her friend Sabina's studio become a success and knew it was a process, albeit a risky one.

Sitting up, she straightened her back, then twisted around from side to side to loosen up. She had to get her head in the game for the day ahead. Opening her notebook, she wrote down the most important next steps: recruit one new teacher, add more classes to the timetable, start planning for the retreat. Staring at the list, she exhaled, feeling more in control and more determined than ever to get the studio to where she wanted it to be.

The bell on the front door chimed, and a gust of cold air came tunnelling through to the office. Angela's mum had insisted on putting a bell on the door so that Angela would always be able to hear people coming and going.

'Hey, are you decent?'

'I'm through the back,' said Angela, getting up and meeting her friend and fellow yoga teacher beside the coffee counter.

'You look tired.'

'Cheers.'

'I need to drop some things off for my class this morning. I've got a meeting in town, and I don't want to lug all this around.' Zoe gestured to the rucksack and two canvas bags she was carrying before putting them in the office next to Angela's bicycle.

Angela leant against the café counter. 'Have you got time for a quick coffee?'

Zoe raised an eyebrow and laughed. 'I love that you always see the need for coffee; it's probably the main reason I love working here.'

Angela shook her head and smiled. 'That's your reason?'

Zoe hung up her coat near the door as Angela busied

herself behind the top-of-the-range coffee machine. Angela glanced up to see Zoe checking her reflection in the mirror on the chest of drawers. When the drinks were ready, Angela brought over the coffees, placed them on the wooden table and sat down.

'Your fringe is looking good today,' said Angela, noticing how straight it was, sitting halfway up her forehead.

'Cheers. I trimmed it.'

'How are you feeling for your class later?' said Angela.

Zoe joined her at the table. 'Great. I can't wait for it. How're the bookings for it? For the studio?'

Angela grimaced. 'Um … getting there. You've got four people for this morning.' Angela shook her head. 'Och, who am I kidding? The bookings are low. But don't worry. We're still new. Still establishing the studio's reputation in the area.'

'I'm not worried. I've been fully booked for years, if anything, this is a nice breather for me.' Zoe paused. 'You've built the perfect space, Angela, and you are the best human being to be around. People will come. I know it.'

'Cheers.' Angela smiled. 'And remember to suggest to everyone this morning that they follow us on social media, will you? I'm going to try and post a bit more.'

'I will. What's this?' Zoe held up a plastic bottle of water with a look of disgust.

'It's my mum's. She left it here yesterday. She's become obsessed with drinking three litres a day and buys loads of them.'

'Wouldn't she be better with a filter?'

'The planet would. I keep telling her to stop buying all that plastic, but she doesn't care.'

'It's hard for people to say no to convenience,' said Zoe, putting down the bottle.

'My mum doesn't like change or trying new things, but she'll never admit that. She knows it's not the done thing to be said any more. Still. I love her. She's my mum, and it was nice of her to come down to visit.'

Zoe looked away. 'Change can be scary. How's the new timetabling coming along?'

'Good, nearly there. It's going to be much better. I'm going to add a Yoga for Anxiety class next week.'

'Great idea. Prompted by?'

'Oh, you know, people. The world. The other day I saw a mum on the school run undertake a white van while shouting obscenities at him.'

'People are so stressed out.'

'They are. God, I am too, half the time.'

'What's your plan for the new class?'

'I'm going to do lots of earthing poses and lots of sequences where we protect the heart.'

'Angela, are you projecting? Are you feeling anxious?'

At this, Angela paused. 'No. I don't think that I am. Concerned, more like, about getting this place off the ground. But proper anxiety, no.'

'Good, good. I'm relieved to hear that. We've known each other for what now? Twelve years?'

'I think it is. Can you believe that.'

'Twelve years. And I know when you're making a good move and when you're making a bad one. Remember Greece?'

'Don't.' They laughed.

'It's so hard starting a new business, but this is definitely a good move for you. Everything's going to work out. I know it.'

'I hope so. I do love it, even if I don't know what I'm doing.' Angela inhaled. 'I'm just going to say it. I hate spreadsheets.'

Zoe belly laughed. 'Say it, sister.'

'I want people to enjoy this beautiful space I've created. I just want to teach yoga. I didn't realise how much of my time would be spent running a business.'

'You've been living and breathing this place. What about the rest of your life? What about your *love* life?'

'I can't think about that right now, Zoe, not until this place is properly up and running. And I don't mind too much anyway. I like not being attached. You know that. I do what I want, when I want. I have time to concentrate on this place. There's no drama when you're on your own. I swear to God I don't have time for that shit any more.'

'Uh-huh,' said Zoe, looking unconvinced.

'Being attached is the root of all suffering. The illusion of what we call romantic love is often just trauma bonding. I need to work on myself more before I enter into a relationship with a woman again.'

'Jeezo, you're getting more Buddhist by the day. Before I know it, you'll have shaved those beautiful blonde locks off and be wearing orange robes and walking about with sandals and socks on.' Zoe took a sip of coffee. 'And isn't getting attached where all the fun is? We're programmed for human connection; it's in our DNA. We're social animals. You can't isolate. You've got to keep an open heart, even if it's been broken before; aren't we always saying that in our classes? Don't you close yours off to love forever, Angela. It's no good for the soul.'

Angela looked down at the table, studying the swirls of a knot on the smooth table surface, trying not to think about what her friend was saying. 'I do believe in keeping an open heart. My heart is open. I'm just focusing on myself for the time being.'

Zoe seemed to understand. A few moments passed. 'Oh, I forgot to tell you,' Angela looked up, 'I have someone coming in to interview for the last teacher position next week.'

'Changing the subject, are we? Nicely done,' said Zoe. 'Are you sure about adding another teacher when you're not quite up to capacity yet? Is that a wise move?'

'The studio needs another dimension to it. It can't just be the same classes by you and me. Every studio knows this. I have to do it. Yeah, it feels risky, but the studio I wanted to set up was a well-rounded one and that's what I'm going to offer.'

'You're brave. Also, right. What's their name?'

'Susie. She says yoga saved her life and has kept her sober for fifteen years. I think she grew up near here. Plus, I think she's even more of an eco-warrior than you are, from the social media stalk I did on her. You'd like her.'

'Susie sounds great, I'm sure I would. But so we're clear, yeah, I'm the biggest hippy, okay?'

Angela laughed. 'Yes, that's your thing. You're the vegan who lives a zero-packaging-waste lifestyle.'

'Not that I'm attached to egotistical labels like that or anything.'

'Course not.'

'And you're the deep, soulful yogini.'

Angela squinted at Zoe. 'Rubbish. I've got so much to learn before I could be called a yogini.'

'Nonsense! You've got your own studio, you walk the talk, you practically hypnotise people with your gorgeous voice. You heal people. It's a skill.'

'I don't know what you're talking about.'

'Take the compliment, Ange. Own it.'

Angela hesitated. 'Okay, I will. Maybe I'll put that as my Twitter bio.'

'Great idea!'

Angela gave her best disapproving look. 'All we need is people through the door.'

'They will come.'

7

'I really hope so,' said Angela, crossing her fingers. 'I hope they like the studio. I hope I've done a good enough job in doing it up.'

Zoe narrowed her eyes. 'How many times have I got to reassure you. It's friggin' awesome. Believe.'

'In other news, I got the new coffee supplier sorted. I hope you'll like it.'

'Which one did you go for in the end?'

'A good one, I think. They're fairtrade, organic and reinvest a lot of their profits back into the production communities.'

'Nice.'

'I'm still undecided about how much Ayurveda tea to order in though. I've no idea how fast or slow it will sell. I wouldn't want to not have any if someone came in looking for it. That nearly happened last week. I was down to my last bag. Thank God they were on their own.'

'Shit gets dramatic down here, doesn't it?'

Angela laughed. 'It was an issue. It's still an issue. I've nowhere to store masses of boxes.'

Zoe raised an eyebrow. 'You still find room for all the coffee.'

'You're right. I should reprioritise. What would you do?'

'Chill, boss. Sounds like you need to make your mind up about it. You don't need my say on the matter.' Zoe laughed. 'Sometimes you really surprise me, Ange.' Zoe shook her head. 'You've got all the confidence in the world and everything going for you as a badass business-woman, then you come out with stuff like that.'

'All I want is to make people happy when they come here.'

Zoe looked at her closely but thankfully didn't grill her any further. 'Are you still campaigning for the Greens this weekend?' said Angela, still undecided about the tea.

'Yep, I'll be out with them most of the day.'

'You're so good,' said Angela. 'I would join you, you know I'd love to, but I have to be here, even if it's on the slow side.'

Zoe nodded.

'It's got to start picking up soon,' said Angela intently. 'It must.'

Chapter 2

Scrolling through a friend from school's little sister's wedding photos on the internet, Emily realised she was holding her breath. Her friend's little sister stood tall in a tailored white suit, next to her glowing wife in a stunning shoulder-less white dress. The little sister always used to annoy her friend when they were having sleepovers, but Emily never minded it. Family and friends surrounded the happy couple in a castle's gardens underneath rolling Scottish hills, posing for photographs and smiling with one another. The pictures were full of dads and uncles in kilts and mums and aunties in gigantic hats. Emily's friend was there with her baby next to her husband and three-year-old. Emily's chest felt tight. She knew she should only be happy for them all, but somehow their happiness only reaffirmed her own misery. It was quite possible she was absolutely failing at life.

What was she doing on social media at one in the morning anyway? Shutting the lid of the laptop resting on her thighs, she put it on the coffee table and went through to the kitchen for another drink. Dishes were piled high around the sink. Looking at the messy worktops, she had a brief notion to clean up, but seeing that she'd run out of washing-up liquid, she ignored it. She poured a large measure of red wine into a mug as there were no clean glasses left. Feeling bad at the state of her flat, she switched off the light and put it out of her mind. She would do it tomorrow.

Back on the sofa, she pulled her favourite red tartan blanket over her legs. The tenement living room was quiet, the neighbours most likely all asleep. The room was dimly lit, which suited her mood perfectly. Her life seemed to be contracting, shrinking, and moving in the wrong direction. She couldn't go on like this: no job, no money, no girlfriend, distant from her family. While she was able to live off her redundancy money for the time being, it was fast running out and she wasn't hearing back from any of the jobs she was applying for. Jobs she barely wanted. Certainly, she didn't want to work for a big company again anytime soon, but the depressing inevitability of going back to the corporate rat race weighed down on her heavily.

In some ways, this was her time out. But it was quickly becoming a descent into squalor and full-on depression. Things that used to come naturally to her, like getting ready in the morning, making plans, or cooking for herself, all seemed incredibly difficult and challenging now. Sometimes she felt like she was wading through mud, struggling simply to put one foot in front of the other. It was more than that, she didn't know what to do with herself. The days seemed endless; something always felt slightly off, like she was living someone else's life, not of her own making, as if any minute now it would all come tumbling down.

With a sharp intake of breath, she remembered the horrible moment she had found out she was getting fired and realised that it already had. Overhearing the news from within a toilet cubicle while her boss talked to a colleague at the sinks about who was and wasn't getting fired in the restructuring process was utterly devastating. It was humiliating opening the door, tears running down her face, walking towards the sinks, knowing that they knew she would have overheard, and knowing that they couldn't care less given the feeble attempt at an apology. All that time spent working – the eighty-hour weeks, the missing out on time with friends, the damage it had done to her relationships, the toll it had taken on her mental health – was for nothing. Never again would she pour *all* her energy and passion into a job. Never. These were the thoughts going around and around in her head.

It was exhausting.

Taking a large drink of wine, she decided enough was enough. She had to take some action. Get moving again. Do something. Another big drink of wine and she was dead set. But the thought of searching the job adverts again filled her with despair. She wasn't ready for it. And if she wasn't working, how could she begin dating again? What would she say? How would she explain herself? *"I sit around all day in a depression and I've lost interest in almost everything, apart from wine and chocolate?"*

She couldn't think of the last time she'd tried anything new, ordering something different than her usual at the Indian takeaway probably didn't count. All that time spent at work really had cost her a lot. Who was she? What did she like? These were questions that she no longer knew the answer to. Maybe she should take her best friend Anna's advice and take up yoga. That way she'd have a hobby that she could say she did. It might even be good for her.

Her laptop was still warm. It hummed into life as she opened the lid. She immediately closed all the useless tabs she'd been wasting time on and clicked onto a fresh Google search page. She watched the cursor blink in the search bar. A few taps later and she was scrolling through dozens of YouTube yoga videos. This continued far longer than was necessary. Finally, she pressed play on a ten-minute yoga for beginners video and put her mug on the table. It was an American woman in a home studio, sitting on a mat in the lotus position next to her dog. This didn't look too hard. What was all the fuss about?

After a minute or so out of the ten-minute video spent talking about what they were about to do, the American began breathing deeply, on all fours, bending her body upwards and downwards in slow repetition in a move named Angry Cat. Fascinated, Emily continued to watch. Towards the end of the ten minutes, Emily realised that she should probably join in and clumsily pushed herself up on all fours on the sofa. At the instruction of the face on her laptop, she "took" Downward Dog pose, pressing her back up in a sort of upside down V position, whilst wobbling on the uneven surface of sofa cushions. The wine wasn't helping either. Off balance, but still trying to watch the cute American woman telling her to witness her thoughts, she found herself tumbling off the sofa. 'Fuck!' she witnessed.

Lying on the floor with her head squashed against the underside of the sofa, Emily was breathing far too heavily for something untaxing. Seeing a remote control under the sofa that she thought had been lost months ago, she sighed. There was no escaping the fact she had become someone she didn't want to be. A mess. Unwanted. Alone.

Is this my rock bottom?

Remembering her resolve to get moving again, she pushed herself up, promptly sat on the edge of the sofa and picked up her laptop. This time, she typed in "Edinburgh yoga class", which threw up tons of search results. A map showed studios scattered all over the city. Never one to click on the top result, she scrolled a little further down the page and came to a rest at Cult Yoga before being put off by the colour scheme. Too clinical. Everyone looked too polished, too smug, and too orange.

Continuing her search, she vaguely clicked here and there but nothing jumped out at her. Unable to picture herself feeling comfortable in any of the studios she took a quick look at, she quit that approach and turned her attention to the map, clicking on a smaller red dot in her area called Heart Yoga. It was a new studio and only a five-minute walk from her flat. Interested, she read on.

The location was on the cusp of one of the rougher areas of the city. Emily respected anyone who thought to open a yoga studio in that part of town. Heart Yoga talked about being an accessible, inclusive type of yoga for the whole community. Some classes were aimed at total relaxation, others at beginners. A candlelit class caught her eye. Clicking through the gallery of pictures, as if choosing a new home, she stopped at a picture of a quote on the wall, written in green chalk on a mini-blackboard, *"Reboot your mind, body and soul with Heart Yoga."*. And, added at the end of the quote in purple, *"Also, we have cake, and lots of it!"*. Emily laughed a little. It had been a while.

Back on the homepage, there was an image of a woman standing on a hillside in a warm country, most likely *not* Scotland, with her back to the camera looking out towards the valley below her. The woman looked like she was deep in thought, contemplating the meaning of life. Guessing from the other pictures on the site, the woman on the hillside was most likely the owner of the studio – same blonde hair, same toned yoga body and trendy yoga clothing. Emily had a good feeling about going there. It seemed … calming. Not too intimidating. Maybe this was the place for her. At the very least, it would get her out of the house. Out of her head. Moments later, she was entering her details and signing up. As the confirmation page flashed up at her, she found herself taking a deep breath, feeling a tiny bit of something quite alien to her now – optimism.

***

Emily finished the last of the chocolates as she sat in her best friend's living room babysitting nine-month-old Russell, who was currently fast asleep. A romcom played on the extra large flatscreen on the wall with the subtitles on and the sound turned down. Everything in the house was of high quality and tastefully arranged. It looked more like a John Lewis showroom than anything else. The house fitted its owners well: neat, thoughtful, and stylish. Anna was on maternity leave from her job in the Scottish Government, and her husband Jason worked in the renewable energy sector.

Russell's soft little face was perfectly relaxed as he slept peacefully, giving no indication of the havoc he was capable of causing. Emily didn't know how Anna had coped – recovering from her C-section, the sleepless nights, figuring out how to look after a tiny human. Hopefully date night was going well. When they'd left the house earlier that evening, Russell had cried for a while. Emily hadn't wanted to disturb them on their first night out away from their baby, and before long he'd settled down.

When Mum and Dad came home, Russell's eyes flew open and Emily sat upright, having nearly dozed off.

'We're back!' said Anna, running through to the lounge to see her baby. She picked him up immediately as his eyes lit up in delight. Jason appeared a moment later.

'Was he any bother? Did he miss me? I mean, us?' said Anna, quickly, desperate for the answer.

'He cried a wee bit when you first went out, but he's been absolutely fine since. Loves his Aunty Emily, he does.'

'He does love his Aunty Emily!' said Anna. 'It's cos you've been around him so much that he's so chill.'

Russell's face crumbled into a cry.

'Give him here,' said Jason. 'I'll change him. My boy's a machine. That arse,' said Jason, shaking his head. 'Thanks for coming over Emily. You're a star.'

'No worries,' said Emily, as Jason hoisted the baby up and put him on his shoulder, before leaving the room.

'Honestly, thanks so much for this,' said Anna, joining Emily on the sofa.

'It's fine. That's what I'm here for. I'm the cool aunt. How was it?'

Kicking her shoes off and stretching, Anna shrugged. 'The restaurant was good, but the film was a bit rubbish. I dozed off once. Christ knows how he persuaded me to go and see a superhero film when we have a baby in the house.'

'Think of the brownie points.'

'It was good to have some adult time with each other.'

Emily raised an eyebrow. 'Adult?'

Anna laughed, waving her away. 'Eh, no. Not yet, anyway.'

'So how did it feel being away from Russell?'

'Obviously, I missed him.'

'You must have.'

'To be honest. I enjoyed having the time away to myself. It was such a relief in a way. Is that awful?'

'Of course not! You need to look after you sometimes, then you'll have more to give.'

'I do feel a bit more human.'

'See. It's important. And important for you guys.'

Anna smiled and gave Emily a thoughtful look. 'You're such a good friend, Emily. I love you. How are you? Are you okay?'

'I'm okay. The job hunt is taking a bit longer than expected.'

'That's totally understandable. These things take time.'

'Yeah, I suppose.'

'You seem a little down. Are you sure you're all right?'

'I've been better.'

Anna looked concerned.

'I'll be fine once I get another job. That's all.'

They both got up when the taxi arrived. Emily put on her coat as they made their way to the front door. Emily's eyes watered with a stifled yawn, before clearing themselves up almost as quickly as they'd glazed over.

'What about the yoga? Have you started it up yet?' said Anna, hovering at the door next to her friend.

'I signed up to a studio last night.'

'Brilliant. Where is it?'

'Around the corner from me.'

'Oh, really? I don't think I know that one.'

'It's new.'

'Honestly, it'll be great for you.' Anna seemed deadly serious. 'Exactly what you need.'

'I'll give it a try.'

'And how's the online dating going?'

'It's not,' said Emily, shaking her head. She pulled her coat closer around her. 'From where I'm standing, it's a cold and lonely universe filled with nothing but empty black space stretching out for eternity.'

'Right. Definitely don't say that on Tinder.'

'I think it's the silence that's the most deafening. I never knew how loud silence could be.'

'Maybe taking a wee break's a good thing then, for now. You never know. There might be a big bang waiting to happen when you least expect it.' Anna's face was hopeful. Kind.

'It was great seeing you tonight, and I'm glad you had a good time out.'

'Thanks for being here,' said Anna, hugging Emily, and then pulling away. 'You take care of yourself, okay? Let me know how the yoga goes.'

'I will.'

Chapter 3

Emily closed the door to her flat and made her way down the two flights of stairs in her tenement. Passing a bundle of flyers on the floor by the main door, she opened the latch to the outside world and let the heavy door slowly close itself behind her. Once outside in the cold air, she picked up her pace. It was a Friday night and she was heading to her first yoga class in years. Walking along the main road, absorbed in thought, Emily passed a string of betting shops, newsagents and old-man pubs. A man who was probably much younger than he looked stood outside a pub having a cigarette, watching Emily walk all the way along the street. Passing him, she averted her eyes, out of irritation as much as anything.

'Smile,' said the man, taking a draw on his cigarette.

'Fuck off, you fucking cunt.'

'Okay,' said the man, visibly shaken.

Emily kept on walking, not even altering her stride, with adrenaline coursing through her. She wasn't sure how pre-yoga Zen it was, but surely any chance to tell a creep to fuck off was worth taking. The satisfaction of being able to say in the moment the perfect answer to that tired form of woman-controlling behaviour gave her an extra bounce in her step. It didn't stop her from looking over her shoulder to check he wasn't running after her with a taste for revenge. Thankfully, he wasn't there any more and must have gone back inside. She quickened her pace anyway and turned off the main road onto the side street where the yoga studio was. Two blocks of high flats stood at the end of the street, looming over them. From the outside, Heart Yoga was unassuming and, if Emily was honest, a little underwhelming. To the side of the building was brownfield land, scattered with broken glass and discarded shopping trolleys. She hadn't realised she'd be roughing it this much. At the door, she hesitated a little. It had been a while since she'd last been anywhere new. Had it been a mistake coming here when all she wanted to do was lie on the sofa with a duvet wrapped around her watching Netflix? She wasn't even good at yoga. What was she thinking?

Giving herself a mental push, but still feeling like an imposter, she went through the front door. A soft bell chimed against itself as she entered and again as she closed the door behind her. A group in front of her was talking. The studio wasn't big. Its small size made her feel like she was almost trespassing in someone's home. Stepping further in, she looked for the quote she'd seen on the website. When she found it on the wall at about eye level above the tables and chairs for the café, she relaxed a little.

Hanging back from the group, she took a good look around. From what she could tell, there were two main rooms, this café reception area, and another room for the main studio. A large chest of drawers sat against the wall dividing the two rooms, facing the small café. It had various items for sale on it: jewellery, gemstones, moon cards, and incense. Her reflection in the panel of mirrors on top of the chest of drawers startled her. When did she get so pale? Smelling sandalwood incense in the air, she noted how beautifully decorated the café was from top to bottom. It seemed as if every detail carried some meaning and had been lovingly thought through.

Returning her attention to the group waiting to go in, she saw what must have been the owner of the studio with her back to her, standing in the centre of the group chatting to the others also there for the class. Emily tentatively wandered further into the action. When a break in the conversation allowed, the owner looked over at Emily and smiled warmly at her. 'Hello, welcome to Heart Yoga. I'm Angela Forbes. What's your name, please?' She held an iPad and was checking names off a list.

In that moment Emily's body did strange things. Her pulse picked up and she held her breath. She couldn't find any words and was sure her pupils had dilated dramatically. The woman in front of her was breathtakingly beautiful. Her eyes were a striking grey-blue, which stood out from subtle but defining smoky eye make-up. Her arresting eyes were like nothing Emily had ever seen. It was like they were looking deep into your soul. Her blonde hair was tied up loosely with some strands falling beside her ears, framing her smile, which was gorgeous. Even her skin was glowing. The owner looked far better in person than in her pictures online, not that they weren't great, but there was something about her presence that seemed to translate much more in person. A goodness and a feeling of calm emanated from her.

'Emily. Emily Mackenzie.'

'That's right, you booked recently for the twenty-one-day pass.' Angela had a posh Scottish accent.

'Yep, that's me.'

'Perfect. It's a great way to find out which classes you prefer. Make sure to try as many of the different ones as you can. Have you been to a yoga class before?'

'No. Well,' Emily shook her head. 'I went to a class years ago, but I didn't really take to it. I've done a couple of yoga YouTube videos since then. To be honest, I'm not flexible at all.'

Angela smiled again and gave no impression that she might be judging Emily less favourably for not taking to the thing that Angela was obviously most passionate about in life. 'Take your time with it in that case. Remember, there's no pressure tonight at all. Just see how you go.' Angela paused and spoke sincerely to Emily, 'I hope you enjoy it.'

***

Emily and the other classmates followed Angela through French doors into the main studio. The colours caught Emily's attention first. With soft purple walls and painted yellow and purple wooden panels on the ceiling, it felt warm and inviting. Counting at least four buddhas of different shapes and sizes, she continued through to a changing room off to the side of the studio. It seemed odd to have to walk through the studio to get to the changing room, but Emily was willing to go with it. The changing room was retro with a twist. Dark wooden benches sat below rows of cast iron hooks that lined most of the walls. A modern white mantelpiece and stove stood at the end of the room. A door led off to a bathroom. Overall, it was much larger than it looked from the front door and outside on the street.

As Emily and her new classmates took off their coats and got ready in a concentrated silence, the teacher, Angela, chatted to a woman she seemed to know well by the entrance to the changing room. Emily discreetly looked her up and down, safely, from a distance. She had a perfectly balanced body that she looked very comfortable in. Her outfit looked brand new, expensive, and expertly chosen. She had on purple leggings cut below the knee showing off long, lean legs, and a figure-hugging white vest top. Emily glanced over at the soft lines outlining the definition of her tummy muscles. Angela was incredibly hot. She could have been on the cover of a fitness or yoga magazine. Her demeanour was also so kind and warm. The combination had left Emily slightly off balance. It wasn't often she came into contact with an actual goddess. And her smile. Wow, that was simply beautiful.

Taking off her oversized jumper, Emily saw that her T-shirt had holes in it and was fraying at the seams. That wasn't ideal. She would throw it out when she got home. Sporting galaxy splashed workout leggings never before worn outside the house, Emily, barefoot, followed the others and picked up a large cylindrical cushion, a yoga mat, a little block, and a blanket from various boxed shelves and crates lining one wall of the studio. Feeling very out of place, she strategically found a space near the edge by the window. The window ran the length of the entire front wall with soft white curtains draping down, tied in the middle, enclosing a long window seat and numerous colourful cushions. Emily had a notion to sit in the window and watch. Instead, she put down her bits and pieces and unrolled her mat onto the floor before straightening it. Unsure what to do next, she looked around and copied the others sitting on their mats.

Once settled on her mat, she saw a picture on the wall which read, "Be happy now". Emily scoffed. A speaker in the corner played soft music but did nothing to help Emily feel less awkward about being there. The teacher was sitting patiently facing the line of students, as if waiting for the right time to begin. The thought of leaving crossed Emily's mind. The teacher rose to her feet and clasped her hands together in front of her as if she was about to start praying. Everyone copied her, so Emily did the same.

'Dear ones. Bringing our hands to heart centre, let's start here in Mountain Pose. Imagine your feet are roots connecting with the earth, your toes spreading out wide. Relax your shoulders down and lift your chest. Stand tall, tall as an ancient tree in the forest. As you begin to centre yourself, notice where you *are* with yourself tonight. Notice your breath for a few moments, but don't try to change it.' She paused. 'Good. Now, let's take a deep breath in through your nose,' she paused again, 'and a deep breath out through your mouth for an equal amount of time. Breathing with your diaphragm, let your belly and chest expand as you breathe in, and let your tummy come back in as you breathe out. Forget everything you've done in this past week, and all that you've got lined up. Let all of the tension and the noise fall from your mind. Yoga is an opportunity to connect with the self. In its most spiritual form, yoga is union. Union with the mind, body, and soul. If we can connect with the breath, we can slow things down, and give our nervous system a chance to align better with the self and be calm.' A few beats of silence passed. 'Now, reaching our arms up, keeping our hands together, imagine you are reaching up to the sky, to the sun and all of the energy it has to offer. Good. Now let's bend forward at the hips, keeping your back straight and pushing the hips back, and ease into a forward fold. Keep your knees slightly bent, so as not to strain your back. Clasp your elbows with your hands. Let's hang out here for a moment and give ourselves a hug. There's no right or wrong way to do yoga, remember. Just see what's available for you today and next time maybe you'll go a little further. That's it everyone. Let it all hang out.'

The row of bodies stayed doubled in two. Throughout what felt like an eternity in the position, Emily's thoughts raced and spiralled. Exactly the thing she was not supposed to let happen. Blood pooled by her ears and she could feel her skin gather around her cheeks. Mostly, her mind kept replaying the moment she found out she was being made redundant and she felt the pain of it all over again. Her eyes glazed over and watered. It was embarrassing. She'd only started and now was failing at yoga. Typical.

The sound of Angela's melodious voice jolted Emily back to her surroundings. 'Bringing your torso back up so that it's parallel with the ground, straighten out the lower back, and let your chest fall towards your legs again. Bend the knees slightly. Use your breath to sink a little deeper on the exhale, creating more space in your body. Well done, everyone. Slowly bring your heart back to standing, bringing your head up towards the sky.' Angela performed the sequence, using her arms like wings, and then straightened out her toned shoulders.

Once back upright, Emily took a sharp intake of breath and held it, wondering why she was putting herself through this. The class was then taken through a number of movements that all seemed to result in a torturous amount of time spent in one position. Emily glared at Angela more than once, not understanding how someone could be so cruel to inflict such pain onto a group of strangers. Her whole body felt tight, especially her lower back and hips. Often, she had to break off from the stretch and sit for a while before she worked up the motivation to get back into it. When she did, she felt clumsy and awkward compared to everyone else. Slow to pick up the instructions over which hand and leg should go where, she was out of step with the others, not moving as one with them, and breaking the sense of flow in the room. It bothered her that she wasn't getting it, making her feel like a failure all over again. Before long, Emily also got the distinct feeling that the repeated instructions were directed at her but disguised by Angela as if she was talking to the whole class. The class, all of whom Emily could see very well, was doing exactly as Angela was requesting. More time passed. Emily glanced at her watch, bored and humiliated.

Please let this be over soon.

No such let up came. Emily studied the colourful ceiling above her, with her arms splayed out either side. It was an especially high ceiling and had a thick, intricately detailed cornice. The whole room felt so freshly done up – and wasn't so bad to be in. The wooden floors were smooth to touch and seemed barely walked upon. She closed her eyes. She was supposed to be focusing on her breath and "feeling the inner body" but she was mostly thinking about the sound of Angela's voice. It had a reassuring tone to it. A soft lilt that made you instantly trust whatever it had to say. It's what got her into the contorted positions in the first place.

From time to time, Angela would walk around the room, serenading the class with words of wisdom and helpful pointers. Sometimes she readjusted people's positions. Emily prayed she wouldn't come over to her. As Emily watched Angela glide about, it struck her that Angela had a bit of a gay walk. In fact, as she twisted her body around to one side to get a better view of her, she realised there was a hint of a lesbian vibe coming from Angela: the way she held herself, her strong jaw line, her confidence. She had long toned legs and strong shoulders and arms like an Amazonian goddess.

Dream on.

'Now let your attention return to your breath. Notice the gentle expansion of your chest, and the opening of your heart. Bring your knees up and let them gently fall to the side, allowing your body to follow, so that you are in the foetal position. Inhale and know that you are safe. Letting your body lead the way in quieting the mind.'

Emily sighed and flopped heavily onto her side with a thud. She watched as the woman next to her did the same but gracefully.

'Take a few moments to connect with the earth. As you lie here, take some nourishing breaths and tell yourself that you are enough. Repeat after me in your head, "I am enough".'

Since when did this become a self-help class?

After that, as the soothing music continued to play in the background, they lay down for a nap under the blankets for ten minutes. This was the best bit. They were then invited to sit up. Angela sat upright, cross-legged in the lotus position with perfect posture. There was a stillness to her that was alluring but also a little unnerving. She seemed almost untouchable, yet very present. It was a strange paradox. A single gong boomed out from the speakers.

'Let's give thanks to our bodies for allowing us to move in different ways tonight.' Angela took a massive inhale, her chest visibly rising, and then emanated a low noise that seemed to last for eternity. The rest of the class joined in.

'Ommmmmmmmmmmmmmm.'

Emily had *not* been prepared for this. Since when was this a thing? Her tummy muscles tensed; it felt like she'd stopped breathing as the giggles rose up in her throat.

Oh no.

She let out a little clenched snort at first, giving way to a quick succession of high-pitched laughs. The omming was just too much. Angela seemed so nice and well meaning, but Emily found the weird noise unbearably funny and so ridiculous. The om noise stopped but Emily kept going. Unable to stop, she continued to sit there giggling and laughing, nervous and disruptive. The row of heads had snapped around, one by one, to look at her. The only sound was of her uncontrollable laughter and disjointed breathing conflicting with the meditative background music. It continued past the point at which it ever would have been socially acceptable. Her breathing felt high up in her neck. Forcing out her belly and letting new air into her lungs, she managed to get it under control and stop laughing. Finally. Looking up, she saw Angela glance over at her. Emily mouthed an apology when Angela looked over again and then clasped her hands over her mouth in shame.

Angela was every bit the professional. She addressed the class and smiled, not acknowledging the interruption. Drawing the palms of her hands together in front of her, she bowed her head, 'Namaste.'

The class copied her movements and returned the sentiment. Emily hurriedly did the same. 'Namaste.'

Angela effortlessly rose to her feet; her movements were light and springy. Emily sat there for a few moments with her head down, avoiding eye contact with everyone as the class dispersed. She got up in stages, using her knee for support. Her body wasn't used to sitting on a hard floor for so long. She rolled her mat up but it went slightly off to one side and began rolling unevenly, so she started again. Unsurprisingly, the others had managed to roll their mats up perfectly first time and were already in the changing room getting changed. Emotional, she quickly gathered the rest of the equipment and hurriedly stored it away where it belonged. Some were chatting a little when she walked through to the changing room. No one spoke to her as she put her shoes on and got her bag and jacket. The rest of the students efficiently gathered their belongings and made their way out of the changing room as Emily hid in the toilet.

***

When Emily emerged from the bathroom and into the changing room, the place was empty and quiet. She didn't think she'd been in there for that long.

'You okay back there?' asked Angela.

Emily's face flushed with embarrassment. 'Yes, thanks.'

Angela came into the changing room.

'I am so, SO sorry about that. It was rude and disrespectful of me. If you want to bar me, I totally understand.' Angela's expression gave nothing away. Emily continued, tense and awkward. 'I got caught a wee bit off-guard there with the chant at the end. It's this stupid thing I do sometimes: UHLS. Uncontrollable Hysterical Laughter Syndrome. It's nerves. It won't happen again. There is a way to get my breathing under control, and I should be able to do that quicker next time – not that there will be a next time.'

Angela's face softened. 'It's all right. The om can bring out different things in different people. It resonates with different chakras. If you do the sound, it might help you release some of that tension.'

'I think I've embarrassed myself too much to show my face here again.'

Angela tilted her head to one side. 'Nonsense. It happens. Did you enjoy the class?'

Emily wasn't convinced. 'Yes, it was great, thank you.' She hesitated, 'I'm not very good at it.'

'First times are always a bit strange. Just do one thing for me. Give it another try? I promise you you'll start to enjoy it and feel the benefits of it if you give it a chance.'

'Okay then, I'll be back,' Emily's voice squeaked, and she was not sure at all if she wanted to come back. 'Thanks for not kicking me out.' Emily looked around the homely studio and realised she might be holding Angela up and should exit the place as soon as possible. 'I'd better get going.' She smiled uncertainly at Angela. 'Have a great night, and thanks again.'

'You're very welcome. So, when will we be seeing you again at Heart Yoga?'

'Oh, um, well, I did have my eye on your Vinyasa Flow on Sundays?'

'Excellent choice. See you on Sunday then.' Angela saw Emily to the door.

Emily pulled open the front door. 'Bye then.'

'Bye. Take care.'

Emily stepped out into the night air. The street was full of parked cars which had settled in for the night. Walking home, she reflected on her sheer inability to do anything right. The class had been an epic failure. She'd been unable to do most of it and had made a fool of herself at the end. The familiar tightness in her chest returned. Defeated, Emily walked the rest of the way back to her flat looking at the ground, not sure where she was going in life or if she would ever set foot in Heart Yoga again.'

Chapter 4

Angela locked the front door, unsure if the newcomer would ever come back. Some teachers would have found the laughter offensive, but she didn't. No one had ever gone off like that in any of her classes before. The quick snort or one-off giggle but never such a performance. It was funny, yoga, in a way, so she couldn't blame her. It hadn't felt malicious. Silly, if anything, and a clear sign that the woman was not able to self-regulate very well and probably had some issues to work on. She wondered what Zoe would think about it. Turning the sign on the door to "closed", she considered running a Yoga for Laughs class. The giggling seemed to have made the others in the class more annoyed than they should have been.

Going through her end-of-day routine, she straightened the chairs in the café, rearranged the seat cushions, and went through to the studio and turned off the main overhead light. Only the Himalayan salt lamps were left on, giving a warm orange glow. Tidying the yoga blocks and blankets inside the shelving unit, she was grateful her students were always willing to put the kit away, even if they weren't particularly good at putting it away neatly. The studio needed to look perfect for when she opened in the morning, so she dutifully got on with the task. Yawning while re-folding one of the blankets, her eyes watered with tiredness. At least she didn't have to hurry home; there was no one there waiting. Once everything was in its right place and exactly how it should be, she stepped back and admired her work. Satisfied, she went into the changing room to turn off the light. Before she could hit the switch, she saw a phone on the bench at the opposite side of the room.

That's a shame, someone's left their phone.

As she moved towards it, there was a knock on the front door. Most likely the phone's owner. Then a few more rapid knocks. She looked towards the door and then back at the phone, before deciding to answer the door where she found Emily the newcomer peering through the window, a worried expression drawn across her face. Angela unlocked the door and opened it.

'Emily, hi.'

Her eyes were wide with alarm. 'Hey. I've lost my phone. Can I have a quick look for it here? I can't believe I could be so stupid to lose it. Have you seen it?'

Angela nodded. 'Yes. Come in. It's in the changing room.'

'Oh, thank God, I thought it was gone. I don't have a landline and live alone, so the thought of not having a phone tonight was bloody awful. I'd have been too worried to stay in the flat by myself without one.' Emily quickly came through the door, looking around as if she shouldn't be there. 'Thanks. I'm so sorry to bother you again. I'll just get the phone and leave you be. I'm sure you've got better places to be than standing here talking to me.'

Angela couldn't believe how negative Emily was being about herself. She tried her best to put her at ease. 'You're not bothering me at all. Wait a sec. I'll go and get it for you.'

As she went through to retrieve the phone, the thought crossed her mind that Emily might not be okay. Re-joining Emily in the café, she found her standing there with her arms folded, looking at the ground. Her long dark hair covered her face, her fringe a little too long, sitting just over her eyes. Her jacket hung off her, as if a size too big. She held herself as if trying not to take up any space in the world. When she looked up, her face brightened a little, but there was still a heaviness to her expression. It contrasted sharply with

Emily's striking natural beauty. Her features were almost perfectly symmetrical, accentuating deep brown eyes that seemed a little sad. Angela had the urge to straighten her up, move the hair out of her face and give her a big hug.

'Here it is.' Angela handed the phone over.

Emily visibly relaxed at having it back in her hands. She brushed her fringe out of her eyes, which had a faraway look in them. 'Oh my God, thanks.'

'No problem.'

Emily looked around furtively as she moved towards the door. 'You work late.'

'I was tidying up and getting the studio ready for tomorrow. I have to do it before I leave, or it'll be playing on my mind all night. There's always something that needs to be done around here.'

'It must be great to run your own business, though.'

'It has its moments.'

'I love what you've done with the place, by the way. It's really lovely.'

'Cheers. Thank you for saying. Did you get all the way home before you realised you'd lost the phone?'

'I did, but I live quite nearby. When I reached into my bag for my keys it wasn't where it normally is. I knew I'd taken it with me, so I figured it must still be here. I can't believe I freaked out so much over a stupid phone.'

'It's understandable.'

'I'm an idiot.'

'You're not. A lot of people would've been upset by that.'

'I think I panicked so much because I live alone and having a phone feels like an essential.'

'Yeah, I know what you mean. I live alone, too.' Angela loved living alone, but suspected Emily did not, and a phone did feel necessary, just in case anything happened.

'Do you?' Emily shook her head. Angela noticed the

freckles around Emily's cheeks, brown like her hair.

'Yes.'

'I bet you wouldn't freak out like I did.'

'You'd be surprised. So, will you be back on Sunday, Ms Got the Giggles.'

Emily laughed a little and half-smiled, showing off dimples in her cheeks. The worry from earlier had lifted from her face. 'I will, but you're going to have to warn me if there's going to be any more of that humming. I'm not sure I can handle it; I'm too … Scottish.'

Angela laughed. 'I'm Scottish too.'

'Yes, but you're a Scottish yoga teaching goddess. Are you some kind of unicorn, or something?'

Angela swallowed at "goddess". 'What can I say, we do exist.'

Emily laughed softly, still smiling at her, but more fully now. Angela, happy that Emily seemed a bit lighter in herself, continued, 'I'll say now that the om is in a lot of classes, so you might have to prepare yourself for it if you want to fully embrace the yoga experience. It's designed to get you tuned into the moment, to operate at the frequency of the noise, and to release all tension in your body. If you do it fully with me, I will have you vibrating from your core before you know it. It can be very powerful if you fully commit to it.'

"Vibrating from your core"? What am I saying?

Emily scratched her head and looked away, as if slightly unsure. Angela felt herself blush a little and shook her head, not knowing where that comment had come from. She'd never said it before.

When Emily looked back up at her, they locked eyes properly for the first time. Emily's brown eyes held so much depth and were soft and warm. Their shape was quite beautiful. Angela found it hard to look away and was unsure why this was the case. For a second or two, it literally felt like time stood still as they stood there looking at each other. This did things to her body, low down in her body, much to her instant disapproval and surprise. The connection was intense. Angela looked away, she had to. It was Emily who broke the silence first. 'Well, thank you again. I better get going. I'm really sorry to have disturbed you again tonight.'

Angela gathered herself, internally scrambling to find her professionalism, and opened the door. 'It really was no problem.' She continued to hold onto the handle.

Emily held up her phone and wiggled it. There was a gentle playfulness to Emily now. It suited her. 'I think I've got it this time.'

'Excellent.'

As Emily slowly brushed past, she looked at Angela as she went out. Again, it felt like time stood still and that something passed between them. The feeling hit Angela in the chest. Given her training in meditation and mindfulness, she was hyper-aware of her emotions and how she was feeling. Being so attuned to her body and in touch with her feelings had its advantages in that she didn't miss a thing. Emily turned back to face her once she was over the threshold and standing out on the street, visibly calmer than when she'd arrived. Had she felt the same thing? Her starry leggings glimmered in the darkness as she smiled at Angela again. Angela really liked it when she smiled.

'Thanks again. See you on Sunday, Angela. Looking forward to it.'

'See you then.'

Chapter 5

Walking along the canal on her way into town, Emily clutched the phone in her pocket. There was no way she was going to forget it, not after the upset of thinking she'd lost it after yoga. The memory of standing at the door to the yoga studio in a panic was a little mortifying. She hadn't been able to hide just how anxious she had been. The whole experience that night would normally have made her run a mile but, having spoken more with Angela after she'd gone back for her phone, she was curious to give it all another try. She'd thought a lot about their chat since last Friday. Meeting Angela felt significant somehow. Being around Angela more would be a good thing, she seemed so lovely and genuine. And a good yoga teacher, too. Yes, she'd go back to Heart Yoga. But when she was feeling more up to it. After a string of failed applications and rejections for interviews, it had been a bad few days. Logically, she knew that it didn't mean anything, and she'd get something sorted eventually, but the sense of fear and failure it triggered in her was debilitating.

With each step, she regretted her decision to stretch her body out by walking into town before catching a bus onwards to Portobello to have dinner with Anna and Jason. Despite having walked fifteen minutes, she still wasn't even halfway there. Her legs felt heavy, lacking the energy they used to have. The malt-scented air from the city distilleries was intense. The distinctive smell clashed with the mint in her mouth. Heading into early evening, the light was fading with remnants of sunshine peeking out behind buildings, sending long shadows out in front of her. Everything felt so bright and loud. She must have adjusted to the indoors a little too much. Swans and their cygnets swam beside her, but she wasn't that interested. The canal sat between long rows of tenements and, as she got closer to town, their new-build equivalents. It was quiet and there wasn't much to look at, but it was better than walking along the busy main road.

Running her fingers through her hair and feeling the silky-smooth texture, Emily was pleased with the effort she'd made earlier. Going to the hairdresser's still felt like a mammoth effort and was either put off or forgotten about, so today, she'd cut her own. Cutting her own hair was always a bit risky, but this time it had gone well, although it had taken her all afternoon using three mirrors and accepting a lot of arm pain from holding the scissors up. Judging from the masses of hair that she'd swept up afterwards, it had been a long overdue situation. It felt lighter on her shoulders, and now she could see without thick dark hair covering her eyes. Her fringe had become like a safety blanket, and she sort of missed it. Still, it was good to open herself back up to the world. If only sorting her life out could be as simple as a few well-placed cuts here and there.

Since it was the first time she'd left the flat in days, it was the first time she'd had to put a bra on. The one she'd grabbed and thrown on was now digging into her flesh whilst doing nothing to support her. The material scratched at her skin and was surely making it red. Somehow it had escaped being thrown out and here she was, repeating the same old mistake. But never again. As soon as she got to Anna's, she would throw it in the bin. Anna wouldn't mind.

A canal boat ambled towards her in the distance. As it came closer, the crowd of women on a hen night became hard to ignore. Music blared over a constant loud chattering. There were glasses and bottles of fizz everywhere. The group were identically dressed as princesses, in revealing baby-pink dresses, with the bride clearly visible in a silver tiara and garish "bride to be" sash. The cold weather didn't seem to be an issue for them. A giant pink blow-up penis rested against the window, pointing at passers-by on the canal path.

Yuck.

Emily kept her head down as the boat passed. The music faded as she and the boat each moved further apart. Towards the end of the canal path, she stepped onto a cobblestone street and rounded the corner. Buses and cars blared past, signalling the end of the peaceful bit of the walk. When she reached Lothian Road, a gust of wind nearly blew her off her feet. Leaning into it like a pro, she crossed at the lights, taking care to watch for rogue cars turning out of nowhere. As she headed down towards the Grassmarket, she found herself looking up at the castle as it came into view. The jagged rock it sat on always seemed so out of place next to the city that had been built up around it. The Grassmarket wasn't busy. From January to March, it was like a different city with fewer tourists. The pedestrian walkway seemed almost closed, with no tables and chairs parked outside the restaurants and bars. There was a flatness to it. Not even many smokers were out.

The quietness suited her today. Pressing further into Old Town, the architecture, the history, the plethora of familiar pubs, restaurants, cafés, and quirky shops were still able to stir a bit of excitement and wonder in her, and for this she was grateful. Memories of epic nights out, of sunny days walking about the city, and of meeting up with friends felt like a warm blanket she could shelter under. Walking up the steep hill of Victoria Street to join George IV Bridge, she felt lighter on her feet with each step. A hint of the summer months appeared in front of her as a small crowd of keen tourists lined the pavement taking pictures in all directions. One was photographing a lamppost, while another was pointing down the street excitedly. Moving past them, she headed over the Royal Mile and down The Mound.

When she rounded the corner, she did something she never did – she stopped, and really looked at the view in front of her. The sun would be setting soon. The disappearing light threw its last beams over the buildings on Princes Street and down into the gardens below it. A soft yellow and orange glow reflected in the windows of the buildings making it a truly spectacular sight. Standing there, she took it all in and appreciated its beauty. This was her city. When had she stopped looking at it? Appreciating it? Too often, she darted past, only ever thinking about what she was doing rather than where she was. She'd been taking it for granted for years now. Maybe that was part of the reason she'd got so depressed? Whatever it was, stopping to smell the flowers, as it were, felt good. To her right, that's exactly what a couple of tourists were doing. She smiled at them and they smiled back. This was living.

Satisfied with her fill of the view, she turned right, and skipped down steep steps towards the National Gallery and her bus stop, a little beyond it. Market stalls lined the pathway at the bottom of the steps. Tables draped with dark cloth underneath makeshift shelters were stacked full. For some reason, she stopped to browse the trinkets, hats, scarves, and odd bits of handmade jewellery on offer. A Celtic necklace caught her eye. It hung on a stall decorated with a staggering number of different pieces of jewellery next to gemstones and postcards. She stepped up to the table for a closer look. The seller, a woman with kind eyes and long dark hair, greeted her. Emily turned back to the necklace. It was a silver chain with a round pendant of a tree and its roots.

'That one's the Tree of Life knot. Would you like to see it out?'

'Em, no, thank you. I'm just looking.' Emily turned to leave. She couldn't deal with a conversation with a stranger. Not today.

The woman spoke quickly. 'They're known as endless knots because they don't have a beginning or an end. The roots and branches of the tree are woven together, showing the continuous cycle of life on earth.' The woman was wrapped up in a thick scarf, hat, and fingerless gloves. There was something comforting in her tone.

People walked past on the narrow pathway behind them. Emily turned back. 'I've never seen it before.'

'Maybe it wasn't the right time.'

Emily eyed her closely. 'No. Maybe not.' There was an openness to her that made Emily stop and listen.

'It means balance, positive energy and rebirth. It reminds us of the continuous cycle of life. Some say it's about a fresh start. It's a very powerful symbol.'

Picking it up and letting the chain sit in the palm of her hand, she stroked her thumb over the pendant and examined the shiny surface. The simple tree and circle stirred something within her. She could see that everything was connected. Nature was all we had. Life went on. Her life would go on. She would bounce back from this. The mere hint of coming through the other side was such a relief, but short lived. She had enjoyed getting out of the house, though, and seeing the beauty of her city again had been pretty special. Maybe she should mark the moment and remind herself of it, and the idea of life going on, by wearing it around her neck? Placing it back on its hook, she addressed the woman, who hadn't stopped watching her, 'how much?'

The seller smiled. 'That one is twenty-two pounds.'

Overpriced. Still, I'll enjoy it.

'I'll take it, please.'

'Nice choice. I'll wrap it up for you.'

'It's okay thanks. You don't need to wrap it. It's only for me.'

Emily handed over the money, grateful that she had cash

in her purse since she was no longer working. For a moment, she didn't feel worried about money or the prospect of having to move out of her flat. The seller wished her the best of luck as she handed her the plain box with the necklace in it. Smiling, Emily put the necklace on straight away, much to the delight of the seller. She waved goodbye and continued on her way, somewhat renewed.

The Crags and Arthur's Seat caught her attention in the fading light. The ancient volcanic hill and ex-quarry sat majestically under a thick brooding cloud. Even in winter, Emily found Arthur's Seat poetic as it loomed over the city like a constant reminder of nature.

She looked up at the giant clock on the Balmoral Hotel. She still had plenty of time. She found her bus stop and stood in the queue of commuters. When the 26 to Seton Sands pulled into the bus stop, the line of people boarded in the exact order at which they had arrived at the stop. The locals' adherence to queuing at a bus stop was probably one of the things that satisfied her most about Edinburgh. Stumbling up the stairs as the bus jerked its way from the kerb, she found a seat on the top deck near the back as the burgundy bus made its way up towards York Place, past the Pink Triangle, and out east onto London Road. As the bus ambled along, she let her eyes wander over the streets of her city. She knew them all so well. Almost every corner, everywhere she looked, there were so many memories and reminders of days gone by: the premises of the company she'd learned to drive with, an ex-girlfriend's flat, the step outside a pub she'd once vomited on at two in the morning. It was like she had been another person then – carefree, optimistic. Young. Someone she no longer recognised.

Chapter 6

The marimba tune went off on Emily's phone at eight. Starting at the sound, she spun over to her bedside table to reach it but missed the button the first time, then opened her eyes properly and finally switched it off. Exhaling from exertion before she had even woken up properly, she lay her head back on the pillow and looked up at the ceiling. Having spent the night tossing and turning, tired yet wired, she didn't feel rested at all. Pushing herself up with one arm, she dangled her feet off the bed. It wasn't like her to be up so early on a Sunday. The urge to look at social media was there but she resisted.

Humiliating herself at the end of the yoga class had been a low point, and she'd spent the last week doing yoga in the flat daily and had even been on a few runs around the park. Admittedly, she'd tasted brief moments of what she could only describe as "what inner peace must feel like" during the class and was curious about it and wanted more of that feeling. It felt like the only thing that might actually be able to get her out of her funk. Hence the sudden obsession. But she wasn't going to worry about it too much because it was a healthy one for once.

Her next visit to Heart Yoga was in two hours. Feeling slightly guilty about breaking the promise of going last Sunday, she tried to reason with herself. She hadn't been back because she wanted to practise on her own, before making another fool of herself. That, and that she had had enough of feeling like a loser. Emily stood up and stretched her arms up high above her head, picturing Angela standing in front of her, both encouraging and gorgeous. Padding down her long hallway towards the kitchen, shooting pain and stiff muscles caused her to limp. Maybe she had been overdoing it.

Her kitchen had no windows. The box room in the centre of the flat had been converted, leaving a small kitchen but a large lounge, bedroom, and guest bedroom for when friends came to visit. It was exactly the type of flat she hoped to buy one day, with its high ceilings and large bay window. Taking her coffee into the lounge, she opened the blinds to the sunshine. Some crocuses were starting to poke through in the park opposite. She looked out at the empty street below. The only person out was a woman walking her dog in the park. With the sun streaming into the living room, she found herself doing yoga *again*. Facing the rug in Downward Dog, she felt the pull on her lower back and hamstrings. Noticing that her heels were a little closer to the floor, she wondered if Angela would notice any improvements in her practice.

As she made her way over to the studio, she realised how out of sync she was with the rest of society in general now and especially with the chilled out Sunday morning vibe. Apart from visiting Anna, this was the first social thing she had done all week. Crossing the bridge and walking down a side road to get to the studio past a large supermarket, she enjoyed the sweet scent of biscuits in the air, wafting over from a local factory. The closer to the studio she got, the flats became less like tenements and more like questionably designed 1960s high-rise council flats. In the early morning glow, they seemed a lot less intimidating.

Being early was a strong point of Emily's. When she was working, she made a point of always being early to meetings. She hated the idea of people waiting for her and of letting anyone down. Emily got to the studio at the same time as an older woman dressed in sports clothing. Standing back, Emily gestured for the older woman to go in first.

'Thank you. Are you joining us this morning?' said the woman.

'I am, yes. Not sure how good I'll be though.'

The woman chuckled at Emily. 'There's nothing to be good at, ma dear. You're here, aren't you?' She went through the door and Emily followed her, feeling slightly confused but also more at ease.

Angela was standing by the café counter, watching them come in. 'Good morning. How were the grandkids last night, Louise?'

Louise put her Edinburgh International Book Festival canvas bag down on one of the tables. Her stance was solid, with her chin up and excellent posture. She did not look like she had grandchildren. 'Wee rascals, the lot of them. How on earth I ended up with six is beyond me. Being a nurse was a walk in the park compared to the weekend I've had. Their mum and dad picked them up at the back of ten last night. It's just as well I'm so flexible, that's all I can tell you.'

Angela laughed politely. 'I bet you're their favourite granny.'

Emily noticed the Tree of Life symbol on the chest of drawers. How had she not seen it before? It was also on a necklace, and on a mug and on a set of rings and earrings.

Louise picked up her bag and moved towards the changing room. 'I was never this soft with my two, so I must be. All this peace and love talk of yours must be rubbing off on me.' Louise shook her head like she didn't know what had become of her life as she wandered off at a steady, slow pace.

Emily joined Angela by the counter, feeling like Angela must be completely on her wavelength given her affinity with her new favourite symbol. With new eyes, Emily saw another side to Angela and wondered what struggles she might ever have gone through. Her happy and calm demeanour suggested that life was always rosy.

43

'You came back,' said Angela, smiling at her with one hand resting on the iPad on the counter.

'I gave you my word, didn't I?'

'It really is great to see you.'

Emily laughed nervously and looked around exaggeratedly. She clocked brown bags of organic coffee on display on the shelves above the coffee machine. She hadn't noticed them before. They looked expensive, artisan, and a little out of keeping with the area. There was a greasy spoon café around the corner that always looked busy. 'This space really is amazing. It's even better in daylight. I can't wait to try one of your coffees later.'

Angela laughed. 'Sometimes I think it's the only reason people keep coming back.'

This, Emily knew, would not be the case. Angela clearly had a big personality that people would warm to. Also, the café always seemed empty. Was it a coffee shop or a yoga studio? Emily decided to park that thought.

'You're early, but would you like to come in and get ready?'

Angela smiled and gestured with a nod for Emily to follow her. It wasn't so much of a question as an order. Angela was wearing salmon-coloured capris and a short, grey muscle tank top with "grateful" written on it. Her visible skin and sports bra at the side was very sexy. Her skin was golden, like her hair. As they walked through, Emily let her eyes wander over Angela's body, especially her perfectly shaped bum. Emily found it hard to take her eyes away, doing so in the end, only to go into the changing room as Angela stayed in the studio.

By the time the class began, there were still only four students. Emily, Louise, and two other women who introduced themselves to her in the changing room – Erin, who looked like an athlete, and Karen, with a wide smile and big curly hair. Emily found the place much more relaxing than the intense Friday night crowd over a week ago. They each had enough space to spread out and move their limbs. This time, Emily ended up in the middle, but it was okay. When she arranged the various bits of kit around her, she watched as Angela settled herself at the front. As Angela seemed about to get started, the bell went at the front door. Angela frowned and quickly went out to see who it was. 'Sorry, ladies. Back in a moment.'

'I think someone's a wee bit annoyed,' said Karen, loving the interruption.

Angela came gliding back into the studio. 'Delivery. Sorry. Now, where were we.'

As the class started, Angela informed them they were going to begin with a sun salutation. Emily watched as Angela effortlessly demonstrated the sequence for them. Her limbs flowed as she moved from standing to crouching to Downward Dog and more, before raising herself back to the start again, bringing her arms out to her side and back up towards the ceiling above her. Emily stared, realising her mouth was slightly open, forgetting she'd have to go next.

The four students got started on Angela's request. Emily got right into it and after ten minutes or so was loving the flow of it all – specifically the focus it gave her, and how it was quietening her anxious and despairing thoughts.

'Well done, everyone,' said Angela.

Emily took the praise personally. It lifted her. There was a totally different vibe to the class that day. Emily didn't feel as intimidated. It felt to her like the space was there for her to use, to enjoy. And she was.

'There is no goal to be reached, just see what your body feels like doing today, how far you can take it, and maybe next time you might go a little further or not. What we're trying to do is to connect to ourselves, above all else. The moves themselves are secondary,' said Angela, with her arms out in a Warrior Pose. 'Your body exists in the present, your mind wants to exist in the past and future, we want them to exist together, now, in the present.'

Emily wasn't quite sure what that meant, but it sounded good. Feeling like she was going to topple over and fail at being a warrior, she fought to steady herself. She looked to her left and saw Louise doing it flawlessly, and to her right, to Erin, also ready for battle. However, the more Emily did the sequence, the easier it got. She knew she wasn't doing it perfectly, despite having practised all week, but she was happy with just okay. With each passing minute, Emily could feel her mind and body becoming calmer. It wasn't easy, she had to concentrate on what she was doing, but being around these nicer classmates and having the motivation of looking at Angela for an hour was also helping.

'Let the body and the mind be as one.'

Angela's harmonious voice was sending Emily into a sort of trance. The light streaming through the windows added extra warmth to the room. It was perfect. She could get used to this. As the yellow haze cast a spell over Emily, she breathed deeper into her stretch and her mind fell quiet. Angela moved them through so many different poses, and Emily went with it – until she couldn't. With one leg bent in front of her and the other stretched out behind her, she struggled to square her hips; her outer hip and thigh of her leg in front burned all the way down to her knee.

'Let's take another full breath in Pigeon before we slowly begin to inhale deeply and drop our chests to our legs.'

Emily smiled to herself. Some of the names had been eye-opening. Taking a deep breath as instructed, she momentarily considered that if she hadn't been as chilled out as she was now, she might well have gone into UHLS for that.

'Finding a comfortable seated position on your mats, place your bolster directly behind your spine and lie down on it.'

Emily copied Angela as she placed the bolster behind her. They were instructed to slowly lower their bodies back onto the bolster so that it was placed under the spine from their tailbones to their heads, bring the soles of their feet together, and let their inner thighs fall open. Emily was in knots and felt completely out of sorts with the position. It was way beyond anything she'd practised in the flat. She didn't dare look left or right; she knew she'd be the only one having trouble. Angela encouraged them to close their eyes and let the move massage their heart.

Emily kept her eyes open, not feeling it at all. Catching Angela's eyes when she should have had them closed like the rest of the class, she quickly looked away. Putting her head back down, she forced her body to lie over the bolster. It hurt and she grimaced. Angela got up and moved towards her. As she approached, Emily felt exposed, lying there with her legs open. Silently, Angela knelt down beside her, picked up Emily's blanket, folded it, and paused for Emily to lift her head up so she could place it under her. The pillow had an immediate effect. Emily's body relaxed with the pressure taken off her spine. Emily swallowed at the kindness of the gesture. It was thoughtful and oddly intimate. Before she could say thanks, Angela had already moved away from her, moving lightly on her feet. Emily watched the soft sway of her hips. It was possible the others didn't know she had got up as they often had long periods of silence.

Angela resumed her place at the front of the class. 'Feel the expansion of your pelvis, and the release of tension in your knees and ankles. Allow yourself to open up, taking a deep breath in.' She paused. 'And slowly breathing out.'

Emily focused on breathing with Angela. Her eyelids felt heavy. Telling herself not to fall asleep, she didn't know if she had ever felt as comfortable. Her mind was blank except for picturing Angela watching her, taking in every inch of Emily's body laid flat out before her, as if it was just the two of them in a more intimate setting. It felt as though Angela's sexy grey-blue eyes could see right through her and were doing just that.

A girl can dream, can't she?

Chapter 7

Angela loved Sundays, and this was starting off as a great one. The mood in the room was serene. The sun was shining. She had four lovely students to spend time with. It might not be everyone's happy place, but it was hers. It didn't feel like a job; she had to remind herself sometimes that she was technically working. If she wasn't taking a class, she'd be at one or doing yoga on her own. If earning money wasn't necessary to live, she'd teach it for free.

She addressed the class. 'Nicely done, everyone. When you're ready, gently bring your awareness back to the room and open your eyes. Please take your time and come back to a sitting position.' The class took a few moments to sit back up. Sitting in the lotus position, Angela watched the class as they got into position. Waiting patiently, she tried not to rush anyone. 'For the last ten minutes, we are going to rest our bodies and minds in *Shavasana*. Lying with our backs down on the mat, let your arms and legs go heavy. Once you have found a comfortable position, allow your body and your mind to relax. That's it. Now slow down your thoughts and just breathe. The next few minutes will be silent.' Four bodies lay out before Angela. During *Shavasana*, Angela liked to hold the space for her students while they rested. For this, she remained as present as she could be and kept a watchful eye out on the group so they could be completely vulnerable. As they lay in front of her, she wondered about their lives: Erin with her mammoth fitness exploits, Louise with her big family, and Karen as a working mum. This was their time to take a time out from all their responsibilities.

Angela had been keeping an eye on her newest student

throughout the class and had seen Emily move into pose after pose with increasing skill. While Emily was still in the phase of getting yoga physically right, Angela could see she was a fast learner. The sight of Emily trying to master basic techniques triggered a longing in Angela for when she had first discovered yoga all those years ago. Yes, her practice had deepened, and she had become a teacher – it was now her whole life – yet that sense of newness would never be there again.

You could only fall in love with yoga for the first time once: that sense of a whole new world opening up; that first glimpse into the spirituality underlying it; the deepening of your practice; the process of caring about not being able to do the moves right, to realising that it doesn't matter; and then suddenly finding that it all clicks one day when you're so in flow with the moves and your body. There was nothing like it. At least for Angela, anyway. Emily had all that in front of her if she wanted it.

There was a difference in her today. Emily, who was now lying very still, apart from the slow, steady rise and fall of her chest, seemed more relaxed. The muscles in her face had gone soft, and her mouth was slightly open. Angela allowed her eyes to linger on Emily for a few moments. This was not something she normally did. At all. Emily was wearing tight-fitting short black leggings and a dark red tank top with a barbell on the front. The clothes hugged her figure in all the right places. Angela's eyes lingered on her narrow waist, before moving upwards to her chest. Emily was attractive. Objectively speaking. At that she caught herself. What was she doing? Looking at a student like that was totally inappropriate.

With a shake of the head, she looked to the rest of the group and refocused. Closing her eyes, Angela mentally cast a white light around each individual, envisioning the light wrap around their bodies, from head to toe and from side to side. Then she imagined the light was around all of them, together, protected, loved and whole. Holding them in the light that she mentally created was probably her deepest spiritual practice, but she never told anyone that she ever did this sort of thing; she didn't want to be considered too weird. It was important for people to like you and for everyone to get along, especially now that she had her own business.

When the time was right, she asked the students to wake up. There was a long pause with no movement and no words. Erin, Emily, and Karen stirred, but Louise continued to lie where she was, not moving anywhere. Angela didn't know if she was asleep and if she should wake her; Louise had fallen asleep in class once before. Karen broke with convention and did it for her.

'Ahem.'

Louise's eyes flew open. 'Oh! Sorry, I did it again!'

'It doesn't matter. Glad you're back with us.' Angela smiled.

'Quite the snore you've got on you,' said Karen, winking at Erin, Emily, and Angela.

'I didn't,' said Louise, normally so dignified, with a look of regret.

'Just having you on; you were fine,' said Karen, looking thrilled.

Emily clasped her shins, grinning. Angela liked seeing her smile. There was something so pure and sweet about it.

'It's no reflection on you, Angela. If anything, it means it's working for me,' said Louise. 'To be honest with you, I feel more peaceful in this hour than I do at any time during the rest of the week. Sometimes I get a little too peaceful, that's all.'

Angela shrugged. 'It's supposed to be relaxing. You're fine.' Bringing her hands together, she bowed her head.

'Namaste.' Opting not to do a sound vibration to end the class, maybe she had been more affected by Emily's giggling than she realised.

'Thanks, Angela. I can really feel my lower back easing up now,' said Erin, standing up, looking ready to go.

'You're welcome. How did the race go?' Angela let the others know that Erin had competed in a twenty-four-hour mountain bike endurance race in the Highlands.

'I was twelfth out of forty, so not bad. I cramped up a bit on the last leg, I don't know if I got my hydration quite right. I wasn't sure I was going to be able to finish, but I made it.'

'Still, it's some feat to have achieved. Well done!' said Karen.

'Thanks. I was quite pleased.'

'You should be very proud.' Angela smiled.

'You young ones, I don't know where you get the energy from,' said Louise.

'Neither do I, to be honest.' Erin laughed. 'I'll see you next week; I've got to head off quickly today.' Erin nipped into the changing room, picked up her bag and dashed off. 'Bye, all. Cheers.'

Karen and Louise went off to the changing room, leaving Emily alone with Angela in the studio. Emily was kneeling down, taking a sip of water.

'Thank you,' said Emily. 'I think I might actually have enjoyed that.'

Angela was grinning. 'You're very welcome. No giggles today?'

'No giggles.' Emily held her gaze. 'I was too busy following your every word and trying to breathe along with you.'

'That's excellent.'

Emily got up and started putting things away then moved into the changing room. Karen and Louise came back through, still locked in conversation. Angela waited for everyone in the café. The three of them came through together, Emily now involved in the conversation and holding herself that bit taller. She was about the same height as Angela, slightly taller than average.

'Would anyone like a cup of tea or coffee? I have an hour until my next class. It'll be on the house.'

'Oh, that's so kind of you, Angela, thank you, but I've got to get back home. We're going to a country park this afternoon. That giant treehouse is all my kids have been talking about all week,' said Karen.

'Sounds like fun,' said Angela.

'I'd love nothing more, but I'm looking after my other daughter's children today,' said Louise.

'Just watch you don't do too much, Louise. Even Supergranny needs a break sometimes,' said Karen.

'I'll have the next few weeks off, so I can't really complain.'

'Oh, in that case, I'd better not keep you,' said Angela. 'Emily? Would you like to stay?'

Emily blushed, which was interesting. 'Yes, I can stay, that would be lovely. Thanks.'

Karen and Louise left. Emily stood awkwardly again, looking around the café, as Angela went behind the counter. 'Did you want to try the coffee?'

'Actually, I'd prefer tea. Coffee would be too stimulating now. I feel all Zen and I don't want to ruin it.'

Angela laughed. Emily was funny. And also very cute. Cute and undeniably sexy.

What the hell are you thinking!?

After a long pause she found some words. Any words. 'What sort of tea would you like?'

'What sort?'

'Herbal tea, normal tea—'

'Oh, yeah. A normal tea with a wee bit of milk, if you have

53

it, thanks.'

'I do,' said Angela.

With some hesitation, Emily finally picked a seat and sat down, obviously admiring the surroundings. It brought Angela so much pride to see that look on people's faces in her studio. Seeing it on Emily's face, for some reason, felt that bit more satisfying. Important.

'It's so peaceful here. I love it.'

'I love that it makes you feel like that. That's kind of exactly what I was aiming for. I also love having the café as well as the studio. I hang out here all day. It's like a second home to me.'

'It's got a great feel about it,' said Emily.

Angela put two mugs on the counter and placed a green tea bag in one and a black tea bag in the other. Both organic, both unbleached and plastic free. She poured the hot water and added some cow's milk for Emily. Angela only drank oat or almond milk but bought cow's milk for customers. Guests. It dawned on her that it didn't feel like Emily was a customer. Why was that? But of course she was! Joining Emily at the table, she gave her the *Star Trek* mug with "Make It So, Number One" written above a picture of the starship *Enterprise*.

'Thanks.' Emily slid the mug towards her and held onto the handle.

'So, you enjoyed the class a bit better today?'

'I did! I really did. How did you get so good at all that?'

'Years of practice. Regular practice. Being unable to cope with life unless I practised. And teacher training, of course.'

'That ought to do it. Seriously, it's like you're a supple leopard.'

Angela laughed. 'Maybe my body's just naturally good at it. And that's why I do it so much.'

Emily took a sip and put her mug back down gently.

'Honest. I like that.'

'And you? What do you like about it now that you've completed two of my classes?'

Emily thought for a moment. 'I like the meditative side to it. I feel quite calm right now.'

'Yoga can be great for helping with one's mental health.'

Emily nodded. 'I see that now.'

'You didn't before?'

'Maybe I always thought it was a bit pointless.'

Angela shrugged. 'That's why it's good to try new things.'

'I have a question though. How do you balance on one foot the way you do? My legs are so wobbly, but you looked as poised as a statue.'

'Push your big toe into the ground.'

Emily laughed. 'Sounds simple enough.'

'And lots of falling over until you find something that works for you.'

'I liked your website by the way. Now that I've met you in person, I can tell it's your voice. Did you do it by yourself?'

Angela blew softly on her green tea to cool it down. 'I did, yeah. It was a bit of a nightmare getting it all organised, to be honest.' She paused, shifting her legs up on the chair to sit in the lotus position. She bobbed the tea bag by the string, trying to get more of the flavour through. 'Do you live quite close to here then? I remember you saying last week you were not far.'

Emily smiled. Angela was struck again by how beautiful a smile it was. 'Yeah, only five minutes away. I've been living here for years. I like this part of town, always have.'

'Me too. Are you from Edinburgh?'

'Yeah. Lived here all my life.'

'You?'

'I grew up in Perth. I've been living in Edinburgh since I was about eighteen. It feels like home to me now.'

Emily smiled and nodded encouragingly. Angela continued. 'Whenever I leave, I can't wait to get back here. I miss it too much. Then when you're on your way back in and you see the Pentlands and Arthur's Seat and the castle and get goose bumps, you know you're home.'

'You sound like a tour guide.'

'Ha! Well, I do like walking up Arthur's Seat. It's a great place to watch the sunset. I go up there when I need to clear my mind or when I'm feeling a bit off. It's a great place to sit. And just ... be, you know. Most people leave it for the tourists, but I still love it up there.'

Emily smiled again. 'I know exactly what you mean. It is such a treat having it there. We're very lucky.'

Angela gazed into Emily's eyes. She knew hardly anything about Emily but had a sense that they were on the same frequency.

'I love the hills around Edinburgh too. I never get up there as much as I'd like.' Emily looked down at her hands. 'I used to love going out on long walks.'

'What changed?'

'I'm not sure. Life.'

'Well, they're still there. All you've got to do is go.'

Emily was quiet for a few moments. Her dark hair fell in front of her face. When she looked back up, she tucked one side behind her ear. 'What made you open your own place?'

Angela liked the directness of the question and was curious at how easy it felt to talk and open up to her. 'It's always been a dream of mine. I've been doing yoga since I was a teenager. I feel so lucky to actually get the chance to have my own place. I took over the lease here after saving for years. I've put everything into this business. It's my life. I spend all my time here, and I mean *all*. I love it though. I guess you've got to, to be willing to take on the financial risk, right?'

'You've got to love it, that's for sure,' said Emily.

'And have an appetite for risk.'

'Why did you call it Heart Yoga?'

Angela smiled, enjoying the depth of Emily's questions. 'Well, my original idea was to have my initials in the title, but then I decided I probably shouldn't call it Yoga AF.'

Emily burst out laughing. Her eyes lit up. 'You should have gone with that.'

They sat there looking at each other, smiling, for a few moments.

Emily cleared her throat loudly. 'I love that you chose this part of town, by the way. Do you get many locals in? Other local riff raff like me?' A playful look crept onto her face for a second. While she smiled and acted fine, Angela sensed an unease in Emily under the surface. The sort of unease that would lead to that negative self-talk Angela had heard come out of her mouth the week before.

Angela laughed. 'Well it was a little cheaper, that helped. And yeah, I do get in the locals. They're brilliant. You're the only one who's caused such a ruckus, though.'

Emily went pale. 'I'm so sorry about that. Honestly, I can't understand myself sometimes.'

Angela shook her head. 'It wasn't that bad, and I'm the teacher. There I've said it. You're off the hook.'

Emily stared at Angela looking sceptical, as if assessing her level of sincerity. 'I guess you're right.'

'It's probably the most interesting thing that's happened around here since I've opened.'

Emily laughed at that and her face lit up. 'Is it, now.' She took another sip of tea, holding Angela's eyes.

Angela felt herself blush and had to look away.

This could be dangerous.

Chapter 8

'Bring the fullness of your energy to this moment. Hold this position now and breathe,' said Angela. The class was lined up in front of her, squatting with their hands together in front of them in a prayer position. Faces were locked in concentration, eyes directly forward. Some were bright red. 'If you have to take a rest from the position, know that you can do so.' No one moved. Angela was impressed at the determination. 'Power Yoga is as much about physically bringing your all to class today as it is about honing and honouring the power within you. This is the power you bring to your life.' Angela had certain things she always liked to say in different classes. She didn't want them to become repetitive and predictable, so she rotated a few lines here and there to keep her regulars constantly surprised and stimulated. 'Let your spine lengthen and bring its natural strength to the situation. Create space when you exhale. Your spine is your backbone and your backbone will see you through the hard times in life. You've got this. Breathe deeply and hold.' Angela sat comfortably in her deep squat position, her bum close to the floor, heels on the ground, her toes pointing straight ahead.

The next section of the class was going to be even harder. Hopefully, it wouldn't be too difficult. She had to push the students in Power Yoga. 'Take one last deep breath in,' she paused, 'and out.' She exhaled loudly to encourage the others to feel free to do the same. 'Putting both hands in front of you on the mat, I want you to walk your hands forward to take a high plank position.' She demonstrated the move and the class followed.

Once everyone was in position, Angela stopped and took watch. Emily's face was crimson and her breathing heavy. She had been moving in time with her fellow classmates, looking every bit as competent as they did today. She also seemed considerably more concentrated. She had been coming to lots of classes and her practice had progressed substantially.

'Make sure your elbows and wrists are in a straight line below your shoulders. Keep your back in neutral spine and try to squeeze your belly button towards your spine. Hold this position while you breathe.' She paused. 'We are going to stay here for two minutes. Now is the time to give it your full attention.'

The class were silent as they struggled. Erin sat down on her mat, which was unlike her. But Angela knew she'd been training hard recently, in preparation for another big endurance race. It was understandable she wasn't pushing it today. Not long later, Louise dropped to her knees too, looking up at Angela, shaking her head in defeat. The clock ticked as the students worked. 'You are doing brilliantly. Keep this going. This is your moment. Keep breathing.' Emily's back was bending upwards and shaking from side to side. Angela expected her to drop to her knees, but she didn't. 'Feel the length of your spine and the strength in your heart. If you start to shake or if you're losing that neutral spine position, please drop to your knees and rest.' Emily didn't drop. She kept going, nearly doing Downward Dog, looking barely able to support herself. Angela debated whether or not to single her out. She didn't. 'There's no harm in stopping if you have to,' she said to the class.

Thirty seconds to go. Most had fallen to their knees. Some sprawled out on the mat, breathing heavily, others were still catching their breath. Only Emily and two others were still going. Emily's face was contorted in pain.

'Not long to go, you are all doing well.'

Angela watched the last ten seconds and called it to a stop. 'That's wonderful class. When you are ready, let your knees fall to the ground and take a few moments to centre yourself. That was a hard one.' The remainder still going stopped immediately and there were cries of relief. But Emily remained on her hands and toes. Angela was slightly annoyed Emily was pushing herself past her limits.

What is she doing?

It wasn't like Emily to ignore her instructions either. Angela went over to Emily and crouched down next to her. Her eyes were closed; her head was somewhere else. A bead of sweat dripped from Emily's nose onto the mat. Angela put a hand on Emily's shoulder.

'Emily.' No response. 'Emily.' Angela tapped her back this time.

'I'm trying to break my record.'

'Your back is rounded and you're shaking all over the place. You should stop.'

'Oh, sorry.' Emily dropped her knees to the ground. She leant forward on her hands, still in her own world.

Angela left her to it and went back to the front of the class. 'Please join me standing up, and we'll get set up for *Vriksasana.*' Angela stood tall in front of the class and began. 'Standing at the front of your mat,' the class moved forward almost in unison, 'that's right, we'll begin in Mountain Pose. Take a conscious breath here.' She paused. 'Now lift and hover your left leg above the ground, then rest the sole of your left foot on the inside of your right leg. If it's available to you to place your foot higher up your leg you can do so, but it's equally fine to place your foot lower down your leg also. Bring your hands together at your heart. Now press your right foot down, pressing your big toe into the ground, and squeezing your core for balance, then stretch your arms up to the sky.' Everyone was getting it. 'That's wonderful, class. Imagine you are a tree, with roots all under the floor.' Angela let the class fall silent and pretended they were a forest.

A thud broke the silence. Emily lay flat out on the ground. Her eyes were closed. Angela was at Emily's side in an instant, as were the others. Angela shook Emily's shoulder and called her name, but to no avail.

'Is she conscious?' asked Louise.

Angela touched Emily's cheek, before checking the pulse on her carotid artery. 'I don't think so, but she has a strong pulse.' She counted for a short while before rolling her over onto her side and placing her in the recovery position. 'Someone, call an ambulance.' Erin was already on it; she came running back from the changing room pulling her phone from her bag. Louise, sitting on the other side of Emily, held Emily's hand. 'I think she's just fainted.'

'Maybe. Let's not take any chances,' said Angela.

Angela was first aid qualified and had gained numerous badges in the Girl Guides, yet, in this moment, she was frozen. Her throat felt thick with fear, and she was sweating and breathing heavily. Wishing she reacted cooler to stress, she consciously tried to calm down and not panic. Louise was most likely right. She'd been warned when she was training that students fainting was a possibility, but it had never happened before in any of her classes. The sight of Emily's limp body below her was distressing. Her other students looked on, worried. Had she really pushed them this far? She kept a hand on Emily's shoulder, gently shaking it.

Emily rolled over.

The class, now crowding around, sighed in relief.

'Emily, are you okay?' said Angela, leaning over her. 'Emily, breathe with me.' Angela made exaggerated breathing noises, even for her.

Emily's eyes were half open, her gaze unfocused. Her head lolled from one side to the other. 'Huh?' her eyes landed on a very concerned Angela above her. 'What's going on?' said Emily, gazing into Angela's eyes.

Angela squeezed Emily's warm hand and held onto it. 'You fainted. How do you feel?'

'What?' She brought a hand up to her head. 'How's that possible?'

'You went down like a sack of potatoes, luvvie,' said Louise.

'Oh. Sorry.' Emily's face and neck started to redden.

'We better get you to a hospital,' said Angela.

Louise looked sceptical. Erin looked on, her face fixed in a permanent grave look of concern and a hint of confusion; she had likely pushed herself to much higher limits on numerous occasions. Angela helped Emily sit up, still holding her hand. 'How does your head feel?'

'Fuzzy … as if it's not attached to my body.'

'Here, sit forward,' Angela helped Emily sit forward. 'Put your head between your knees and give it a few minutes. It should pass.' Angela knelt over Emily. 'Did you call an ambulance?' Angela asked Erin.

'I was about to, but then she came around.'

'Hmm,' said Angela, unsure, watching Emily closely.

'I'm fine,' Emily lifted her head and looked around at the worried expressions surrounding her. 'Thank you.' She went to stand up, then stumbled slightly.

'No, no. I think you should stay down for a bit longer,' said Angela.

Emily frowned. The blood and oxygen almost visibly returning to her brain, fuelling her back to normal. 'Please don't let an ambulance arrive. Really, I'm fine.'

Angela looked around. As the class was nearly finished it didn't feel appropriate to continue. She addressed everyone else. 'I think that's all for today, folks. Do take your time to cool down before you leave. And please help yourself to water.'

Louise stood over Emily with her hands on her hips, still surveying the situation intently. 'I've seen my fair share of fainting in my time. You'll be fine. Make sure you get plenty of rest and have a biscuit or two.' Louise spoke with a degree of finality on the matter, and seemingly satisfied, she walked off to get changed. The others in the class took Louise's lead, casting sympathetic looks Emily's way, as they put their equipment back and went about their normal routine for ending class. As the class dispersed, Angela let go of Emily's hand, moved back, and resumed a normal personal distance. She was lost for words for a few moments, and it didn't escape her attention how easy it had been to move into Emily's space. Emily spoke first.

'Thank you. I've never felt so safe coming around from fainting before.'

'Have you fainted many times before?'

'Once or twice.'

'Look, I don't have another class for a few hours. Will you let me get you home, at least?'

'That's really not necessary; I live around the corner.'

'No, I insist. But first I think you should rest here for a bit before we get you moving.'

'Well, if you insist.' Emily smiled at Angela and looked directly at her now.

The hairs on her body stood up as she swallowed hard. What was happening to her? Emily was in a vulnerable state. It was Angela's duty to take care of her, yet her feelings felt totally out of her control and were quite unwelcome. Why was she unable to stop it? 'Good,' said Angela hesitantly. 'Wait here, I'll go and check everybody else is getting away okay.'

'Not moving a muscle,' said Emily, holding her hands up.

As Angela walked away from her, she got the feeling Emily was watching her leave. It wasn't an unpleasant feeling. At the door, Angela made the usual pleasantries and waved people goodbye. The door swung open and shut continuously. Louise hovered, then turned to Angela with a serious face. 'I'd watch her for a little bit. Do you know if there's anyone you could call for her? I don't think she should be on her own.'

'Oh my God, I should have—'

'You're on it, Angela. We can all see that.'

Angela wasn't convinced. She was getting it all wrong. Emily made her feel different. Like she wasn't just looking after a student. Like she was her responsibility. Even though there was absolutely no reason for that to be the case. They barely knew each other. 'I'll ask her who to call. I'll sort it. I might even cancel my next class or get someone to cover.'

'You'll work it out.'

'Louise, thank you. You're so wise.'

'Forty years as an A&E nurse does that to you.'

After seeing Louise away, Angela went back through to find Emily flat on her back with her knees bent, still on the pale side.

'How are you feeling now?'

'Oh, hey. I think I'm back to my normal self again, if that's ever an achievement.'

Angela could tell Emily was pretending to be better than she was. 'I'm glad you're feeling a bit better, but I still need to keep an eye on you for a bit. Is there anyone I can call? Let them know you've fainted and need a wee bit of looking after today?'

Emily's face went paler; a sad look crept across her face. 'No. I don't want you to call anyone.'

'Um, your parents?'

'No.'

'Oh. Okay. Well, I'm more than happy to get you home and see that you are okay.'

'Don't you have things to do? Honestly, it's fine. I'll just take it easy.'

Angela sat down next to Emily. 'Emily. I'm taking you home. In fact, I'm calling a taxi.'

Emily looked like she was about to protest and then stopped, as if internally accepting the offer. 'Okay. Thank you. I live near the park.'

'Good.' Angela smiled. 'Two secs.'

Angela called the taxi company's number. There was a long pause on the line when she told the person in the taxi office where it was going to.

'It will be with you as soon as possible,' said the taxi operator.

Angela thanked her and hung up.

'Did they agree to such a short ride?'

'Just about. Now, let's get you up.'

Emily pushed herself up but stumbled again, unsteady in her movements.

Angela stepped closer to her. 'Can I help you at all?'

'No, it's all right.' Emily headed towards the changing room.

Angela's phone rang twice. Taking a quick look out of the window, she saw the black cab pulling up. 'It's here. But take your time.' Angela dashed about turning things off. She grabbed her bag and checked she had her keys. Emily walked slowly to the door, almost dragging her feet.

Angela allowed her to go out first, and then she put the alarm on. The two women approached the taxi. Angela opened the door for Emily. She peeked her head in from the pavement. 'Hi. Sorry, we'll just be a sec.'

The driver turned and spoke through the hole in the

barrier, mostly addressing Emily. 'You doin' all right?'

'Yes, thanks. Just embarrassing myself,' mumbled Emily as she got in.

'She fainted,' said Angela, still at the door.

'Sure she doesn't need to go to A&E?'

'I don't need to go to hospital. Sitting for four hours in a waiting room is not going to help. I'm fine. A little lightheaded if anything.'

'What is it with you girls and fainting?'

Angela got into the taxi and slammed the door shut, perhaps harder than necessary. The smell of taxi hit Angela's nose. It struck her how all black cabs seemed to smell of the same cheap air fresheners.

'Where to ladies?'

'Homer Drive,' they said together.

'You know where I live?'

'Yeah,' she paused. Why had she remembered her address? 'I remember your address from when you signed up. I guess it stuck in my head.'

'That's weird.'

'Sorry, yes. It's a bit weird. I don't know why, but I remembered.'

Emily smiled, showing those dimples in her cheeks. Her eyes lit up, framing her face as the colour continued to return to it.

'That's very observant of you.'

Chapter 9

The taxi pulled out and they sat there in silence. Angela was very conscious of Emily sitting next to her. Emily closed her eyes and Angela turned her head to look out the window, aware of her desire to keep looking at Emily. The taxi proceeded to take the long way around to get back over the train tracks. A few minutes later, the taxi jolted around the corner onto Homer Drive. Using her tummy muscles to fight against the momentum, Angela prevented herself from being thrown over onto Emily's lap.

'Just here's great, thanks,' said Emily.

The taxi came to a halt and the driver punched the meter button. 'Four pounds, please.'

Emily reached for her bag.

'No, let me,' said Angela.

Emily sat back in her seat shaking her head and puffing out her cheeks. 'It's really not necessary.'

'Please,' said Angela, poised at the edge of her seat. Not waiting for an answer, she gave the driver a five-pound note. 'Thanks. Keep the change.' Angela stepped out first and held the door open. Emily got out slowly, holding onto the handle until she had placed both feet on the pavement. The taxi pulled away. A cyclist passed them. It was enough to threaten Emily's balance.

'Can I help you there?' said Angela.

Emily smiled again. 'Yeah. You could, thanks. I'm still a bit unsteady.'

She held out an arm, and Emily linked her arm in hers, then led them towards the flats.

'I'm over here. Number seventy-six.'

They went into the tenement and up the two flights of stairs to Emily's flat. The building was similar to Angela's, with its wide staircase and patterned tiles on the walls. With each step Angela grew less sure of why she had insisted on taking Emily home. Emily was fast getting back to normal but seemed a little awkward as well, as if she was purposefully walking slower. Still, it still seemed as though it was the right thing to do, and it was good to know Emily was okay. But deep down she knew she was just thrilled to spend a bit of time with Emily away from the studio. Angela waited as Emily rooted around in her bag for her keys, giving a shy smile when she pulled them out and half held them up in a sort of victory.

'Found them.'

Angela followed Emily in and waited as Emily shut the door. She took off her coat, glanced around the large hall, noting the box of empty wine bottles in a tub by the door and the wooden floors with a Persian runner she quite liked. The style of the flat wasn't unlike her own.

'Can I get you anything?' said Emily. 'Tea?'

'No, let me. That's why I'm here. Why don't you sit down?'

'I will. But first, I'm going to get you a drink and then get changed. Take this sports bra off.'

'Okay then, sure.'

Emily walked into the small kitchen. 'What would you like?'

'Just some water, please.'

Angela watched Emily run the water from the tap and fill two glasses.

'There you go.' Emily smiled brightly as she handed a glass to Angela.

'Thanks.' Angela felt so out of place. 'I won't stay long.'

'Don't rush off. You've just got here. You're very welcome

to stay. It's so nice of you. I can't believe I fainted at yoga; who does that? And then my yoga teacher kindly escorts me home. This is awesome.'

'I'm just glad you're okay. Do you have any biscuits? Chocolate? Help get your blood sugar back up.'

'I do. Good idea.' Emily got out a packet of biscuits and offered her one.

'No, thanks.'

Emily took one for herself and left the packet beside the kettle. 'I'm going to get changed first. Do you want to wait in the living room? I'll be back in a sec.'

'Sure.'

Emily wandered off down the hall after showing Angela where to go. Moving into the airy living room and sitting down on the well-used sofa, she heard a drawer thud shut from down the hall. Angela looked around the room. Cushions of various shapes, sizes and patterns were scattered everywhere. One was on the floor beside the coffee table. Another one was on a chair at the table by the window. Mugs sat on nearly every surface, and a single empty plate with a sad-looking fork resting on it lay on the tabletop. A box of Nag Champa incense sticks, the same type she had in the studio, sat on a shelf in the Edinburgh press. A notebook was open beside her on the sofa, but Angela didn't read what it said. Emily reappeared, wearing soft black leggings and an oversized green woolly jumper. She seemed better than before. Her face softened as she took in Angela sitting in her living room.

'Sorry to keep you waiting. I brought in the biscuits.' Emily wiggled the packet before placing it on the coffee table.

Angela took a biscuit from the packet, out of politeness. 'I like your place. It's lovely.'

'It's not bad sometimes. But it's a mess today. I would have tidied but … um. And now I've no energy to pretend like it was in order, so I'm just going to sit here for a bit. Normally, I'd be stressing about something like that by the way.'

'Don't stress. It's fine, you should see my place.'

'Where do you live?'

Emily caught sight of the open notebook beside Angela and promptly picked it up, closed it, and put in on the coffee table.

Angela pretended she hadn't noticed. 'Around the corner, actually.'

'No way.'

Angela nodded. 'My flat's a lot like yours. They're all so similar, aren't they, around here?' She took a sip of water.

'It's not mine. I wish it was. I'm still renting. I'm not sure when I'll ever be able to afford to buy a flat in this area.'

'It's an awesome flat to call home, though,' said Angela. 'Whether your name is on the bit of paper or not, you get to enjoy it.'

Emily laughed, good-naturedly. 'You always look on the positive side, don't you? I like that about you.'

'Thanks. I guess I don't know how to switch off from yoga teacher mode.'

'Maybe it's just who you are.'

Angela took another bite of her biscuit. 'How's your head now?'

Emily copied her and picked up another biscuit. 'Much better.' She chewed for a few moments. 'I don't know what happened. One second, I was doing a plank; I was pushing it a bit but ... and the next, when I stood up, I felt my head go all weird. It's such a strange sensation, the oxygen leaving your brain ... have you ever fainted?'

'Yes. Twice. I know how scary it can be. It takes me a while to recover.'

'It's icky, isn't it?'

'Yeah. I'm glad you're recovering quickly. You probably should rest up for today though. Did you have any plans?'

'Nope. No plans.' Emily paused. She seemed sad. 'No life. Things haven't been going that great lately.'

'Do you want to talk about it?'

Emily looked off to the side.

After a few moments, Angela held her hands up. 'Or if you'd rather not that's all good too. But if you change your mind you know where I am. I'm all about bringing some light into people's lives, as corny as that sounds, that's why I do what I do. To help people.'

'No, yes, thanks. I … I wasn't expecting this. I thought I'd go to yoga and keep to myself. But you've been so nice and welcoming and lovely.'

'I aim to please.'

A quiet fell between them. It wasn't awkward. If anything, it felt entirely natural and Angela was starting to relax about being there.

Emily puffed out her cheeks. 'I was made redundant right before Christmas and I've been stuck in a rut ever since. I was at the company for a long time. I got a redundancy package which is helping to keep me going while I figure things out.'

'Losing a job is one of the most stressful things that can happen to someone. It's okay if you're struggling with it.'

'Thanks. I wasn't in a good place before I got sacked though. When things at work started to tank, it got worse. Well. It was a horrible company to work for, but that's by the by now. For ages leading up to it, I was lurching from one day to another. I was constantly on edge, even though I was absolutely killing it in the job. I worked my arse off for them even when I was really struggling with my mental health. The stress of it all really took its toll.'

'What was going on with your mental health?'

'I'd been struggling with anxiety and depression. I still am. I don't think I have a mental health condition, but I've been struggling with symptoms, if you know what I mean. I know it will pass. Anyway, when I got sacked, I couldn't cope. I know I reacted badly to it, but I couldn't help it. Who knows, maybe I'm just another whingeing millennial.'

'Of course you're not.'

'People think I'm moping around. I've heard "just snap out of it" way too many times.'

'Some people can't understand about mental health issues. It's not their fault.'

'My mum has depression. Which makes me anxious. You know.' Emily paused. 'I guess I worry that getting it is inevitable or something.'

'That must be difficult.'

Emily blushed. 'I feel like I'm baring my soul to you, and we've only just met.'

Angela smiled warmly. 'I've been told I have that effect on people. Yoga teacher and therapist, all rolled into one. You don't need to talk about anything you don't want to though. I just want to know that you're okay.'

'No … I like talking to you. And I'm not – okay – I guess.'

Angela genuinely felt pained to know that she wasn't okay. Emily was quiet. After a minute or so she spoke again. 'I've had this feeling, this sharp pain in the centre of my chest. It comes with the thought that I'm falling behind, that I'm losing at life. I don't have anyone: no partner, no children, no pets to look after. No one needs me. All my friends are busy getting married and having babies. Sometimes it feels like I'm drowning. Like literally, drowning. I can't shake it. All I had was my career and now I don't even have that. Some days, I haven't even been able to get out of bed.'

'Have you been to your GP?'

Emily looked at her, full of unexpressed pain. 'I don't want to get stuck on medication. I know there must be a way to sort my life out that's healthier than that. My GP suggested I should start exercising and my best friend Anna kept recommending I do yoga and start meditating. So, I started running again and joined your studio. The only problem is that I'm running and yoga-ing every single day now, sometimes twice a day. Maybe that's why I fainted.'

'It's understandable you want to try and get better. I know it will get better. In my experience dealing with stuff at the root of the problem is much better than taking pills. So, I commend you for taking the approach you're taking. But I do get that medication works and is necessary for some people. And it's good to have the option.'

'It's a lot of work managing my mental health. I know that sounds crazy. But I'll get there.'

'You will. How's the meditation going?'

'Well, since your classes I've been getting into it a bit. I try to meditate here, but I'm not really sure what I'm doing, and I don't know if it's helping. I mean, when I try to sit and empty my mind, I can never do it. It brings up too much stuff. It's too hard.'

'What do you think helps the most?'

Emily crossed her arms and spoke softly, curled up on her sofa, the colour now back in her cheeks, looking as youthful and fresh as she'd seen her. Still, Angela sensed there was something deeply troubling her and that she hadn't yet got to the real root of the problem.

'I don't know. Your dulcet tones during class.'

Angela blushed.

'I know that I want to feel good about life again: to reach my goals, handle stress better. I just feel like a total failure, Angela ...' Emily looked away and bit on her bottom lip.

'You're not a failure. No one is. Failing at things is actually a good thing. The more mistakes you make, the more you

73

learn.'

'I must be a genius then.'

Angela tilted her head. 'And it's the getting back up that counts the most.'

'Yep. That's the toughest part.'

'We're a lot stronger than we realise. No matter what's happened to us in the past, we can recover from it. No matter what it is.'

'I do hope you're right about that.' There was a pause. 'My girlfriend of three years cheated on me with our friend last year. This may have been the trigger. The whole thing sent me into a spiral. I'm totally over her now by the way. That's for sure. Some things just can't be unseen.'

Angela stopped breathing for a second and let Emily's words sink in. The hairs on the back of her neck stood up. She recognised that she was far too excited to learn about Emily's sexuality than she should be. 'That's horrible. I'm so sorry to hear that. That sounds very painful.'

'Cheers. It was all a bit messy. We used to live together. Here. I threw her out.'

'Her loss, I mean you're—'

'Yeah, I'm a right catch. An unemployed twenty-nine-year-old with issues, who faints in yoga ... sure.'

'Emily. That negative self-talk isn't going to get you anywhere.'

'How do you do it?' asked Emily. 'How are you so calm and confident and positive? When I look at you, I see perfection. You've got everything going for you. I wish I had just a slice of what you've got.'

Angela mulled over what Emily had said and felt herself go into teacher mode again. 'You really shouldn't compare yourself to others. There's so much we don't see; we'll never know what it's like to have lived someone else's life. All it does is completely rob us of happiness.' Stopping, she took a breath and remembered she wasn't in front of a class at the moment. It was just the two of them, in Emily's home. 'I am most certainly not perfect. I'm just a person. I'm flawed and have insecurities like anyone else.' She paused. 'And the studio is not doing that well, for example. So, there's that.'

Emily gasped. 'I'm sorry. I had no idea.'

'Hopefully, I'm a better yoga teacher than I am a small business owner.'

'You're an amazing yoga teacher. I'm sure it's just the tricky start up process you're still going through, right? That's all.'

'Thank you. I hope that's all it is.'

Emily smiled at her. She really loved seeing that.

On a roll now, Angela continued. 'And I've not been in a relationship for years. Society tells us successful people couple-up, and I'm not. I'm on my own, and I'm happy with that.'

Emily nodded empathetically.

'Also, I'm quite femme so people often assume I'm straight. I actually identify as a lesbian.'

Emily kept a neutral face, seemingly not as flustered by the same information as she had been about her.

'But I am grateful for my life and I know that I am in a privileged position.'

Emily was still quiet.

Angela felt vulnerable. What was she doing in a client's house talking about herself, her life, her business?

'Well now I just think you're even more amazing.'

The dimension between them had changed. Angela felt she had crossed an invisible boundary in their relationship.

Angela stood up. 'I should get going.'

The colour drained from Emily's face, but she recovered quickly. 'Okay. I really am grateful that you helped me get home, Angela. I'm sorry I fainted; it must have upset everyone. And sorry I went on a bit; I tend to talk too much when I'm nervous. And I get nervous around you. Um, or maybe I'm still just a wee bit lightheaded, it's probably that, that would be better.'

'Emily, I'm happy that you're okay,' she could feel her voice grow more distant, 'I really would get some rest today if I were you. And call your parents. Take your time coming back to yoga, maybe a few days off it and the running might help. You have been doing a lot recently. It might be your body's way of telling you to slow down.' Angela winced internally at the matter-of-fact way she was talking.

Emily cleared her throat. 'Thanks, Angela. I can see you out.'

'Don't worry about it; you should stay resting. I'll see myself out. I hope you feel better soon.' Angela spun on her heels and headed for the door. 'Bye, Emily, take care.'

Chapter 10

Sitting at the table next to the bay window, Emily tapped a pen on her notebook. Fainting in yoga had been, ironically, a wake-up call. One minute she was fine, albeit working hard, and the next lightheaded and nauseated. It was like her head became disconnected from her body. But if she was being honest with herself, not feeling quite right had become so familiar. Feeling a little off was now so normal to her. She didn't sleep well, either suffering from insomnia or waking in the middle of the night with bad dreams. Nightmares. She always fell asleep on her back and when she woke up it felt as though her heart was exposed to the room, all the energy seeping from her chest, her heart racing. The only thing that made it better was to sleep on her front, arms below her body, protected.

With everyone at work, there was a serenity to the street and park below and, in some ways, within her. Without the usual to-do lists of work, her mind was free to wander where it liked. When she wasn't stuck in a negative spiral, she sometimes wrote in her notebook. If she was feeling good, she'd write about her five-year plan and endeavour to will it into being.

These days, however, she'd been thinking a lot about Angela and a full-blown crush had now developed. Getting to know her a bit better had been exhilarating. The confirmation that she was indeed into women was thrilling. That she had spotted a femme lesbian brought her great satisfaction. It was always good to get her gaydar validated. But that wasn't just it. There was something so healing and soothing about Angela. Chatting to her had felt so safe and honest. Angela was both vulnerable yet unreachable. Emily wanted to crack through that tough exterior somehow. There was so much more that she wanted to know about her now. Yes, she'd been fantasising about getting close to her, of doing naughty things on those yoga mats. It was leaving her breathless at times.

Being unemployed had its advantages: bingeing on Netflix and organising the music on her laptop – it also allowed her to make impromptu daytime visits to hot yoga teachers. Her plan was to go into the studio today and see if Angela was around. Mainly, she wanted to thank her for looking after her after she'd fainted. Having checked the class schedule, she knew there was a few free hours in the middle of the day with nothing on.

Surprising herself by following through with her plan, a couple of hours later she was peering through the window of the studio hoping in that moment she didn't look like a stalker. The sign on the door read closed. Angela sat at one of the tables, cupping her hands around the mug she held. Loosely wrapped around her neck was the most elegant scarf, very posh, and very expensive looking. How could someone look this good when they were not even trying? Tapping gently on the window, Angela flinched then smiled and relaxed when she saw that it was Emily.

Angela got up and opened the door, looking slightly confused. 'Hi there.'

'Hey,' said Emily, 'I'm not here for a class. I was hoping to have a quick chat?'

Angela's demeanour instantly changed, and she smiled the warmest smile Emily had ever seen from her. 'Of course! Yes. Sorry, I was in a paperwork hole. How's your head today?'

'Yeah, it's still on, just about.'

'Good, heads do come in handy sometimes.'

Emily laughed nervously. 'Not if yours is as highly-strung as mine, they don't.' Emily paused and looked into Angela's eyes. 'I wanted to say thank you properly for yesterday.' She handed Angela a box of chocolates. 'I was in a bad way and you were brilliant.'

'Oh wow,' Angela took the chocolates, and examined the luxurious square box with a wide beaming smile. 'These are so lovely; you really shouldn't have. It was the least I could do, given that you came to my studio and lost consciousness.'

'It wasn't your fault that I fainted. And you got me home safely. That was above and beyond.'

Angela shifted on her feet, still looking slightly caught off-guard and as if she wasn't used to visitors during the day. 'Sorry, sorry, come in. Why are we standing at the door?'

As Emily stepped in, the smell of freshly ground coffee reminded Emily of any other coffee shop except that this one was empty. Why was the sign on the door set to closed? Angela had an office. Piles of paper were sprawled across the table; glasses with thick tortoiseshell rims sat atop one. Emily sat down across the table from the seat that Angela had been working on, still feeling like a bit of an intruder. Angela took her seat, putting the box of chocolates on the table between them. She stretched an arm out to the side and rested it on the top of the next chair, oozing a seductive mixture of self-confidence and kindness.

'So, how's your day going?'

'Oh, me, I'm good. Really good. I had a long bath earlier. Epsom salts.'

'That's good.'

'It doesn't feel like I fainted yesterday.'

'You've recovered, then.'

'Yes. I'm sorry I … was so depressing. In my flat. Things are a bit … weird right now.'

Angela nodded, empathetically. Kindness seeped from her.

Emily felt so seen and so safe around her. 'At least you've got some time to yourself to work things out for a while.'

'True. And I do manage to fill the time, even though I'm not actually doing anything.'

'What were you doing before?'

'Business development and marketing.'

'Awesome. You must be very clever.'

Emily shook her head, dismissively. 'These days all I do is watch Netflix on the sofa. So, not very clever, really.' Emily realised how poor her self-esteem sounded when she verbalised what was going on inside her head.

Angela gave her another one of those empathetic looks.

'I don't know. I think not having anything to do is making me worse. I'm getting nowhere with job applications either. I can't tell if I'm in the middle of a mini-breakdown to be perfectly honest with you.'

Angela nodded again, still concerned, still listening.

'I've been so career focused and it's gotten me nowhere. All that effort I put into that company and they just threw a bit of money at me and tossed me away. It's the rejection that hurts the most. Fuck, I think I've spent the last five years recovering from one rejection after another.' Emily inhaled. Why did she always end up oversharing so much with Angela?

Angela's face was still kind, despite the instant offloading that Emily had unleashed on her again. 'I'm sorry things haven't turned out like you wanted them to.'

'It's okay. I can't even look back over the last few years and say it didn't all work out for the best. I'm starting to feel like I've been needing to go through this.'

'How so?'

'I've always been really worried about my ability to support myself. I don't have any sort of safety net from my family, so the pressure's always been on. I've probably been living in survival mode for a decade. On the plus side, it's driven me to achieve things, but on the downside, I haven't been entirely happy with what I've been doing. I've never had a spell like this before, where I can just be. Like lying in bed until noon like a teenager again and properly resting … like doing yoga. It just so happens that a lot of trauma and repressed emotions are coming up, so it's not the jaunty experience I thought it was going to be.'

'Wow. I think it sounds like you're exactly where you're supposed to be right now. The universe has a way of giving us the things we need the most, rather than the things we want. All we really need to do is to stay in the present moment, in total acceptance of what is.'

'Is that the new age yoga chat again? I love it. Honestly, it keeps me going during the classes. It gets me thinking, like really thinking. Sometimes I leave your classes not knowing what my name is, too busy contemplating the meaning of life and my very existence.'

Angela laughed. 'I didn't know it was having such an effect on you.'

Emily smiled and sat back in her chair, putting an arm across the back of the chair next to her, unconsciously mirroring Angela's position.

'Oh, I think you do.'

They held each other's eyes for a few moments before Angela glanced down at the table, breaking the connection.

'You made me faint.'

Angela returned her eyes to Emily's. 'Yes, right. I know, I'm really sorry about that.'

'I'm joking! I made myself faint really. You need to stop apologising.'

Angela laughed. 'Okay, we both need to stop apologising.'

A few moments of silence went by.

Emily broke it. 'I've come to the end of my pass now. Or

it runs out tomorrow. I wasn't sure if I should pay as I go or buy the ten-class package. I'd really like to keep coming.'

'Oh, sure. Did you need any help with the different options?' Angela sat forward, putting on her glasses.

The glasses really suited her. Emily stumbled over her words, distracted at how beautiful Angela was. 'Actually, I wasn't sure if your pricing options were as strong as they could be.' Emily paused, attempting to gauge Angela's reaction. Not seeing any negative signs at the comment, she continued. 'In all honesty, what you've got doesn't encourage me to commit. I want to, mind. I thought you might find the feedback helpful?'

Angela furrowed her brow. 'I do. But what do you mean? Tell me more.'

'Well, if I buy the twenty-one-day pass – and that's a huge amount of time by the way – when it runs out, like it has done now, then I can either go for the pay-as-you-go option at twelve pounds a session, which is quite a lot, or ten classes for one hundred. I see that you're trying to get people to go for the ten classes, but you can take six months to use them. Neither requires me to think of Heart Yoga as my go-to weekly or more yoga class.

'I see.'

'Sorry. I hope that's okay of me to say?'

'It's fine. It's good. Really. I need to know these things.'

'Well, I know that you are just starting out, and that you said the studio isn't doing so well. I guess I was wondering why you don't offer a monthly membership. I'd definitely sign up, and I'm sure many of the others would too. You already have a lot of regulars. It would mean changing your pricing structure completely, but I think it would give you more of a competitive edge.'

Angela seemed interested. 'Go on.'

'You need to start charging more and you need to tie

people in for longer; attract some of the core yoga-goers in Edinburgh, prise away some customers from those stuck-up-looking places, and while at the same time offer flexible options that might suit more people around this area. Tiers. It's all about tiers. Give three options. One super expensive, for all inclusive access, one quite low for just the basics, and one in the middle to attract the bulk of your customers. That's the one you really want to sell. It's what I would go for.'

'Because?' said Angela.

Emily paused. 'Because I think I might be falling for yoga.'

Angela blinked. Did she swallow? 'I told you you'd love it.'

Emily could feel her heart rate picking up and her head beginning to spin. *Have I really just confessed to having fallen in love with yoga? Was it just the yoga?*

Angela was lost in thought, nodding her head. 'What you said about pricing totally makes sense.'

'It's pretty basic marketing.'

'No, it's brilliant. You know, I'd pay for this advice. I have in the past, but I didn't find it that good. Put me off, actually.'

'What? Seriously?'

'Yeah. Have you considered consulting? Going in and fixing people's businesses? I've been to a few small business events and your advice is ten times better than anything I've heard there.'

Emily was speechless. She had not thought about consulting.

Angela continued. 'And I like your manner. You don't patronise; you just tell it straight without seeming judgemental. It's actually kind of motivating.'

Emily smiled, happy that she was able have such an impact on her yoga teacher. '*I* motivate *you* now, do I? That's quite the role reversal.'

Angela laughed, running a hand around the back of her

neck, baring the inside of her arm, and knocking her scarf out of place. 'Stranger things have happened.' She took her scarf off and put it down beside her.

Emily smiled, enjoying their conversation, and enjoying the soft definition of Angela's muscles underneath her V-neck T-shirt. She was having a hard time not glancing down at Angela's cleavage but managing.

'I've never seriously thought about setting up my own business, no. I've always been attracted to the idea but never really thought it would be something I'd actually consider doing.'

'You should. There's a huge demand for it. And people like it coming from well-meaning women rather than stuffy men in suits nearing retirement.'

Emily laughed, then took a moment to consider Angela's suggestion. It chimed with her. It made her feel ... expansive. And excited. She *had* always been frustrated at her ideas not being heard enough at work and having to report to a boss. Being a freelancer would mean more flexibility and the control to implement her ideas. Plus, she could add her personal touch to solving every client's unique problem. Combined with the latest technical know-how, she'd successfully seen numerous new business ideas through to fruition, albeit from the safety of a large organisation and with the resources it provides.

'What's the main business problem you face?'

'Apart from the fact that I just want to teach yoga rather than do the business side ... I'd say location. We're not in an area exactly known for a love of yoga. We don't get many passers-by that notice us and come in. Everything's driven from the website, and there are loads of other yoga studios in the city in more prominent locations.'

'So, you need to do two things: be more visible in the area and drive more traffic to your website.'

Angela nodded. 'Yes, but it's a lot harder than that.'

'Is it? Have you ever done any direct sales promotion in the area?'

'Well, no—'

'And are you using SEO?'

'What's that?'

'Angela, you must know about optimising search engines so that you get seen on Google.'

'Oh yeah, that's right. The website builder said something about that, but it was a right faff and I think I gave up on it.'

'It sounds like you need to look at it again, in that case.'

'I already have a million things to do, I don't have the time.'

'You need to make the time.' Emily sat forward, clasping her hands together on the table like she used to do at work. 'What sets your studio apart from all the others?'

Angela did not answer straight away. She closed her eyes. 'Community.' She took a deep breath in. 'I wanted to make yoga more accessible. The idea was to engage with the local community and play a positive part, help bring people together, run yoga events, retreats, social stuff. That's why I've got a pay-as-you-go option.'

'What have you done to engage with the local area?'

Angela looked off towards the window. Sunlight shone onto her face as a recognition of something came across her expression. 'Nothing. I opened the place and hoped for the best.'

'You've been busy getting to this stage, it sounds like. Now you've got to push to the next level.'

'By doing what?'

Emily thought for a few seconds. 'First of all, you've got to sort out what makes you special and then focus on that. Tell people all over your website who you are and what you are all about. If it's community, show them. Make it more obvious.

Second, get on top of your SEO and look into what else you can do to attract more of your ideal clients. Do you know who your ideal clients are? Can you start a blog? Run offers? Be more active on social media? Are you even on social media?'

'I post a bit … as and when I can.'

'That's not enough. You've got to be strategic about that stuff. It connects you to your audience and it's a great way to engage with people, create that community you feel so passionately about.' Emily paused. 'Do you want me to go on?'

'I do, but I feel I'll need to pay you if you say any more.'

'Don't be silly, it's nothing. I'm sure you would have picked this up in a podcast or something at some point.'

Angela shook her head. 'Not a great line if you ever want to do this for a living.'

'Oh, yeah.' Emily agreed instantly. 'That'll be my first bit of advice to myself: know your own value and don't give it away for free. Except to friendly yoga teachers who help you get home when you faint in front of them.'

Angela's eyes lit up as she laughed softly.

'And then you need to get out there.' Emily looked towards the window. 'We can do door-to-door leafleting, put a big chalkboard out the front with FREE YOGA handwritten all over it and stand there handing out flapjacks or something.'

Angela looked at her papers and pen as Emily was speaking. In Emily's pause, she picked up the pen and started writing notes. Emily smiled, glad she was able to help. 'And last but not least, run a free yoga morning or two. That will get them all in. People love freebies. And then you can upsell them if it's appropriate and they can afford regular yoga classes. Sorry, I hate myself for talking about money like that.'

Angela continued to scribble then stopped and looked up. 'Seriously, Emily. Never say that you hate yourself. You've got to be so careful with what you put out into the universe and bring into your life. Even words.'

'There you go again. Blowing my mind. Challenging and inspiring me in ways I never thought possible.'

Angela looked lost for words.

'Sorry. Too much?' said Emily.

'Look, I don't know what to say. You've suggested great ideas. I've been so caught up in getting the yoga part right – getting the studio up and running and hiring other teachers – I've not even thought about this stuff. But now that you're saying it, it's exactly what I need to be focusing on now.' Angela looked around at the empty studio. 'I don't even have a choice. What's the use in having a lovely studio if no one is using it?'

Angela had totally ignored her question, but that was okay. Emily didn't mind. She could be too much sometimes. 'Like any new launch, any new business or product, it takes time to get where you want to be. A lot of people want quick wins and smooth paths to success, but what they don't realise is how much work it takes, how adaptive you have to be to the challenge.' Emily scratched her head. 'I heard that one on a podcast, I'm not gonna lie.'

Angela laughed brightly again, 'I like your honesty,' and folded her arms. 'It's way easier being a freelance teacher going into a studio than being the driving force behind one. It's just as well my business is in yoga – managing stress – or I'd be all grey haired by now.'

'What makes it fun for you? All this work … what's in it for you, Angela?'

Angela looked away and Emily worried if she'd been too direct again. She wasn't accusing, she was just interested. She wanted to know what motivated someone like Angela.

'I guess it's me who wants to connect with people. I genuinely care about people and I want to help them flourish in some way. I think it's what I love doing, it energises me, brings me right into what I'm doing … like flow or something.'

Emily waited patiently as Angela trailed off, with a wistful look in her eye. 'You mentioned retreats, social stuff … did you have anything in mind?'

Angela looked back at her. 'I want to take a group of students up to the Highlands for a long weekend or a week. Maybe every quarter. There are a few centres that welcome groups, or it's possible to hire a venue and have it all to ourselves. We'd bring a chef, a counsellor, and a massage therapist, or there would be those services there. And most of all, we'd ask some of my favourite yoga gurus to join us. They'd help us all to deepen our practice, take guided meditations. I already have my own teacher lined up.'

'That sounds like heaven. I would so go to that. There, you've got your first student. How many would you want in the group?'

'It depends but I think no more than twelve. You want to get the right balance for group cohesion. Any more than that and it risks becoming too clinical. Any less and it can be too small. I was also thinking of starting a weekend supper club and that might spark off a close-knit group, might create the demand for retreats.'

'I'm there. Honestly. These are great ideas.'

'And along with your ideas, this place might actually stand a chance.'

'Well, as I've got nothing but time on my hands, I'm more than happy to help chat through all this in more detail. Help you make a plan? I could even do some leafleting for you. Would get me out of the flat.'

Angela sat up straighter and squared her shoulders. 'I'd

really like that, but you'd have to let me pay you. There's no way I can benefit from all your time and advice and not.'

'Let's see if any of it works first.'

'I want to do this properly, regardless.'

'It's fine, it's fine. Honestly, I'm not expecting to get paid. You've already done so much to help me start to feel better in myself. It would give me a purpose. Maybe even get my arse in gear for my next step. My only thought is when do you want to start?'

'I feel like I'd be taking advantage.'

'Take it.'

Angela's cheeks flushed and she looked down at the table. Emily got the distinct sense she was not thinking about the business. 'If you put it like that then okay. Is there a good time this week for you?'

Emily smiled softly. 'Like I said, any time's fine.'

Angela bit her bottom lip. 'Um, are you free now? I have another two hours to work on the paperwork, but this feels much more important. Would you stay? I'll feed you lunch.'

Emily was thrilled. More than thrilled. Ecstatic. 'Okay, why not. I guess we're on a roll.'

Smiling, Angela got up from her seat, and rested a hand on Emily's shoulder. 'I'm happy you popped in.'

Emily felt a spark flow between them. Angela removed her hand and visibly shook herself as she walked away.

'Can I get you a drink? Sorry, I've just realised I didn't offer you anything when you came in.'

'Coffee would be great.'

Angela smiled and busied herself behind the counter. Emily looked around the empty café, catching sight of the quote on the wall that had captured her imagination from the website only a few weeks ago. Inhaling deeply, she got her mind back in gear about the business. Happy to help, she already knew she was going to look into setting up her own business as a possible next step.

Emily smiled at the sight of Angela making the coffee and revelled in the feel of the studio without anyone else with them. She felt like she had somehow got a little bit closer to Angela and that the day was turning out to be one of the best she'd had in ages.

Chapter 11

The studio was closed up for the day and it had just gone ten at night. Emily had spent most of the day right next to Angela at the desk in the little office at the back of the studio. The proximity had been exhilarating. They stared at the orange tinted screen intensely, trying to work out how to make some fixes to the website. Their voices pierced the silence of the studio now and again.

Angela sat with her elbow on the table and her head resting on her hand. 'I really should get a stand for the laptop and a flat keyboard. It's bad enough knowing how not good this is for my own posture but seeing it affect yours is too much.'

'I don't mind.'

'You should. Your thoracic spine is quite kyphotic in this position. I can see it when you stand in Mountain Pose. It takes you a while to get yourself into neutral spine and this is the cause.' Angela ran a hand up and down Emily's back, coming to a rest where it was most rounded. 'Right here.'

Emily froze. Angela's touch sent a wave of tingles through her body and she did well not to tremble. She wasn't entirely sure what kyphotic meant but, if it made Angela touch her, was thankful for it.

Angela removed her hand and looked away.

Emily sat up straight, stretching her shoulders back and twisting around a couple of times. 'Busted.'

Angela laughed. 'You don't have a hunchback. I'm just a perfectionist when it comes to posture. We're not in class now so feel free to ignore me.' She yawned. 'It's late. We'd better stop. We've been at this for hours, well … days.'

Emily had been there for most of the week doing a thorough review and revamp of all of Angela's processes and plans. Now they were working on the website. Having gladly thrown herself into the new challenge, she realised how much she'd missed not having any problems to solve or any projects to work on. With each passing moment, she could feel her drive and motivation slowly coming back to her. And putting her skills to good use, for someone who both needed her help and deserved it, brought her so much satisfaction. 'This is my thing. It's giving me a purpose again. I'm okay to keep working on this for a wee bit longer and then make some notes. Do you mind?'

'No. Are you sure?'

'I am. We're almost there now, this is the most important thing to get right. People need to know if they can afford to come here before getting all excited. Or they need to feel excited about treating themselves for once. Whatever. How much does it cost? Is it clear what you get for it? Now I think it is.'

They got back to work. After a while, Emily took to writing on a notepad and Angela took over on the laptop. Emily was summarising what she'd done that day and making notes on what she had to do tomorrow.

Angela sighed. 'I still need to change the last row but it's not lining up right. I want it to look absolutely perfect.'

'Here, let me.' Emily moved in closer to Angela, their fingers brushing as she took control of the mouse. Again, the contact was electrifying.

'You have to click save twice before it lets you make any changes for some reason. I only figured this out in the last half hour.' Emily felt the side of her leg graze Angela's as she got into the right position to work the computer. Angela did not move away.

'Clever,' said Angela softly.

'Dumb luck, more like. You know, I like how I'm teaching you things now.'

Angela tilted her head towards Emily almost imperceptibly, but Emily saw it. 'You're doing more than teach me. You're wowing me with all this.'

'Don't you think you wow me too, up there with your mantras and your flexibility?'

Angela laughed quietly. 'I didn't realise you were paying that much attention.'

Emily's breath caught in her throat. 'I pay attention. Haven't you seen my progress?'

'It's been a beautiful thing to watch.'

'Then you'll know that I can be very observant,' said Emily, turning her gaze to the contents of the office as if demonstrating. Scanning the small room, Emily fixed her eyes on a picture frame sitting on a shelf then picked it up and sat down again. 'Who's this adorable puppy?'

'Oh, that's my first dog, Patch.'

'He's so cute. I love his little face. Look at his ears and his white stripe. Collie?'

Angela half-smiled. 'Collie-cross. Collie and Spaniel. Fiercely intelligent, highly energetic, and completely neurotic.'

Emily held the frame closer to her face. 'Aww. Who's the gorgeous baby?'

'That's me.'

Emily laughed. 'Now this is too much cuteness. Not sure who's more adorable here. It's a close call.'

Angela shook her head and a small smile crept onto her face. She beckoned for Emily to hand it to her. Emily shook her head, still looking at the picture frame in her hand. 'You're quite playful, aren't you?' Angela took hold of Emily's wrist holding the picture. Her grip was firm. Holding eye contact with her, Angela took the picture from her with her free hand. She put the picture frame back on the shelf, and sat back down, flustered.

Emily swallowed hard and turned back to the computer, but she couldn't focus on what she was doing for thoughts of Angela taking hold of her wrist again.

Angela stood up, stretching her arms high above her head, before taking her bobble out and letting down her hair. She ruffled it up when it was set free. Fluffy blonde locks came to a rest on her shoulders. 'That feels better. Ever just need to do that sometimes?'

'It's like taking your bra off as soon as you get home, isn't it?'

Angela laughed. 'Yeah.'

'That "bras aff" moment is *everything*.'

Angela laughed again. 'You're probably right. I do do that as soon as I get home.'

'That sounds so good right now.'

Angela raised an eyebrow. 'You want to take your bra off?'

Emily laughed. 'Um, no. I was thinking more of getting home and taking it off and putting my pyjamas on. But I can take it off now if you like?' There was a playfulness to her tone.

Angela's eyes grew wide in alarm.

Emily laughed again. 'Don't worry, it's staying on.' Angela visibly relaxed at that. 'Now's probably a good time to stop. I do feel a bit stiff from sitting all day.'

'No wonder. You've been in here beavering away. God, that makes me feel like I'm pushing you too hard.'

It was Emily's turn to raise an eyebrow.

Angela gestured towards the door. 'Come with me.' She led Emily through to the main studio where the only light was from a couple of salt lamps. It made their being there feel sort of illicit.

'Wait here.'

Angela returned with two yoga mats and placed them on

the floor next to each other directly underneath the main wall.

'What's all this?'

Angela gracefully sat down on her mat, setting her arms out behind her on the mat to support her weight, she gestured for Emily to sit down with her. 'We're going to do a very advanced yoga move called Legs up the Wall.'

Dropping to her mat beside Angela, Emily almost bashed into her as the mats were very close together. 'Sorry.' Her heart rate picked up. Her earlier confidence was waning. Facing Angela, her eyes fell on her long neck and shoulders. She watched as Angela lightly got herself in an L-shape position with her back on the mat and legs, literally, up the wall.

Turning her head towards her, Angela went into yoga teacher mode but was definitely more relaxed with it. 'Skoosh up to the wall so your bum is flush with it. Then scoot your legs up. This helps relax your back and stretch your hamstrings, and it's a good recovery position. Helps you calm down and aids circulation. Try it. It'll help your back.'

'Okay. Here goes.'

Emily threw her legs out to the side and slid her hips forward in the most ungainly fashion. With some effort, she windscreen-wiped her legs onto the wall. Hopefully, Angela had not seen that. 'Right. I'm there.'

'Good.'

'Now what.'

'We stay like this.'

'Oh.'

'Your feet might go a bit tingly after a while. That's from numbness. You might want to drop out of it if that happens, and it might give you pins and needles. I usually hang out here for about fifteen minutes before I get that.'

'Cool, I'll see how I go.' Surprisingly, it felt good to let it all hang out. Emily could feel herself relax and was enjoying how close Angela's hand was to hers on the floor.

'Great.'

They were silent after that. The only thing on Emily's mind was their proximity, how good it felt and how much she loved being around Angela. With a glance to her left, however, it seemed Angela was unfazed and pretty chill.

She couldn't help it. 'What are you thinking about?'

There was a long pause. 'I'm not, really.'

Emily let her head tilt towards Angela, not even trying to hide that she was looking directly at her. 'How do you do that?'

'I meditate. Do you want me to take you through a guided meditation?'

'What, now?'

'Why not?'

'Um, because it's just us … Wouldn't that be weird?'

'Okay, we don't have to. It was just a thought.'

'No, let's do it.'

'Okay. Just be the witness of your thoughts and focus on your breath.' There was a pause. 'Close your eyes.'

Emily closed them.

'Bring your attention to your toes, and then your feet, then your legs,' she spoke slowly, 'and your hips, working all the way up your body, and then focusing on your hands, and the tips of your fingers.' There was a long pause. 'Then turn your attention to your face. Your eyelids. Your nose. Your mouth … your lips.'

Emily swallowed. This was turning her on and it shouldn't have been.

'Open your eyes. And just look at whatever's in front of you. In our case, this wall.' Angela laughed a little. 'That's the mindful bit. Now we just stay lying here.'

They lay in silence with their legs up the wall for a minute or so. Emily's legs felt surprisingly okay. 'I'm witnessing my mind.' Emily paused, unsure of how much to reveal. 'It's noisy.'

'Let your thoughts be as they are. Accept whatever comes into your head and try to notice the blank bits in between each thought. Try to stay in that space.'

'I'm focusing.'

'Good.'

As time went on most random thoughts fell away leaving Emily consumed by those darker, negative thoughts telling her that she wasn't worthy and pulling her down. She slid her feet down the wall, dropping her knees towards her chest.

'What's wrong?'

'It's not working. The more I focus on what's going on inside, the worse I feel.'

Angela reached out and put her hand over Emily's. The touch made her tremble.

Angela noticed it. 'It's all right. Focus on your breath. Breathe with me.'

With Angela's hand on hers a warmth spread through Emily's body, causing a gentle throbbing between her legs. When Angela's hand left, she wished she could grab it back. Angela closed her eyes again and so did Emily. Emily followed Angela's exaggerated breathing, and they did this for a minute or so. The energy coming from Angela felt almost tangible. Somehow, it felt like Angela was bringing her back to life and patching up the edges of her wounded heart. The room was dark, but Emily was starting to feel lighter somehow.

'You are more than the pain you've experienced, Emily.'

'I am?'

'You're a unique, beautiful, kind, amazing human being.' There was a pause. 'There's something special about you.'

'There is? Not from where I'm looking. I feel like I'm at

rock bottom.'

'Or you could be going through a spiritual awakening? Our troubles can teach us so much.'

'I have learned a lot about yoga. I didn't expect that.'

'No, I mean, about ourselves. Deeper insights into who we are and what makes us tick. The trick is to listen. To get curious.'

Emily let her mind go blank. 'I know that I've been feeling shit about myself. And I'm not really happy with who I've become. I know that for sure.'

'Do you want to know what I see?'

Emily wasn't entirely sure that she did. 'Yeah.'

'You're an incredible human being, Emily. You have the universe inside of you. Think about what your body does for you without you even thinking about it. And it does it all for you – so that you get to live this wonderful experience called life. Think about it. Your lungs breathe for *you*, your heart beats for *you*, your liver functions for *you*, your ears listen for *you*, your toes work for *you*, your eyes see things for *you* – beautiful things, and they see the beauty in you, too.'

Emily let Angela's beautiful words sink in. She felt a couple of tears run down her face and into her hair. Wiping them gently, she realised that if Angela had seen she wouldn't have minded. A silence settled between them as Emily bathed in Angela's energy. As her mind slowed down, a heaviness lifted from her. Unable to put her finger on it, Emily closed her eyes harder, trying to hold onto the sensation, the moment.

'Emily.' Angela's voice matched the quietness of the studio.

Emily turned her head and found Angela's kind eyes looking right at her, as their heads faced each other only a short distance away on the mats. Her grey-blue eyes were so soulful. Intense. Sexy, even though she clearly wasn't trying to be. It was Angela who broke the connection first, and they both scooted away from the wall and sat on their mats, legs crossed.

'How do you feel now?' asked Angela.

'Wonderful. Thank you. I haven't felt this good in a long time.' Emily rested a hand on Angela's knee.

Angela moved back as if she hadn't noticed. She spoke as she was getting up to her feet and her voice was a slightly higher pitch. 'Great. Hopefully you're won over by the power of really going within now. Yoga and meditation. It's all about that union with the self, remember.'

'I think it's you who's won me over,' said Emily, softly, still on the mat. 'I don't know what it is about you, but just being here with you makes me feel like a different person. I don't feel stressed right now. About anything. Or sad. What you said was really beautiful.'

Angela was quiet for a few beats. 'That's lovely of you to say. I'd hoped it might help you feel a bit better.'

Emily got to her feet almost falling over herself as the blood returned to her legs.

Angela gasped. 'You're not going to faint again, are you?'

'No. Not at all. Just adjusting to vertical life.' Emily steadied herself in front of Angela and then they locked eyes. Emily could feel the heavy beat of her heart as adrenaline coursed through her veins. There was so much in their silent communication.

Emily did something unexpected, even to her. She stepped forward and hugged her. She kept a polite distance and simply wrapped one arm around her shoulder as Angela awkwardly did the same. It was not a particularly long hug, but in that moment, the energy shifted between them. Being that close to Angela felt amazing, however brief. 'Thank you,' said Emily, over her shoulder.

Angela stepped out of the embrace. 'You're so welcome.'

She avoided Emily's eyes. 'Well, I'd better get closed up for the evening.'

Emily nodded. 'Of course, I'll leave you to it.'

Angela smiled. 'Thank you for all you've done today. I really appreciate it.'

'Sure, it's no problem. Again, thank *you* for the legs-up-the-wall pep-talk.'

Angela laughed nervously at that and they parted ways. Emily saw herself out. The empty street outside was bathed in patches of bright white light from new energy-efficient street lighting. As she strolled home, in no rush, she stroked her wrist and thought about Angela the whole time. She was so wholesome, so kind, gentle and thoughtful. And the way she had been during the meditation felt very loving. But that unnecessarily rough grip when she was taking away the picture frame suggested so much more: a darker, extremely sexy side that Emily could not stop thinking about.

Back in her flat, she locked the door and slipped off her trainers, leaving them scattered in the middle of the hallway. Walking through to her bedroom, she took off her bra under her T-shirt and threw it on the bed. Her phone beeped.

It was Angela.

Thanks again for today – for this week. I feel like I'm learning so much from you. You've made business stuff actually kind of fun. That's talent.

Emily smiled, texting back immediately.

My pleasure. See you tomorrow!

She plugged the charger into her phone and made herself some tea. Her flat usually felt cold and lonely when she arrived home, at least until the heating came on and she switched on numerous screens to keep her company. But tonight it was fine, and she didn't need to drown out the silence. She was already excited about seeing Angela so soon and comforted by thoughts of what had just happened at the studio. Even though Angela was not beside her, she could feel her presence with her. If she didn't know any better, she would have to say that it felt a lot like love.

Chapter 12

Angela stood on the street outside Heart Yoga clutching a bunch of leaflets, which Emily had designed. The crisp sunny day hinted at promising things to come, much like the past few weeks she had spent on her business. The business was starting to take off, and Angela had been barely able to sleep with excitement. She and Emily had spent hours together going through everything and had implemented some of the ideas straight away. First of all, they'd changed the pricing and membership options. Already, there had been a thirty percent rise in new clients. The biggest pick up was during the mornings. Every class had been full for the past week. Emily had been coming in every day to work with her in the office and had helped her deliver leaflets to every home in the vicinity of the studio. It felt like she had a business partner, and she hadn't even known that she needed one until now. All she had to do was figure out a way to pay Emily for her time and input. But Emily had been having none of it, saying that she was more than happy to help and that it was helping her to get motivated for her own next step.

Today was a beautiful day to be engaging with the local community in advance of the new free classes. Angela kept having to run back into the studio to see to clients coming and going from classes with other teachers. It was packed. She had never seen it like this, not even at other studios she'd worked at over the years. Looking around the street she had chosen to open her studio on, she felt closer to it. Simply taking things outdoors had brought in a whole new dimension. The street never had high footfall as it was just off a main road. Only flats and a dog grooming shop shared the street with them. With the help of Zoe and Emily, they'd set up a table in front of the studio window, complete with gingham tablecloth, cakes, biscuits, and clipboards. Between them, they'd been talking to people on the street for hours and had generated a good amount of interest.

A smartly dressed woman, perhaps a social worker, came striding up the street like she meant business.

'Hi there! Are you interested in free yoga?' said Angela, holding out an A6-sized leaflet made from recycled paper.

The woman walked straight past with a faraway look in her eyes, barely acknowledging her.

'Not today, apparently,' said Angela, turning around, undeterred.

The street grew quieter. Angela stood beside her newly acquired A-frame chalkboard. It gave her a sense of security to stand next to something in the middle of the wide pavement. As she canvassed the street, a small part of her was constantly aware of Emily, thinking of Emily and feeling that Emily was stealing quick glances at her. And she too was stealing quick glances at Emily. Sometimes, she was sure Emily was openly gazing her way. One time she turned around after a long chat with the next-door neighbour and caught Emily looking away abruptly. There was no mistaking what she had seen. Emily had been looking at her. There was no doubt. And Angela had *enjoyed* it.

And why wouldn't she enjoy it? The more Angela allowed herself to think about all of Emily's great qualities, the more things she realised she absolutely adored: the relaxed way Emily held herself when she was in a good place, her warm, playful personality, her smile. Her intellect had wowed her even more. Emily wasn't pushy with her cleverness or even with her opinions. Through spending more time together, Angela had realised how deeply Emily cared about things, and other people. She had that exuberant confidence that

Angela found so attractive. And she was sweet. If she thought Angela was good at something or liked something she'd heard, she'd let her know. She saw through Angela's yoga teacher front, to the real her, or so it felt.

Angela knew that she had allowed herself to indulge in Emily's company – perhaps a little too much. It was dangerous. That night they'd gone into the studio after dark had been the turning point for Angela. It was then that she realised that maybe all this thinking about Emily, and this instant physical attraction might be something more. She was more than capable of appreciating a beautiful woman from a distance, to appreciate that she might be physically attracted to someone without ever acting on it. But Emily was more than just those things. Angela was now craving her company and wanting to get to know her better. And this was where the conflict was sitting within her; Emily was first and foremost a student, and Angela was her yoga teacher.

Looking off into the distance, she took a deep breath, which ended with a sigh. It was absolutely forbidden to get romantically involved with one of her yoga students. It went against the values of her training, her peers and most importantly of all, her mentor, Jackie Hay, an internationally acclaimed yoga and spiritual teacher whom she deeply respected and admired. It was something her mentor talked at length about in her training, about the potential for feelings to develop, given the circumstances yoga created. They'd discussed and agreed on how it was a yoga teacher's job to create a safe space, an atmosphere where the mind and body can become one, to fully open up and connect. To become one with body and mind. This naturally facilitates the potential for warmth and empathy that could be misinterpreted by either party. She'd never once in the past looked at her students that way. Not until now. Emily was off-limits and there was nothing she could do about it.

Sometimes, maybe, the universe didn't have her back. That thought alone was a little deflating.

Angela took another deep breath and refocused on her surroundings and what she was there to do. This was in good time as well, as there was a young woman walking towards her pushing a pram. Angela smiled at her and waved. 'Hello. Interested in free yoga?'

The young woman stopped and eyed Angela suspiciously. She looked down at the leaflet and back at Angela as if she'd been offered an invitation to join a cult. 'That's no really ma kinda hing.' She took a step to leave as Angela took a step closer to her.

'It could be. Have you ever tried it?'

'Naw.'

'Well, why not give it a try?' Angela looked at the baby in the pram smiling its head off. Her insides melted and the familiar yearning in the pit of her stomach reared itself. Pushing down the feeling, she looked back up at the baby's mum. 'Yoga helps you relax, like, really unwind. That's my studio, right here,' Angela gestured with her other hand to the front of Heart Yoga. Emily was standing beside the table, watching them, and Zoe was talking to a mum with a toddler. 'We'd love to see you pop in sometime. You'd be very welcome. We're running a free yoga class tomorrow morning and we also offer a community yoga class that's based on donations only. That starts next week. You only pay what you can. And the little one can come too.' Angela tried to give her most welcoming smile and I-am-not-a-threat face.

The young woman looked over at the studio. Her expression was sceptical, but there was also a hint of curiosity. She swallowed and looked back at Angela. 'Sorry, it's no fur me.' She left, leaving Angela looking after her with a long face.

'If you change your mind …' Angela called out after her.

The young woman had looked at her as if she had no idea what her life was like, and she felt misunderstood. In Angela's mind, everyone was equal, no matter what background they came from. Plus, she had a baby, something Angela desperately wanted. With each passing day she felt the dream slowly slipping away from her. Mostly, she tried not to think about it, but when she saw babies it always came flooding back. Angela was in a peculiar situation of not wanting a relationship but still wanting a child.

Maybe I should just go it alone?

Given that her spirits had dropped, she decided to take a break. She joined Emily and Zoe by the front door. Emily was beaming at her, and she wasn't sure why. Zoe had a smirk on her face and suddenly it clicked. Zoe had no doubt mentioned something salacious from Angela's wild past. Zoe knew too much. Angela eyed them both suspiciously. 'Any more takers? I saw you guys talking to that group.'

'They all signed up. And not even for the free yoga but for real paying classes. See,' Emily held up the sign-up forms brimming with blue ink. 'They just needed a wee nudge.'

Angela smiled. 'Of course people would sign up if you were talking to them! You're incredible. And so clever. I would never have thought of all this.'

'Let's be real, Angela. It was the free cake,' said Emily.

Angela laughed. 'Even that was wonderful. Thank you so much for baking. I don't know what I did to deserve your help.'

'I had time to bake; it was nothing.'

Angela tilted her head and narrowed her eyes in disagreement. 'It's everything. These cakes are pretty much turning my business around.'

Zoe had her hands in the pockets of her oversized hemp jacket staying quiet as she observed the interaction. 'Angela's right. You got loads of people interested. I barely got any.

Turns out people are intimidated by yoga teachers. Weird, cos we're the friendliest, most chilled out people I know.'

'Well, you guys are so warm and lovely that I can't stay away.'

Emily and Angela stood beaming at each other. Angela was aware of Zoe looking between them, which made her slightly nervous.

Zoe had a knowing look on her face as she spoke next. 'You have been here a lot recently. Are you sure you're not on the payroll? Or moving in?'

Angela shifted on her feet and shot Zoe a look. Clearly, she suspected something. One of the many reasons she needed to nip whatever was going on between her and Emily in the bud.

Emily addressed Zoe's comment. 'I guess I have been getting unlimited free yoga,' she laughed awkwardly.

Something caught Angela's eye in the distance. Two older ladies were ambling towards them, both carrying a shopping bag in each hand. Angela had recently booked a new teacher, Grace, who was going to run one class a week for senior citizens. They would be ideal candidates.

'So, what were you two laughing about earlier?'

'I was telling Emily how much of a stoner you used to be.'

Angela winced. For some reason she didn't immediately want Emily knowing anything like that about her. Picking up a bit of shortbread and taking a bite, she realised that was foolish. 'So what? It was ages ago.'

'Quite right,' said Emily. 'Nothing to be ashamed of.'

'Okay. I'm off.' Angela approached the two older ladies slowly.

'Good morning, ladies. Beautiful day, isn't it?'

'It's too hot,' said the shortest lady. 'It said it was gonnae rain but then we get this,' she held her hands out as if catching rays of sun was a bad thing. 'Just dinnae ken where ye stand. Never dae.'

'Can I interest you in some yoga at my studio here? We're running a class every Tuesday morning that I think you both would enjoy.'

The two older ladies looked at her. 'Yoga. Are ye kiddin me? Ah havenae bent doon since 1992.'

Her friend let out a huge belly laugh and spoke in the same accent. 'Whit are ye suggestin, hen? That we go in there wi you young hings? Throw oot a hip puttin on thae funny claes. Whit wid ye want that fur? We'd only cramp yer style.'

Angela warmed to the pair. 'We would love to have you. We already have quite a few,' she paused, unsure of how to put it, 'mature ladies, so you'd be in very good company. Here,' she handed them each a leaflet. 'This tells you more about it and what to expect. Again, don't be put off by the young woman on the front; we have a great mix of ages.'

They held the leaflets up to their eyes so that they were nearly touching their noses. 'It's you, dear, is it no?'

'Yes, I'm afraid it is.'

'Ye're quite the picture, hen. Whit ah wudnae gie tae huv ma youthful looks back. Ah used tae make heids turn, ah tell ye. Ah was always first tae be asked tae dance. But look at me the noo. Naebody's lookin any mair.'

'That's no true, Ah'm still looking,' said her friend.

She waved her hand in dismissal. 'You dinnae count.'

Her friend sighed and shook her head.

'Whit've ye got over there?' said the old lady, no longer concerned about the issue.

'Free cakes. Please help yourself. We normally do healthier snacks in the café, which, by the way, you don't need to be doing a class to use. You can pop in anytime.'

The pair looked at each other in mutual recognition of a fantastic piece of new information. 'That's very good. Ye might see us back, after aw. Dae ye mind if we take a wee bit o' cake there, dear?'

'Help yourselves, that's what it's for.'

The pair made their way over to the table, dropped their bags and picked out two small brownies. They ate whilst eyeing up the studio, looking in towards the café and not trying to hide it. After sampling a couple of the other types of cake on offer, they politely waited for the socially acceptable minimum amount of time before they could leave and then picked up their bags.

'Thank you for the cakes, dear. When was your OAP class again?'

'Tuesdays at nine. Hope to see both of you lovely ladies there.' Angela smiled.

'Thanks for asking, dear. Ye never know,' she said, with a twinkle in her eye. The pair moved on, looking down at the leaflets in their hands, perplexed and curious.

Zoe was talking to a teenage boy in tracksuit bottoms and a hoodie. Angela joined Emily by the table. The sun was hot on her Scottish skin. 'Are you sure you're not getting bored? Surely—'

'Eh, like I keep saying, it makes me feel like I'm doing something useful.' Emily held her eyes. 'There's nowhere else I'd rather be right now. Really.'

Angela had the urge to give Emily a hug. Instead, she stood where she was.

'On that note, I'm just going to check something on the computer.' As she walked away, she saw Emily discreetly look over her shoulder at her and watch her go. She felt the hairs on the back of her neck stand up and found herself clenching her jaw. This had to stop.

Why is it so exciting to feel her gaze at me like that?

Once inside she glided past the studio and into the office. Susie was taking her first Yoga for Runners class and it was nearly full. Shifting a cup of half-drunk herbal tea out of the way, she wiggled the mouse and logged back into her computer. After she had answered a few emails and put in a fruit order from a nearby organic farm, she clicked through to the backend of the website and the sign-up page, and almost fell off her seat.

Dumbstruck, her first thought was if the studio could handle so many people. The changes she'd made had been good, but she didn't realise how good until that moment. The gentle tinkle of the bell on the door sounded and Zoe and Emily came in, interrupting her calculations.

'Wee bugger had me chatting to him for ten minutes and all he wanted was a bit of cake. I should have seen it a mile off. See what I was saying about us yoga teachers being too nice,' said Zoe.

'He did show an interest for ten minutes; you have to give him that. You never know, he might turn up one day,' said Emily.

'You guys, you're not going to believe this. Bookings are blowing up! We've got fifty new sign-ups – that's double in the last two weeks, and the retreat has sold out!'

'Fuck, yeah!' said Zoe. 'See, I knew it would take off! I'm so pleased.'

'It's unbelievable,' said Angela. 'I can't believe it.'

Emily smiled. 'It was only a matter of time.'

Angela smiled back at her, feeling so grateful for all that Emily had done to help.

Zoe coughed. 'I'd better get going to my next yoga studio, but not my favourite, mind, you know this place is my home. Well done, Angela. Emily, what can I say, you're a genius. Thank you.'

The look of pride that beamed out of Emily in that moment made Angela's heart happy. Once Zoe had left, Angela faced Emily, wanting to savour the moment a bit longer. 'How can I ever repay you for this? You've

110

completely turned this place around. Without you, this would not be happening.'

'I only suggested a couple of things. The studio, and all you've built up, was ready for the next level. I didn't do anything.'

Angela looked at her seriously. 'This modesty has got to stop. You're clearly good at what you do. I'm thanking you for it. Now, will you please let me?'

'Okay. I will. I'll let you thank me. Just buy me a drink sometime, that'll do.'

'A drink, of course. Let me take you out. We'll get champagne!' said Angela, telling herself that it was a purely professional invitation.

'Sure, yeah. That would be lovely.'

'Are you free this Saturday? It's my night off.'

'Okay. Saturday it is.'

Angela blushed. Why was she blushing? It must have been obvious. 'Perfect.'

'Perfect.' Emily repeated. 'Let's do that.'

They stood there grinning at each other for a few moments like excited teenagers.

'Where do you want to go?' asked Emily.

'Pub? I've not been out in ages.'

'We could go to the Village? Why don't you ever go out?'

'I'm so busy with the studio.'

'You must be. I'm amazed you've even got enough time to sleep.'

'I make time to sleep, that's the one thing I don't mess about with.'

'You look like you sleep well. What *do* you mess about with?' said Emily, eyes twinkling. Angela loved it when Emily was like this. Sweet and a bit flirty.

'I do sleep well, thanks. Anyway,' Angela felt giddy and nervous. It had been a long time since she'd felt this way around someone. 'What time do you want to meet up?'

'Half eight?'

Angela had to think about it. She usually went to bed at ten-thirty.

'Or another night or time would be fine?' said Emily, quickly.

'No, tomorrow is good. It's just that it's quite late. I was thinking more like six-thirty?'

Emily looked confused. 'Half eight is early, no? Half six is more like the afternoon,' she paused. 'Is that you still prioritising your beauty sleep? Going out early?'

'I'm in my thirties, what can I say.'

'How old are you again?

'Thirty-three. There's only four years between us and I'm already past it.'

'I highly doubt that.'

Angela was having a hard time looking Emily in the eyes. 'Right. Half eight it is. I do want to celebrate, and I want to show my appreciation,' Angela looked up at Emily, and then away again. 'I've waited so long for this. Now it's here, it feels … it feels surreal.'

Emily looked at the café behind her and towards the class that was now starting to finish. 'There's nothing surreal about this. You built it. It's a fantastic place full of warmth and great coffee. You are the heart of it all. You touch people.'

Angela absorbed Emily's words. She opened her mouth to respond, not quite knowing what to say. The sound of Susie's class finishing, and belongings being collected, came through. A stream of students came piling out. Angela smiled as the café filled up with people. Observing it all, she let the feeling of success finally sink in. It felt wonderful.

Chapter 13

Emily stood beside the entrance to the Village waiting for Angela to arrive. The pub was full of rugby fans. It was the last day of the Six Nations Championship, and Scotland had won the tournament. Emily was no major fan, but she knew that it was a big deal – and quite unusual – for Scotland to win it. The mood on the street was triumphant, the pub not far from the national stadium. Looking in the window she could see loads of Scotland jerseys, men in kilts, and not a table in sight. They would have to go somewhere else. At least, she hoped they would.

She wasn't sure what kind of an evening it was either. On one hand she got the feeling that Angela saw their relationship as strictly professional and was genuinely just looking to celebrate a win and politely thank her for helping. On the other hand, Emily felt like it was something more. It was a small inkling, but it was there. She knew it wasn't a date, but she couldn't shake the feeling that Angela was starting to like her. Angela had definitely opened up to her since she'd started helping her with the business. The big giveaway was the way Angela had become so flustered when she'd asked Emily out for a drink to celebrate. She had blushed fiercely, which Emily had not expected, and she could hardly look her in the eyes when Emily had said yes. This was quite unlike Angela. Very unlike her.

And Emily's excitement levels had been sky-high ever since.

Overall, life was getting better again. Hanging out with Angela, getting into a routine, doing yoga every day, cleaning the flat, the odd run – it was all helping. The more she learned about yoga and meditation – the more she let herself be open to new ideas and ways of looking at things – the better she'd been feeling. It was the one thing that had changed in her life, and it was working. No longer was she telling herself that she was a failure. The dark cloud above her was ever so slowly moving away. But improving and managing her mental health was now her full-time job, or so it felt.

Being out on the town again, while a bit unfamiliar given that she'd become a social recluse of late, felt really good. She was appreciating everything more. People's faces as they walked past her were fascinating. The joy in the air at having won the rugby was also almost tangible. Smiling at nothing in particular, Emily noticed she was seeing her city for what it was again – thriving, alive, dynamic – and not getting stuck in the past. Having chosen her outfit carefully – her best smart fitted ankle grazer trousers and green top underneath her loose going-out blazer – she felt happy in herself. Her Toms softened the look, giving a casual feel to her now mostly unused good clothes. Being back in them gave her confidence a boost too. Glancing down at her wrist, she realised Angela was a bit late. The thought of Angela made her tummy flip.

'Hey.'

Emily turned to find Angela walking towards her, looking exceptionally radiant and stunning. Her hair was down and styled straight. It suited her. It wasn't often she saw Angela with her hair down, and she had never seen her out of her yoga gear. She wore a blazer, a black one with the sleeves turned up, and blue skinny jeans. Her white top showed a healthy amount of cleavage. Goosebumps spread across Emily's limbs as her eyes wandered over Angela's body. She couldn't help it and didn't particularly try to hide it. 'Hey,' said Emily, moving in closer and hugging her warmly.

Angela's body felt rigid, reciprocating only with a single arm going over Emily's shoulder.

Facing each other in the street, Emily still felt nervous, but hid it well. 'It's full of rugby fans.' She nodded towards the crowded pub.

'I bet it is. Can you believe we won!?'

'No. It's pretty special, right? Are you into rugby?'

Angela nodded, enthusiastically. 'Big time. I was jumping up and down screaming in celebration in my living room earlier. My neighbours must have thought I'd gone mad. We won by one point. A try in the last play of the game, which was then converted for the win. It's usually us giving games away in the last second.'

Emily laughed, but also felt her heart sink a little, assuming Angela would want to join the celebratory crowd. 'There's a lot I've still to learn about you. Yoga teacher, rugby fan … what next? You don't have a secret double life or something, do you?'

Angela jigged a shoulder like an exaggerated TV presenter trying to entice the audience. 'Maybe. I guess you'll have to keep watching if you want to find out more.'

Emily laughed again. Angela was adorable. Cars drew to a halt at the traffic lights next to them, and she heard the loud beeping of the pelican crossing.

'So, should we head somewhere else?' said Angela back in her normal style. 'I know a good place. It's a no-go in there.'

'Yes! Let's do that.'

Before long, they arrived at the new place and it was, unquestionably, date-worthy. Angela held the door open for her, and she stepped past her into the upmarket bar that wasn't very busy. Chandeliers with hipster squirrel-cage light bulbs hung down from the huge high ceiling. With only the odd rugby fan, it was a major improvement. Angela led the way towards a secluded booth near the back. Emily immediately noticed the private nature of the table. One curved seat lined the semicircular table.

'It's perfect,' said Emily, taking a seat on the plush fabric.

Picking up the wine menu but looking out the side of her eye, Emily marvelled at Angela's elegant movements as she slid into the booth and came to a stop actually quite close to her. Angela put her bag down on her other side and leant over it, maybe trying to find something. The shape of Angela's back was so slender, easily maintaining that perfect posture in a compromised position. Satisfied with something in her bag, she turned back to Emily and they locked eyes for a second.

Angela broke the connection. 'Drinks. How's the champagne menu?'

'Enticing.'

'May I see it?'

Emily slid the menu the short distance over to her. For such a classy place it was strange they only had one menu on the table. As Angela sat next to her reading through the menu, Emily realised she felt happy. Being around Angela had that effect on her. Everything felt better when she was with her. The thick blanket of despair was nowhere to be seen. The pull of Angela's calming and soulful personality was strong. It was like the world had fallen away and it was just them, in a pub, sharing a booth, choosing wine. It was.

Angela slid the menu back towards Emily and reached for her purse.

'Have you found one?' Emily got out her purse this time.

'Yes. This is on me.'

'No, no. It's your celebration. You have to be bought a drink, not the other way around.'

'It's my celebration because I'm doing so well and have lots of money to spend on champagne, thanks to you. I'll be back in a minute.' Angela got up and went to the bar. Emily watched her every step as she crossed the room. She loved the sway of her hips and the elegant poise of her back. Emily saw her put one hand on the shiny surface of the bar and effortlessly get the attention of the man behind it. Angela gestured to the person who was at the bar before her that he should be served first. As the barman served him, Angela waited patiently. After a minute, she slowly turned her head and looked over her shoulder at Emily, revealing a look Emily hadn't seen from her before. Open. Vulnerable. Free. Almost as quickly as the look came, it disappeared, and Angela turned away. Emily felt her pulse pick up. The intimate setting, the classy bar, the lighting – it felt like a date. But was it a date? She let out a long heavy breath as her thoughts competed for clarity. Glancing up at the bar again, she saw Angela making her way back, with two glasses and a bucket with a bottle sticking out of it.

'That looks expensive.'

Angela was still avoiding eye contact with Emily. 'If you can't treat yourself when things are going well, when can you?'

'Very true. Don't they do table service here though?'

'They do, but I don't want us to be disturbed. Especially not by some hipster guy who thinks I want him to flirt with me. I am in no mood for male energy tonight,' Angela took her seat next to Emily. 'I've had more than enough of my fill for one day from watching the rugby all afternoon.'

Emily felt her insides go weak and her face relax, unconsciously pursing her lips, and channelling all her nerves into her mouth. Angela's assertiveness was thrilling. Emily inhaled deeply, wanting to be very intentional about every single word she said to her.

'What type of energy *do* you want to be around tonight?'

Angela slowly poured them each a glass of champagne. 'Um.' Angela paused for a few moments. 'Lesbian energy will do just fine.'

Emily felt her jaw clench at that and some tension in her neck. The real Angela had finally shown up. Before Emily could reply Angela handed her a glass and smiled, drawing a line under her comment. They clinked glasses. Emily was so pleased for her. 'Congratulations to you. Now you can focus on the yoga side of things again.' Angela had picked up the business advice quickly and been able to implement changes to get it done, but Emily knew her heart lay with the actual teaching of the yoga. That was probably a good thing, as Heart Yoga was becoming magnetic.

Angela smiled, still holding up her glass. 'I know I've said it quite a few times now, but I really mean it. Thank you so much for all of your help with the business. You're a literal genius.'

'On this topic, I might just be. You're welcome.'

They both sipped from their glasses before putting them on the table. Angela spun the stem of her glass around in her fingers. 'Have you given any more thought to your consulting?'

'I've done a little bit of digging.' In truth, Emily already had a draft business plan. Apart from Angela, it was all she had been thinking about recently.

'Is it something you're going to pursue then?'

Emily smiled. 'Actively.'

'Oooh. Tell me more.'

Emily shook her head. 'It's a work in progress and not exactly scintillating chat for a Saturday night. Besides, tonight's about you. How does it feel to take the Scottish yoga world by storm?'

Angela beamed. 'Yep, amazing. I love what I do. Every day feels like a gift,' Angela looked down. 'Sorry, that's so cheesy.'

'No, it's not. I love that you're like that,' Emily paused, 'that you're doing what you love. Your studio gives so much to people. So, I'm glad to hear that you feel that way about it. To be honest, it shows.'

'It does?'

'Your passion, your belief in yoga. How much of a good time you're having ...'

'All that?' said Angela. 'I must be an open book.'

Emily smiled graciously and took another sip of champagne. Angela was clearly a very private person and Emily had just been watching closely. 'What do your family think about it?'

'My mum is very pleased. She's telling everyone she knows that the studio has finally "taken off". And my dad, well, he knows something good has happened but he's not really that interested.'

'I'm sorry—'

'He's always so busy. He's a businessman. I don't really know what he does.'

Emily nodded.

'He's your typical emotionally unavailable father. He does his best, though. He's very good to us, really.'

'They must be so proud of you.'

Angela smiled. 'How're things with you? Are you feeling any better about stuff?' She took a drink and seemed to check herself. 'Is it okay if I ask you that?'

'It totally is. Thank you for asking. I'm doing much better. Better than I have in ages. I think having been made redundant is doing wonders for me, actually. And the yoga, can't forget that.'

Angela's eyes were kind. 'I'm really pleased to hear that, Emily.'

'I now see that my mental health is something I have to actively work on. To manage. It's not easy, but not doing it is so much worse.'

'You *have* become quite the yoga enthusiast.'

'I'm obsessed. I can't wait to go to the retreat either. I so need something like that right now to look forward to.'

'It's only in four weeks. God, I've got so much to sort out for it.' Angela gulped down some champagne.

'Come on. It's going to be immense. And you are organised, if I remember correctly when you told me about it.'

'The big stuff is mostly done, but not the million other little soft touches that make retreats so magical.'

'I can help, if you want?'

'Emily. There is no way I could take your time again. I would have to pay you, but I haven't budgeted for that. So, I can't afford you.'

'No, you probably can't.' Emily laughed. 'Honestly, if you do get into a pickle, you know where I am.' Emily smiled, awkwardly, and leant forward to pick up her glass.

She saw Angela regard her profile. The pub was still quiet. Emily had noticed the professional veil start to creep back onto Angela's face as she talked about the retreat. She wanted more glimpses of Angela's off-duty personality. She wanted to know the real Angela and what made her tick. Her hopes, her dreams. What else she loved. To take things one step further.

'So, what does a virtuous yoga goddess do to switch off? I'm rather shocked to see you having a drink in all honesty. I thought you were all herbal tea, "my body is my temple".'

Angela threw her head back, laughing.

Emily continued. 'I mean, the *revelation* about the pot was shocking enough, but I put that down to you being a wee hippy trying to fit in in the big city sort of thing. *Grown-up* Angela is a different story. You're so composed, so calm. I can't imagine you breaking the rules.'

Angela was still laughing. 'Then you've a lot more to learn about me. And I fucking *love* how much you've psychoanalysed me.'

'We're saying "fucking" now, are we? I don't know what's going on,' said Emily, belying her sudden arousal at Angela using that word.

Angela took another large drink of champagne and then poured more into the glasses. 'I can do a lot more than swear.'

Emily gulped. What was that? She didn't know what to say and instead found herself staring at the beautiful woman next to her. She glanced out towards the rest of the pub, noticing again how secluded they were from anyone else and wondered why Angela had chosen this seat, out of all the others.

'Oh, I have no doubt. I've seen the way you get through those herbal teas. You're a right hedonist.' Emily had no idea where that had come from.

'So, what else have you noticed about me?' Angela shifted in her seat.

Emily gulped. 'Well, I can tell that you're very capable and independent. You seem to know who you are, and you seem okay talking in front of people every day. You're confident.' Emily could have gone on but stopped herself.

Angela smiled. 'Thank you. Yeah, I guess public speaking doesn't faze me. I've always been quite good at that.'

'It shows.' It was true, seeing the way she took her classes and how she interacted with people was really something. Angela moved her. At least Angela was trying to make the world a better place. She meant well and she was so great with people. The chat with the old ladies in the street, in particular, was quite touching. Angela was obviously from a wealthier background, but she could talk to anyone. Emily felt excited just thinking about all the fun times they could have together, all the friends they could make together. Yes, she'd been fantasising about them building a life together. A great life. 'I think you're probably the best person I've ever met. Definitely the kindest.'

At that, Angela swallowed, looking shy. It was very cute. Not at all the reaction that Emily thought she might give.

'And again, thank you. That's such a sweet thing to say.'

'I'm only telling the truth.'

Angela went quiet at that. They sipped their champagnes and smiled a little tentatively at each other again. Emily could tell there was a lot going on in Angela's head. It contrasted with her usual poise and yoga-teacher-self-assuredness. Could it be that she was feeling the same way as her?

After Angela had switched the chat back to safer ground, and a long discussion about how well the ideas Emily had put forward had helped Heart Yoga, Emily reached for the bottle of champagne only to find that it was empty. Frowning, she looked over at the bar, and then back to Angela, not wanting the night to end. Thankfully, she didn't feel too drunk. 'Look what happened,' she held up the empty bottle.

'We should get another.' Angela got up, hitting her knee on the table as she did so. The glasses on the table shook but didn't fall over. 'Oops.' She sat back down, laughing loudly at herself. The type of belly laugh that was uncommon for the normally so reserved, serious, Angela. Emily had never seen this side of her before: carefree, guard down, animated. She loved it. Her face was gentle, and she was looking at her the whole time with soft, gooey eyes. They literally sparkled and Emily found it hard to look away. So she didn't. Neither of them did. Angela's grey-blue eyes were lingering on Emily for so long, her mouth, her body, that Emily was becoming increasingly convinced at the possibility that Angela felt something towards her, too. It couldn't have been the business chat because they'd pretty much said all of those things to each other already. If nothing else, it was turning out to be one of the best nights she'd had in years. Possibly ever.

Emily stood up. 'My turn.'

When a little smile broke out on Angela's face, Emily picked up the bucket and headed towards the bar. She exhaled deeply as she walked, hoping that Angela was watching her as attentively as she had her. Emily ordered swiftly, as the bar was still not particularly busy, with her back to Angela the whole time. She couldn't bring herself to look around. Maybe she was on her phone and uninterested? Angela had just spent the better part of half an hour singing Emily's praises, and not just about business ideas. That had to be a good sign. When she did turn around, bucket in hand, Angela was sitting up brightly, following her path back to the table. Relief washed over Emily. It felt good.

Time flew as they made their way through the second bottle of champagne. They both seemed to have so many questions for each other, and they talked quickly, covering many topics. What was both a surprise and not a surprise was how many things they had in common. When Emily asked her how long it had been since she'd last had sex, Angela sat back, taking a moment. Emily continued. 'I only ask because for me, it has been … far too long.'

It looked like Angela was struggling to formulate an answer. The directness of the question seemed to have thrown her off balance.

'Sorry, that's a personal one. Forget I asked.'

'No, um, it's okay. Six months ago, maybe seven.'

'And you?' Angela's eyes were curious.

'About a year.'

'Oh.' Angela had her arms folded across her chest, with her head resting on the wall behind her, her head tilted slightly in her direction, watching her. Emily put her glass down. Angela continued to gaze at her from the side. The champagned fizzed. Every inch of her wanted to reach out and touch her.

So she did.

Nearly a bottle of champagne helped. Emily brushed a strand of hair from Angela's face that had fallen forward. 'You're beautiful, you know.' She left her hand cupping Angela's jaw and lightly stroked Angela's cheek with her thumb. Angela took a sharp intake of breath and tensed up, but Emily continued to caress the side of her face.

Angela relaxed her shoulders, and her face softened, looking into Emily's eyes as she did so, sending a wave of electricity through Emily's body. Emily almost forgot to breathe. Her heart pounded in her chest. She mapped out the shape of Angela's grey-blue eyes and recognised something in them. A desire. Yes, there was a definite look of longing from Angela. Emily could see she was struggling not to show it, but it was there.

Emily leant forward into Angela's personal space. Her silky hair smelled like coconut. After a few agonising seconds, Angela swallowed hard and then tilted her head. Emily looked down at Angela's mouth, seeing Angela discreetly lick her own lips. Emily inched forward, checking for permission from Angela to continue. She tilted her head and gently put her lips on Angela's. She kissed her softly but sensed a rigidity in Angela's body. Angela's tension didn't dissipate, so Emily pulled back slightly and met Angela's eyes. The desire in them was now obvious, but there was turmoil.

Emily waited, not knowing what to do next, then Angela kissed her. Emily felt her whole body tingle as Angela kissed her slowly and deliberately. Angela went from gently kissing, to opening her mouth and finding Emily's tongue. Angela's long blond hair was getting in the way. Emily brushed it out of the way again. All Emily could focus on was Angela's mouth on hers and the feeling of finally being close to her. The kiss held so much promise of so much more. When

Angela pulled away, Emily had no idea how long they'd been kissing for. Angela fixed her hair behind her ears and sat back a little. She smiled tenderly at Emily as she straightened out her top and picked up her champagne glass. Emily swallowed hard and inhaled deeply. She put a hand on Angela's thigh as she picked up her own glass and took a big gulp. Just resting her hand on Angela's thigh was so exciting. 'Wow … that was,' Emily puffed out her cheeks.

'Lovely,' Angela stroked Emily's hand with her thumb.

Emily was still in a sort of daze about the kiss. A silence fell between them. She wanted to remember every little detail and re-ran through it again in her head. Angela finished her champagne. That was the second bottle gone.

'Do you want to go?' Emily wanted to ask her outright if she wanted to come back to hers but didn't want to push it. Angela still hadn't said much and was avoiding her eyes.

'Yeah. Let's get a taxi.'

Out on the street a taxi happened to be passing almost as soon as they got outside. They flagged it down, and it pulled up outside the bar.

'Where to?' said the driver.

As Emily climbed in, Angela gave instructions to the driver, making it quite clear that there were to be two drop-offs. At this, Emily's spirits sank low in her stomach. Angela wanted to actually go home. They sat in complete silence as the taxi sped back along the road they had walked along earlier that night. A few rugby fans were still visible, mostly outside pubs smoking, but the numbers walking along the pavement had dwindled significantly. Emily still felt giddy from the kiss. And it had been some kiss. Like nothing she'd ever felt before. Certainly, it showed that Angela liked her. And that she was an excellent kisser.

It didn't feel over.

Angela's arms and legs were now crossed, facing in the

opposite direction. The only sound was the engine moving through the gears and the indicators whenever they took a left or right. The taxi turned onto Emily's street and made its way towards her door, before coming to a stop.

'Thanks,' said Emily, to the driver.

Angela had barely moved the entire ride. Emily paused before getting out. Taking a deep breath, she looked at Angela straight in the eyes. 'Do you want to come in?'

There was a long pause. Angela's mouth opened slightly. She uncrossed her legs and arms, sat up and faced Emily. 'Yes.'

Chapter 14

As Emily turned the key in the main door to the tenement, Angela stood behind her fighting with herself over what she was doing there. The kiss was amazing. Emily had her completely hooked. She wanted more. And it was only going to go one way if they got up to Emily's flat. But she couldn't want that. Emily was a student. A client. And she was off-limits. But was Emily just a client any more? It felt like they'd pushed past that barrier. She couldn't think clearly. The alcohol was making things blurry. Her body wanted one thing, but her mind was in such chaos. Emily went through the door and she followed. Emily turned to face her. The door took forever to close and Angela hesitated, nearly tripping over huge piles of leaflets and old phonebooks on the ground.

'I'm glad you're here,' said Emily, taking her hand.

At this small gesture, Angela broke. She took Emily's face in her hands and kissed her deeply feeling Emily's need for her through fast, hot breaths. She walked Emily back against the wall, pinned Emily against it, and placed one arm up over the wall behind her. They locked eyes. Emily trembled at this, and Angela wanted to devour her then and there. She was aware of the ferocity of her desire for Emily even then, and it shocked her a little.

Angela leant forward, stopping centimetres from Emily's lips. Emily tilted her head up towards Angela, who looked down at Emily's mouth again. They kissed slowly, both finding themselves in the embrace. Angela kissed Emily's top lip and gently opened her mouth, feeling another wave of pleasure go through her as they got lost in the kiss. Emily moaned quietly. Angela planted kisses all over her cheek and neck as Emily wrapped her arms around her shoulders. She kissed Emily on the mouth again as if they'd been kissing this way for years as her fingers found the button on Emily's trousers and lingered there. In that moment something in Angela clicked shut. In a sudden realisation at where this was going, she stepped backwards.

Emily was still breathing heavily. Her eyes were dark. She was so sexy, Angela had to force herself to look away.

'Emily. I can't.'

'What do you mean?'

'I'm sorry. I can't come up.'

'Why?'

Angela met her eyes and shook her head. 'I'm your teacher.'

'My *yoga* teacher,' said Emily, half-smiling. 'It's not the same.' She reached out towards Angela who took another step back. The look of hurt on Emily's face was sad.

'It's taking advantage. I'd better go. I'm sorry. Please don't tell anyone at the studio about this.'

'You're worried what people will think?'

Angela turned her head away, feeling awful for what she was doing. 'I want to … but I can't.'

'You just did.'

'It's unethical. You're my student. I don't date students. Clients.'

'So, I'll leave the studio,' said Emily, raising her voice. 'And I'm not just some client any more, am I?'

'That's not the point. I feel like I am going against my values here, and I'm not sure how I feel about it. Maybe I just need some time.'

Emily recovered herself, stood up straighter, and simply nodded in resignation.

A door opened and closed on a floor above. Footsteps

came clicking down the stairs. Emily looked pained. A tight knot started to grip Angela's stomach. Her emotions and body wanted one thing, but it threatened her whole world. Her breaths were shallow and unconscious. She looked towards the door and felt relief. 'Emily, please don't take this the wrong way. This is my fault. I ... I've got to go.' She left Emily at the bottom of the stairwell. A hot ball of emotion bubbled up inside her; she felt like crying. How could she do this to Emily, who was so sweet and kind? She pushed down the feeling and pulled open the main door. She sped along the dark street trying to outwalk her conflicting emotions. She quickened her pace even further and tried not to think about the look on Emily's face as she'd left, but she was not successful. Emily was all she could think about and she was all that she couldn't have.

What have I done?

Fine drizzle caressed her face. She allowed a single warm tear to join it.

***

Rooted to the spot, Emily's heart sank. Her neighbour from the floors above skipped past her, barely acknowledging her presence. As she dragged herself back up to her flat, her legs feeling like jelly, the absurdity of what had happened started to sink in. Clenching her fists, she couldn't understand how Angela could be so cruel. Emily was obviously fine with her saying no at any point, but she was less fine with Angela saying it shouldn't have happened in the first place.

When she got back into her flat her head was spinning, thoughts racing. The familiar surroundings jarred with how triggered she was feeling. She found it hard to believe Angela's reason for leaving was because she was her yoga teacher. Surely there must be more to it than that. Could she

129

ever go back to the studio after this?

She had to lie down. Walking down the long corridor to her bedroom, she felt her spirits drop with every step. Once inside her bedroom, she lay on top of her bed in the dark, with her feet dangling off the end. Memories of the evening came flooding in. It had been magical, up until the point Angela had left her in the stairwell.

She sighed, loudly, blowing all the air out of her lungs. As she thought back to her previous relationships, at least she knew from hindsight that they hadn't been quite right, and it was probably for the best they had ended. But what if Angela was *the one*? She had never felt this strongly about someone. Ever.

She couldn't understand what the problem was; they were both single and clearly very attracted to each other. The last thing Emily wanted to do was to upset Angela or make her feel uncomfortable. If being a student at her studio bothered Angela so much then she had to respect her boundaries about it. It was her livelihood and her purpose in life that she was worried about after all. With that realisation, Emily felt her spirits plummet further and that same, heavy, hopeless feeling taking hold of her again. With no desire or energy to get up or do anything, she stayed lying on her bed, still in the dark.

Out of nowhere, she found herself starting the deep breathing techniques she'd learned from Angela in class. This was the first time she'd used anything from class in real life at the time it was happening. She could hear Angela's voice telling her to open her heart and fill her lungs with loving energy. How odd that she should have to conjure the words of the person who was making her feel like this to try to calm down. Being angry at Angela wasn't what she wanted, that was for sure. She could hear Angela's voice instructing her to release all the tension in her body with each deep breath out.

Exhaling for longer than normal, she tried to release her pent-up feelings of unworthiness. The more she did this, the more it helped. Emily pictured herself wrapped in a cocoon of white light. Unsure of where the idea came from, it felt good all the same. She knew it was strange, but she could almost feel Angela's presence with her. Emily didn't just find her unbelievably physically attractive – real feelings had developed. Meeting Angela had been life changing. Their connection felt primal and authentic. Almost spiritual. Angela had got inside of her soul and had helped her clear out old destructive patterns of thinking and replace them with a self-compassion Emily had never had before.

Emily lay there quietly for over an hour going over things in her head. By the time she got up, she felt less stressed and less anxious about the whole thing. A favourite old saying popped into her head as she got changed into her pyjamas: *Whit's fur ye'll no go by ye.*

Chapter 15

The ground underneath Angela's feet was muddy and soft. With each footstep she accumulated more mud that stuck to her walking shoes like glue. A Sunday morning walk up Arthur's Seat would help to clear her mind. The view over the city usually helped her get things into perspective. Coconut scented air swirled up from each gorse bush as she passed, the bright yellow blooms extra vibrant after the rain. Recognising one or two people, and most of the dogs, Angela felt quite at home, loving the dedication of dog walkers despite the thick dark clouds brooding above them.

Finding a rock to sit on to look out over her city, Angela inhaled deeply, and tried to deal with the guilt that she felt from last night. A double whammy of guilt: for having and acting on desires and for how she had treated Emily at the end of the night. While she may not have broken any laws, she'd gone against her own ethical principles and the yoga values that she held so dear. She had behaved with neither compassion nor restraint towards Emily; it was crushing. Emily had come to her studio in a vulnerable state. As a teacher, in a position of power, overstepping that boundary, especially in the way she did, was deeply troubling to her. It was classic base chakra behaviour. The opposite of what she expected of herself.

The part of the city where Emily lived drew her attention. How was she feeling? She hoped she was okay. For all she knew, Emily would never speak to her again. It pained her to think that she had hurt Emily's feelings or acted like she didn't care. She cared a lot. The realisation of that was huge. But she wasn't looking to let someone in again, so it scared her.

She hadn't told anyone and was in no hurry to. If it got out that she was the sort of yoga teacher who preyed on people who came to her classes, she might as well quit her business now. Worst of all, she feared the disapproval of her mentor, Jackie Hay. It was she who had taken Angela from being an average teacher and made her into the teacher she was today. Before Jackie, Angela felt she merely dabbled with her practice, teaching the odd class here and there, and getting far too distracted and sucked into things that didn't serve her. She was where she was in her life because of her mentor, and her mentor had always been very clear about the rules when it came to getting involved with one of your students.

And then there was Cult Yoga. They had been getting more than a little aware of the business Angela was taking from them. Angela knew this because Zoe had overheard some gossiping among the staff when she had gone in to cover a class for them. Zoe was not a big fan of their studio but did accept invitations to guest teach there from time to time.

Angela was grateful to have such a trusted friend working for her – especially on days like this where Angela had effectively called in sick for the morning. Emily sometimes came to class on Sunday mornings. There was no way that Angela could risk facing Emily in class so soon after their kiss. Their *kisses*. It was still too raw.

Angela walked home, fast. Once back in her flat, she took off her clothes and let them fall to the ground. Standing naked in her bathroom, she washed her hands, unable to look in the mirror above the sink and unsure if it was shame or guilt which she was feeling the most. Every fibre in her body wanted to ignore and numb the feelings, but she knew it was important to fully feel, recognise and deal with them.

As she touched her cheek where Emily had caressed her so

133

gently the night before, she realised that she also wasn't able to ignore who she had feelings for, however inappropriate. There was a connection between them, something powerful. Walking back through to her bedroom, she checked her mobile to see if Emily had got in touch, but she had not. Turning the phone off, she sighed and sat down on her bed, looking at herself in the full-length mirror in front of her wardrobe.

Why would she have? It was you who was the arsehole.

The clothes she had on last night lay crumpled in a pile on the floor. The knot in her stomach twisted further. Seeing the clothes made the events more real. The feeling of Emily's lips on her own, the eagerness of their touches all burned through her mind and both excited and alarmed her. Things had escalated so quickly that she still couldn't work out exactly when things had gone that way. Part of her was still a bit shocked. She hadn't meant for it to happen. Under no circumstances could she allow herself to get excited about what had happened because she knew where it would lead to. If she was being honest with herself, she had flirted with Emily all night. For this, she was ashamed. Disturbed by her inner turmoil, she bumped into the bed and almost fell as she pulled her leggings on.

***

Angela arrived at Heart Yoga just after the one o'clock class had begun. Two women were chatting at one of the tables over coffee and cake. Zoe's mellifluous voice came through from the studio. One of her younger teachers, Samantha, was looking after the café. Samantha often came in on Sundays to help out, on top of her three classes during the week that she taught. She was young and wanted work experience and it allowed Angela to have a bit of a weekend if she wanted or to catch up on some paperwork in the office. Plus, the new business plan was to allow her more time to teach, and not to always be stuck at the café or in the office. Having discussed at length with Emily about where she felt she was right now with the business and where she envisioned it going, they'd worked out a plan for how she would get there. It also included things to stop doing and things to start. Asking Samantha to work on Sundays had been another of Emily's excellent ideas. It was costly but her health had to feature in this new life she was trying to build for herself. Burnout was a legitimate business risk. Angela did a quick peek into the main studio to see if Emily was there. Seeing that she wasn't, Angela felt relieved but also a little disappointed. Her shoulders dropped and her head went down just as Samantha came out of the office grinning about something.

'Hey,' said Angela. 'How's it going?'

'Excellent! It's been very busy all morning, just thinning out a bit now. I'm really getting the hang of these smoothies,' said Samantha, pouring a generous amount of green liquid into a pint glass.

'Brilliant.'

'Yeah. I like hanging out here, you know. It's got good vibes.'

'Thank you, Samantha. I'm glad you feel that way. Your being here is a big part of that.'

Samantha smiled at her and tilted her head to one side. 'You're so nice. No wonder this place is doing well.'

'Cheers.' Angela was still getting used to the idea that the studio was doing well. The main door opened, and the bell rang predictably. A young mum came into the café, holding a baby in a sling on her chest, and hovered by the door. Not making eye contact with Angela or Samantha, she looked dangerously close to leaving again. Angela didn't think she was any older than eighteen. The baby stirred and she spoke quietly to it and then Angela remembered. It was the young woman from the street when they did the community engagement.

'Hello, please come in,' said Angela walking towards her. When their eyes met it was confirmed that it was one hundred percent the same young woman from before. 'It's lovely to see you and your little one again. I'm glad you've popped in.'

'I hope it's all right.'

'Of course it's all right! Everyone is welcome here. What can I do for you?'

'Mind the free class you were talking about, is it still on?'

'Yes, it runs every Wednesday morning from ten to eleven.'

The girl frowned. 'Oh. That's days away.'

'We have a class that's running this afternoon that I'm taking and there's a discount running. If you buy something from the café you can try a free class.' This wasn't strictly true. Emily's business brain had rubbed off on her. Before her input, Angela would never have been able to come up with stuff like that on the spot or have the courage to talk about money so openly. However, she desperately wanted the young woman and her baby to stay.

'Right. I might take that, thanks.' She looked up at the blackboard above the café. She studied the menu. 'What time does it start?'

'At two.'

'Okay, I'll wait. Is there anywhere I can change his nappy if he needs to go?'

There wasn't. Mentally putting "install baby-changing area in the bathroom" to the top of her to-do list, Angela looked through to the back office. They hadn't had many mums with babies in. That needed to change. 'Would my desk through the back be okay? I haven't got anywhere else yet, but I'll be getting one in as soon as possible.'

'Ta. He might not but it's good to know there's somewhere and that I won't disturb anyone with it.'

'We love babies here, so you won't be disturbing anyone.'

Angela peeped around at the baby swinging comfortably in the sling. Angela became transfixed on the large eyes twinkling before her and the miniature wriggling arms and legs.

'He's gorgeous. Would he like a cuddle?' said Angela.

The girl shrugged. 'If you want,' she picked up her baby and handed him to Angela.

Taking the baby in her arms, Angela felt the pull for one of her own. She made funny noises and silly faces at the baby and quickly elicited a smile from the tiny human in a white onesie.

'He's heavy, isn't he?'

'He was ten pounds.'

Angela did a double take. 'Ten. That's amazing. He's so lovely.'

The girl, tired, smiled slightly. It was the first time Angela had seen her do so. She thanked his mum and reluctantly handed him back to her.

'Have a seat and I'll let you make your mind up about what you want.' Angela left her to it and rejoined Samantha behind the café counter. The pair of them stood quietly behind the counter observing the young girl and her baby. The girl sat down near the window and furtively looked around her. Angela watched as she interacted with her baby and got herself comfortable.

'That baby is so cute. I want one,' said Samantha, absent-mindedly.

'Yeah. Me too.'

As Angela washed her hands, she thought about starting the baby yoga classes and what that might involve. Walking back over to the mum and baby, she could feel it was an idea worth pursuing. 'Do you know what you'd like to have?'

'A hot chocolate.'

'Would you like some marshmallows and cream.'

The young girl paused. 'Yes, please.'

'Coming right up.' Angela smiled.

The young woman smiled and turned her baby to face Angela. 'See the nice lady.' Angela looked into the baby's large round eyes again and made a silly face. The baby giggled and Angela nearly died. Leaving them at the table, Angela got to making the hot chocolate, suggesting to Samantha that she take a break. Samantha quickly found her phone and sat down scrolling through it with a herbal tea next to her. The two women who had been chatting were now enthralled with the young woman and her baby. Angela smiled at the scene. The girl was smiling and making conversation with the two women who sounded like mums themselves. It was exactly what she wanted the café to be about. People interacting and making social connections that otherwise wouldn't happen. She put a generous helping of chocolate powder and some milk into a silver jug and let the nozzle heat it up. She tilted it at the top and brought it into a frothy foam. Pouring it into a large mug, she topped it off with marshmallows, lashings of whipped cream and sprinkles of chocolate. Stepping back, she realised how infrequently she'd made it at the café. Most of her customers were either herbal tea, coffee, or smoothie drinkers.

The door chimed its way open again as someone else came in. Angela's happiness disappeared as soon as she saw who it was. It was the owner of Cult Yoga. Donna Smith. Her rival and one of her least favourite people. They'd both trained under Jackie Hay, but had gone off in completely different directions. Donna had gone down the route of the commercialised image-conscious watered-down version of yoga that Angela so despised. Angela liked to think that she'd followed a more ethical route, and that her form of yoga held true to her teacher and to the ancient principles of the practice. Donna walked slowly into the café, taking in every detail of the room but not finding anything that pleased her. Dressed head to toe in a designer outfit, her perfect hair, nails, and fake tan looked quite out of place in the down-to-earth studio.

'Hi Donna. I'll be with you in a second.'

Angela walked over to the young mum and placed her drink on the table beside her. She turned to find that Donna was right behind her.

'I hear you've turned this place around. Riding a little high this week? That's great. Let's hope it lasts, though, and doesn't fizzle out. You learn these things when you run an established studio, you see. The peaks and troughs, well, we only ever seem to have peaks, but you hear about so many little studios folding within their first year.' Donna gave an insincere smile. 'What sort of back-up plan do you have for when this little flurry dies down?' Donna glanced around looking underwhelmed and superior, running a finger along the chest of drawers. 'Why have you got a chest of drawers here? You could easily get another table on this wall if you used the space better.' Donna shook her head and smiled thinly. 'See, that's the difference between the professional studios and the amateurs. It's the commitment to making a profit that wins the game. People want to know they're spending their money in a place that takes itself, and its yoga, seriously.'

Angela was stunned by the passive-aggression. Part of her wanted to fire back similar cutting remarks, but, after spending the morning meditating up Arthur's Seat and trying to get back in touch with her yoga principles, she resisted the urge to stoop to that level. Samantha stood by the till with her mouth wide open, having never met Donna before. Angela envied anyone who hadn't met a character like Donna before.

'How can I help you?' said Angela.

'Oh, I'm not here to buy anything. I just wanted to see what all the fuss was about.'

'What fuss?'

'You are the talk of the town. Little studio in a shit part of town that draws customers from the city centre. I'm surprised it hasn't been featured in the *Evening News* yet.'

'Donna. What do you want? Why have you come here?'

'Angela. I'm here to congratulate you. I didn't think you had it in you. You were always so … I don't know, airy-fairy. You must have got some help. Who was it?'

'Okay. Thank you. Now I think you should leave.'

'Kicking me out? Wait until people hear that you lost your cool at a friendly bit of competition.'

'I'm not kicking you out. I am asking you why you've come here when all you seem able to do is to mock me and my studio. So, yes, I am suggesting that you are not here for a good reason and should therefore get the fuck out.'

'Ha. There. I've got it,' Donna held up her phone, which was on video. It had been recording the entire time. 'Bet this won't help you after I put it out on YouTube. I'll do a gif on "get the fuck out".' Donna laughed, unkindly.

The young woman and the two friends had stopped chatting long ago and were watching the scene, aghast. Angela gritted her teeth, trying not to say something else that she regretted, and tried to figure out why her impulse control was failing her these days. Donna was such an odd yoga teacher and Angela had found it very difficult to see where she was coming from most of the time when they were students. She could see now that Donna had grown into a mean-spirited woman who had no business teaching yoga and making money off its name.

'Get out,' said Samantha.

'Jeez. Don't get your knickers in a twist, or has Angela already done that for you? Nice little hunting ground you've got here for yourself.'

Angela screwed up her face in anger. Donna turned her attention to the class schedule on an iPad on the chest of drawers. Samantha walked over and stood beside her, in a show of support. Donna put down the iPad and raised an eyebrow one last time in Angela's direction. The baby started to cry. Donna turned and left, barely glancing at the people she had disturbed in the café. Angela was so angry yet also felt calm. She was older now and could see through little demonstrations of nastiness. Not that she came into contact with such behaviour much any more. That was the main thing, the surprise of what Donna had said. They'd not seen each other in over a year yet that was how she saw fit to speak to her. Angela knew it was laughable. Yet, Donna's comments about her sexuality were still cutting. When Donna had found out Angela was a lesbian, she had weaponised the information, and she was still doing it.

Angela looked over at the group in the café and hoped they hadn't heard the exchange. Their voices were quiet. Did they know something? Had it got out that she'd been inappropriate with a student? She thought back to the pub and realised that someone might have seen her and Emily. She thought they'd been in a private spot, but she couldn't be certain. Anxiety started to rise in the pit of her stomach.

'Who was *that*?' asked Samantha.

Angela jerked her head around. 'She owns Cult Yoga. She was a student with me when I was training with Jackie Hay.'

'What's her deal? Why's she being like that? That was downright abusive.'

'Who knows. I can't imagine we've gained that much of

their business. I think she believes that there's not enough for everyone to go around. That if other people do well it somehow takes something away from her. The only – other – reaction she's going to get from me is compassion.'

'She shouldn't have said that about you being sleazy. You're the least likely person to,' Samantha lowered her voice into a whisper, 'sleep with a student.'

Angela felt a wave of guilt flow through her. Instead of carrying on the conversation, she cleaned the coffee machine and wiped down the entire counter while the full force of what she had done hit her. The truth was, she had breached that line. She acted on her attraction to Emily. Reluctantly, she forced herself to accept that it might get out about what happened, but she vowed that it would never happen again.

'I'm going to get ready for my next class.' Angela fled to the sanctuary of her office and shut the door.

Chapter 16

Emily waited by the steps down to Portobello beach for Anna to arrive for their walk. She had got there early after cycling there a bit quicker than she anticipated and was content enough to wait and gaze out at the stormy sea. Being at the beach always reminded Emily of family holidays in Spain as a child, although the memories were sunshine filled and not like the grey skies that sat above her now. There was a thick mist in the air. As it started to rain, she put her hood up and shoved her hands inside her pockets, cursing the fact she didn't own a jacket that was actually waterproof. Some sand lay about her feet after having made its way up onto the promenade from high winds. Thankfully, the tide was going out. Anna had checked the tides before agreeing to meet there, weeks earlier.

'Hello!' said Anna, coming in for a bear hug.

'There you are,' said Emily, turning around and hugging her friend easily.

'I've missed you!'

'How're you? How's Russell? How's Jason?'

'Grand. I couldn't get out the door fast enough though. I was so looking forward to adult conversation. And I do hope it's *adult*, if you know what I mean, hey-hey!' Anna winked, terribly, at Emily. Emily laughed. Anna continued. 'I have to get my kicks somewhere.'

Emily didn't want to disappoint, as she did have a spicy story to tell, but she was going to wait to spill the beans until coffee.

'Well.'

Anna regarded her closely. 'Something's happened.' Anna

squealed. 'You have a look about you.'

'Shall we walk?'

'Oh, yes. Let's. It's not the best day for it but who cares, eh? You know what they say: there's no such thing as bad weather, only the wrong clothes.'

'Yeah. I agree. I hope my showerproof jacket doesn't let in too much.'

'A wee bit of rain won't hurt us. Anyways, it's so great to be outside and to see you.'

'How's it all going at work? How's it being back?'

'Traumatic.'

The pair marched briskly down the steps and out onto the sand. The tide had left rocks and shells and wet sand in its wake. They walked out towards the shore before turning right to head east along the beach. A pyramid-shaped hill further down the coast could be seen jutting out of the landscape in the distance through the mist. The rain lashed down, but they marched along the beach regardless. Anna filled her in on her baby's pooping schedule as the waves raged against the shoreline, sending them on a long gentle curving walk, and the houses on the shore grew further away. After over an hour of walking through the muddy sand they approached where they had started.

They climbed up the same steps and headed into a beachfront coffee shop. It was warm inside, with steamed-up windows and lots of people. Emily felt her cheeks sting as the heat hit her cold skin. Catching sight of herself in a mirror by the door, she looked dishevelled with matted hair and bright pink cheeks. Anna's face was also pink, but her hair seemed remarkably unaffected. Standing in the doorway next to a pile of umbrellas, they peeled off their jackets, and hung them up. Emily's Kathmandu jacket had fared okay, and her clothes weren't too sodden. It had cleared up halfway through the walk, which had helped. Tiers of pastries and cakes lay out on the counter. The sound of indiscriminate chatter filled the air along with the screech from the coffee machine. They found a table by the window and ordered. Emily felt very at home in the café, as it was one of her and Anna's favourite hangouts.

Emily bit into a pastry as Anna's mouth fell open.

'You did what?'

Emily chewed, still in disbelief about the situation herself.

'You nearly had sex with her in the bottom of your stairwell?'

'It was going there.'

Anna flopped back in her seat, flabbergasted. 'And then she ran out and left you? Doesn't sound so namaste or whatever to me ...'

'I didn't expect anything to ever happen with her. I'm thrilled it did. Even though she made such a dramatic exit.'

'Emily. Jeezo. I thought my life was getting a bit boring but hearing this makes me feel like a fossil.'

'Your life is amazing. You have a wonderful husband and baby, a job you love, and a proper family home. A *forever* home. I could go on and on about how good your life is. You wouldn't want to be in my shoes. Not for a second.'

'Says the woman having it off with her hot lesbian yoga teacher. Hot *single* lesbian yoga teacher.'

'At the moment, apart from you, that's all I've got.'

Anna's face softened. She squeezed Emily's hand briefly. 'You've always got me.'

Emily smiled then took a sip of coffee.

'Why do you think she got cold feet on you?'

Emily considered the question. 'She said something about not wanting to get involved with a student, or a client, or whatever she thinks I am. That it's unethical.'

'Yeah. That's a complication.'

'Is it? We're so much more than that now. The fact that

she still sees me that way, I've got to tell you, is kind of annoying.' Emily paused. 'But also kind of hot. I'm not going to lie.'

'Don't hate me for saying this, but I'm getting the warning signals.'

'Why? I'm a grown-ass independent woman and so is she. What's holding her back if she wants to take things further? This sort of stuff happens all the time. People wouldn't judge her for it. I'm not sure why she even cares.'

Anna tilted her head at Emily. 'It seems to make her feel uncomfortable. What was it you said? Unethical? That might be hard to come back from. Clearly, she's not in a position to start dating someone who goes to her studio.' Anna sat forward and placed a hand on Emily's wrist. 'Oh, honey, I don't want to see you getting hurt again.'

In moments like these Emily cursed how well Anna knew her. She didn't want to be reminded of how badly things went with her last girlfriend.

'I don't know what's going on. We have a connection, and not only *like that*. I've been helping her with her business ...'

'You've been working for her?'

'Yeah, I've been helping her business get back on track. It was struggling. It's not like *work*.'

'Has she been paying you for your time?'

'What!? No. Of course not. That would be weird.'

'Oh dear. This is more complicated than I thought.'

'I care about her. We've been hanging out afterwards. At the studio, late, and stuff.'

'Hmm. Tricky. What if she really likes you but she's not able to act on it? That must be hard.'

'I hope she's okay.'

'Look at you. Planning the wedding in your mind, aren't you?'

Emily was indignant. 'No.'

'I knew it. Written. All. Over. Your. Face.'

'I've not even texted her or called her once since.'

'Yes, good. Try not to do what you normally do.'

'Thanks.'

'No, I say that with love. If you push her, she will disappear. Can you play it cool?'

Emily paused and thought about Angela and what it must be like for her. She could feel her anguish. 'I can. I don't want to upset her. It's not my fault if she finds me irresistible.'

Anna laughed. 'Modest, aren't you?'

'Let's face it though. She fucked off *during* ... you know, and that was a bit rude. If I need an excuse to be mad at her in order to play it cool, I'll just keep remembering her walking away from me.'

'Don't overthink it. Let her come to you.'

'You're right. I guess I'm getting carried away with the excitement of it all. And it was, very exciting, if you know what I mean.'

Anna laughed. 'I'm getting the picture.'

Emily finished her pastry. 'I like her but I'm not stupid. I'm not going to go all crazy on her. It was just a kiss. I'll pretend like nothing happened. Give her time and space to see how unnecessary it is to push me away.'

'Are you going to go back to yoga?'

Emily contemplated her response and decided to be brutally honest with Anna. 'I was planning on going tonight.'

'Tonight? That's hardly giving her space, Emily.'

'I know but I really want to see her.'

'You'd be chasing her. Doing the exact opposite of what you just said you were going to do.'

'Hmm. Yes, but if I leave it too long it might get too weird and then I'll never go back. Better to get the awkwardness over with and try to move forward in whatever direction.'

'You mean seduce her again?'

Emily laughed. 'No! I don't know. Maybe.'

Anna shook her head like a disappointed teacher. 'I order you to keep me updated.'

Emily laughed. The café chatter buzzed around them. She felt good and hopeful, despite knowing deep down that her chances with Angela were slim. 'I can do that.'

'Honestly, all this has been having a good effect on you. You seem lighter. Last time we caught up, I was a bit worried.'

Emily avoided Anna's eyes. 'I went through a wee rough spell, but I'm past that now. I think.'

'Losing a job is one of the most stressful things that can happen to someone. I'd say you've coped pretty well, actually.'

'Aw, thanks, Anna. I honestly don't know what I'd do without you. I'm certainly distracted these days, that's true. It's hard to be on a downer when you're crushing on someone. And I've had an idea. Well, Angela had an idea and it's genius.'

'Did she now.'

'I'm exploring the idea of setting up as a business consultant. Basically, helping small businesses to grow, consult on their strategic development, save them from going under. That sort of thing.'

'Like you've been doing for Angela?'

Emily chewed on her lower lip. 'So, it's synchronicity? We bring out the best in each other.'

'She's certainly brought something out in you.'

Emily burst out laughing. 'Don't.'

'I've not seen you like this in a long while. And the business idea sounds fabulous. You'd be so good at that. Being your own boss. Coming up with you own ideas and seeing them through. Isn't that exactly what held you back at the last place?'

'At Bawsac Incorporated, yes.'

Anna laughed. 'You named them, I see.'

'Obvs.'

'I don't blame you. What they did to you after all those years wasn't right.'

'You know, I'm over it. I see now that I was just wasting my time and energy there anyway.'

'When one door closes ... that's all I'm saying.'

'Three more slam in your face?'

'There's a world of possibilities out there. You have the power to manifest *whatever* you want.'

'You should be a life coach.'

'I consider that as a dream job, thank you very much.'

'You'd be amazing at it.'

Anna agreed and then focused on her coffee and pastry. Emily finished her coffee and looked out the window towards the uninviting sea. Touching her necklace, she realised how much better she was feeling in general since the day she bought it. It was as if throwing herself into yoga and her business plans were the only things holding her together.

What if it's Angela?

Anna stood up. 'I'll get the bill,' she said, already on the move.

Chapter 17

Candles illuminated the studio as Angela carefully selected the music to go with her most soothing class. She pressed play at a familiar playlist of slow gentle gongs and flutes over intermittent sounds of waves lapping at shores. The music courted the room and helped set the mood for what was to come. It was Angela's least active class as it mostly involved lying down and listening to Angela whisper soothing words of comfort and helpful reminders. Often, she based it around things she herself was going through or needed to hear. One week it was all about having faith in the universe, another week she focused on letting go of ego and attachment. The class only took place once a week. Any more than that and she feared her words would become trite. Tonight she wasn't entirely sure what to focus on. Part of her wanted to focus on having healthy boundaries, but she couldn't think of a way to tie it in enough with the principles of yoga that underpinned the sessions. Perhaps she could talk about having integrity and standing by your highest values? Taking her place, she decided to keep it generic. It could be unwise to let herself get talking about the subject and risk oversharing in the moment.

As the students came in and put their mats down, Angela didn't recognise a single person. The class was nearly full at fourteen. Double what she used to think was a good turnout for this class. A small rush of nerves flowed through her body. She wanted them to love the class and keep coming back. This was all she wanted for her students, and anyone who did yoga. Since they were at capacity, space was a bit tight. The basket for the blankets had been pushed aside and plant pots moved up onto the window ledge. One more person could fit in, but that was pushing it. As the class found their places and sat down, the atmosphere was rather tense. As far as she'd heard, no one had said a word to each other, or to her. Perhaps she should have waited until the class officially started before putting the music on. A gong banged out from the speakers as she bowed her head and pressed the palms of her hands together in front of her chest, making it look planned though it wasn't.

Angela smiled. 'Hi everyone.'

The students smiled back nervously.

As Angela went into her teacher mode, her nerves disappeared and she fixated on creating the levels of safety and relaxation that were required. 'Thank you so much for joining me this evening. We'll be going into some deep relaxation during our time together, taking the opportunity to feel good, de-stress, and bring a wee bit of balance to our bodies and also to our minds and our emotional selves as well. You've all got your blocks and blankets, I see, so you are all set to go. Take this time at the beginning to find a sitting position that works for you and we'll begin.'

The class repositioned themselves and got more comfortable. Sensing their defences come down a notch, she felt the energy in the room lift a little. One thing that always struck her when teaching was the willingness of students to follow instruction and to try to please her as their teacher.

The bell on the front door chimed. She checked the clock. They were two minutes in, and she had no one covering the café to meet the person.

The French doors moved, and Emily tiptoed through. 'Sorry to interrupt. Is it okay if I join the class? I know I'm a bit late.' Emily, almost whispering, seemed genuinely apologetic. It was unlike her to be late.

Angela felt her breath catch in her throat but knew she had

to remain calm. 'No, it's fine. We'd only just started. Please come in. There's a spot in the corner over here.' Angela pointed at the last space in the front row, beside the basket and the pots that had been moved.

'Thank you.'

Emily moved quickly, taking off her jumper, shoes, and socks at the back of class. She placed her shoes against the back wall, and haphazardly folded her jumper and put it on top of them. Angela watched as she piled her phone and keys on top of her jumper, then swiftly grabbed a mat, block, and blanket before laying it all out on the floor. This all took a matter of seconds. Already dressed in leggings and a T-shirt, she seemed hurried but also cool and confident. When Emily sat on her mat and faced the front, they locked eyes. Angela remembered the night before and felt her cheeks burn hot. At least it wouldn't be visible in the candlelit room.

Angela cleared her throat and began the class again. 'Um, so yes. Are we all settled in now?' Nods and smiles answered her question, and no one seemed too bothered by the interruption. 'I want you to get comfortable and get set up in a way that feels good.'

The class visibly readjusted themselves yet again, each time getting more and more at ease in their surroundings. Angela remained in the lotus position with a hand on each knee. 'Let your head drop to your heart and then slowly lie down on your mat. As you lie here, I want you to find your breath and let it be as it is. Don't try to modify it just yet. I'm sure we've all had enough of trying this week. I know you all try so hard in life, so take this time to offer some time for you and let go. You know you deserve it.' Angela was quiet for a few moments. 'Finding that inner smile, I want you to breathe in love, lengthen the spine, and be kind to yourself. Life can rush past us so quickly, and we can sometimes feel as if it's all a dream. Take this time to anchor yourself in this moment.

Feel your fingers and your toes. Bring your awareness to your arms and legs. Close your eyes and listen to the waves as we occupy this space.'

The class lay on their mats completely silently with their arms and legs languidly hanging off from their bodies, ears tuned in on Angela's every word. 'There really is nothing except this moment. All the experiences of this past week are behind you. Centre yourself in the now and let tomorrow happen when it does. You'll move forward in your life when the time comes, with love, being kind to yourself and others.' Angela said all of this at her usual slow pace. However, this time she had her eyes closed too.

Angela opened her eyes feeling slightly vulnerable and caught Emily gazing at her. Emily looked away and closed her eyes. Angela's mind went blank. She didn't know what to do or say next. Her whole attention had now turned to Emily and her presence. She decided to get the class moving and took them through an exceptionally slow sun salutation. By the time Angela finished the class she had regained full control of what she was doing, but inside she was freaking out about what to do about her feelings for Emily. There was an invisible pull, silent, but strong. She hoped that it wasn't noticeable to the others. Feeling almost naked and still fighting an internal struggle, Angela guided the roomful of women towards the end of the class and to the final namaste. As the women casually and quietly left the class, Angela felt exhausted and very much glad that it was over and had gone well.

'Thanks,' said one student as she rolled up her yoga mat. 'That was so chilled out. Beats any weed.'

'I'm pleased you got something out of it. This is probably the most relaxing class we have. We have a full range of others, too.'

'Yeah, they seem good … but are they not a bit hard, what

with all the planks and stuff?'

'Some are a bit more demanding than others. I'd avoid Power Yoga if moving too much isn't what you're looking for. You might want to try *Hatha* by the sounds of it. We have classes on throughout the week.'

'Cool. I'll check it out,' said the young woman as she put her things away. 'See you next time.'

After seeing the last dreamy-eyed students out the door, Angela went back through to the studio. Emily hadn't moved from her mat. Angela turned off the gongs. The studio was quiet.

'Hey,' said Emily, with hope in her eyes.

'Hey.'

An awkward silence began as Angela fidgeted with her hands. 'Emily.'

'Yes?'

'What happened last night … it can't happen again.'

Emily's face fell in disappointment.

'I don't want to lead you on. I don't date my students and it was wrong of me to act the way I did.' As the words left her mouth, one part of her agreed and wanted her to believe in what she was saying, but another part of her instantly regretted it and was screaming out to be heard.

Emily was quiet. After a few moments she replied. 'Don't worry about it.' She picked up her things. 'I completely understand,' she hurriedly put on her jumper, socks, and shoes. When she was dressed, she looked directly into Angela's eyes. 'I just have one question.'

'What's that?'

Emily took a few moments to ask her question. 'Did you enjoy kissing me?'

Angela's breath caught in her throat again. It was up high in her neck and she had to force herself to exhale. She swallowed hard and felt the need to speak her truth. 'Yes.'

Emily nodded like someone absorbing vital new information. 'And you're quite sure you don't want to do that again?'

'I am.'

'Right, well. If that's how you feel …'

'I don't want things between us to be awkward.'

'Look, Angela. We kissed and … stuff. It happens. It's not like we agreed to marry or something.'

'Yeah, um, that's right.'

'Is it still okay for me to do yoga here? And can I still come on the retreat?'

Angela felt awful. 'It's just also that I'm … I'm not looking for a relationship.'

'Honestly, Angela. I get it. I hope we can still be friends, and that you'll still let me in here.'

Angela could tell Emily's defences were up and she had to respect that. There was no way to communicate how she was feeling without causing further confusion and hurt. 'Of course you're still welcome here.'

As Angela followed her to the door, all she wanted to do was to reach out and hug her tightly. She couldn't find the right words to say. She couldn't see an alternative to saying no to being with her. Emily hovered by the door, then took her hand and squeezed it. 'It's okay, Angela.' Emily gave her a sad, half-smile as she let go of her hand, and then left.

As Emily walked away Angela felt herself splinter inside. If this was the right decision, then why did it feel so painful.

Chapter 18

As the back doors of the minibus opened wide, the retreat officially started. The group stood eagerly outside Heart Yoga, waiting to load up the vehicle which would take them to the Highlands for their much-anticipated inaugural yoga retreat. Bags and suitcases were piled up on the pavement ready to go on. The morning dew was lifting, and everything was finally coming together. Even though it was early May, it was still chilly in the shade. Adding to the excitement was the fact that it was due to get to twenty degrees later.

With expectations running high for an amazing weekend, Angela was on edge but hopeful that everything would go smoothly. The build-up to the retreat had been so frantic. Everything had been thought through to the smallest detail, paid for, and put into an extensively detailed itinerary. After an already crazy start to opening Heart Yoga, which she had yet to recover from, organising the retreat had drained Angela's energy levels. At this point she was looking forward to enjoying some of the benefits of the retreat along with her students.

Zoe was working the retreat with her. Angela had pitched it to Zoe that she would lead the weekend overall, take most of the sessions, run most of the activities, and be responsible for making sure everyone was being looked after, and Zoe would be in charge of making sure it all ran to plan and on time. It would be a combined effort. Zoe was happy to take on this role and had organised the transport to the venue, getting an amazing deal on the minibus from a friend of hers who ran an outdoor adventure company. Zoe had also volunteered to drive the bus – a four-hour drive to the

Highlands with a van full of people. Angela couldn't have been more grateful, and she showed it by covering Zoe's costs and paying her well.

Rushing about from person to person, Angela checked everyone was okay and hadn't forgotten anything. She had a clipboard but kept forgetting to check things off. The retreat would be a dedicated long weekend of yoga, relaxation, and socialising with fellow "Heart Yogers" at a beautiful venue overlooking the Isle of Skye. This would be a retreat in every sense of the word. Angela craved the peace and tranquillity waiting for them there – a chance to slow down, connect with nature and get off grid. On top of this, she would be sharing it with her most loyal and enthusiastic students.

Karen was driving up in her own car, and Jackie Hay would be joining them there, flying in from Germany, making the total party size eleven. Angela was so excited to spend time with her mentor again. It had been nearly two years since she had last seen her, when she joined her in Thailand for a similar style retreat. It was what had inspired Angela to finally open her own place.

The only thing missing was Emily. Yes, she was coming on the retreat; but, after Angela had told her to back off, she most certainly had. Not only had she not been coming to the studio as much, but when she had come, she'd kept her distance. Now, on the cusp of the retreat, Emily was there in the group, fresh-faced and chatting away in the bright morning sunshine, but distant. A pang of regret shot through Angela's belly. Angela had thought about what had happened between them often, of their kissing, of the hunger in their touches. And that was worrying. Not only did she find Emily physically attractive, there was no doubt about that, she knew that she cared about her more than she had done about any other woman in a long time. She simultaneously desired and feared the beautiful woman standing on the pavement not making eye contact with her.

Angela faced Zoe after they'd finished loading the luggage. 'That's us. Are we ready to go?'

'I think so. You ready to pull the plug on them?' said Zoe.

'It's now or never,' said Angela, gravely. 'Hey everyone.' She waved her arms in the air to get their attention. The chatter stopped and a quiet fell as all faces turned to her. 'One last thing before we get going. As you know, the one rule for this retreat is that it's going to be a phone-free zone. Since you've all signed up to this and agreed, that means I'll be confiscating everyone's phone until the end of the retreat and leaving them in the locked studio where they won't be able to tempt you. Any emergencies will be handled via this wee Nokia 3310,' Angela waved the basic phone in front of her. 'The owners of the retreat are fully connected via landline, wifi, and satellite. Did everyone complete their next of kin form?'

A round of nods and agreements came back at Angela.

'What is that you're holding?' said Olivia. 'Is it a toy phone? Is it even real?'

'Yes, it's a real phone,' said Angela, looking at it. 'Actually, I think this was my first ever phone.'

Louise was first to drop her phone off, letting out a long sigh of relief as it hit the inside of the box. 'Finally free from that bloody thing. Thank you, my heavenly darling.'

'They'll be well looked after,' Angela held up the box and dangled it towards the reluctant onlookers, 'in the safe inside. You won't even know they're gone. Think of it like a holiday for your phones, too.'

'I already feel like I've got a limb missing,' said Olivia, placing her phone down carefully.

'All the more reason to part with them for a few days,' said Angela.

'Easier said than done,' said Emily, stepping forward and

swiftly placing hers in the box, glancing briefly into Angela's eyes before stepping aside to let everyone else turn theirs over.

Angela felt a pang of disappointment in the pit of her stomach, again. Pushing it down, she refocused on the party, addressing them like their mother. 'You'll thank me for it one day. I'm going to put the phones in the safe now and do one last check we're all locked up and everything's turned off.' Angela turned to Zoe. 'Do you want to start loading people on?'

'Yes, ma'am. I'll herd these cats.'

'Great, thanks.'

Angela strode into the studio, put the phones into the safe, locked it, re-completed the last-minute checks on plug sockets, and set the security alarm. Shutting the door behind her, she tried the handle a few times. Telling herself that all was well and the place would be fine without her, she took a deep breath and went back to the minibus and hovered behind Emily and Louise as Louise tried to negotiate the step up to the minibus.

'Can I help you up there?' asked Emily.

'Och no! Away wi yersel. I'm as limber as they come, thanks to all this yoga nonsense.'

'The driver says we'd better get a move on,' said Zoe, tapping the steering wheel, unable to sit still. 'That's me channelling my inner bus driver, people. His name is Big Tam and he's got a schedule to keep.'

There were a few surprised chuckles from the group.

'Big Tam?' asked Angela, raising an eyebrow.

'He's a bald-headed white guy. I sometimes think of him as my shadow self.'

'Are you driving us all the way, dear?' asked Louise, ignoring the chat.

'All the way. Don't worry I'll take it easy on those sharp

159

bends.'

'We're in good hands, I can tell.'

Louise heaved herself up onto the front seat beside Samantha and Zoe and got out an Ordnance Survey map. In the back there were three rows of two seats beside a narrow passageway. There was a sliding door on the passenger side and two doors at the rear, but Zoe had advised the group to keep them closed since their luggage and Heart Yoga branded canvas bags and yoga mats were stacked up against it. Emily climbed through the sliding door.

Angela boarded last, realising that her vision of sitting near the front was now gone. Olivia and Meghan were sitting together, and Erin was sitting beside her friend Faye, who was also very into her fitness. Angela was pleased they were all coming to the retreat, which was going to be a social media free zone, since she often saw them glued to their phones immediately before and after class. Finding the last available seat, she stopped before sitting down, seeing that it was beside Emily. She gulped. 'Do you mind if I sit here?' Angela couldn't look Emily in the eyes.

Emily looked up at her, expressionless. 'No. It's the last seat anyway so you don't have much choice.'

'Thanks.' Angela carefully took a seat next to Emily, noting how small the seats were. Emily moved further over towards the window slightly to give Angela more room and let her put her seatbelt on. 'Not much room, is there. You know, in some of the buses I rode in India you pretty much had to sit on your neighbour's lap,' said Angela, immediately getting an image of Emily sitting on her lap, straddling her, with her arms around her neck.

'Well let's be grateful that's not the case here,' said Emily.

Angela felt a stab of rejection, fully aware that her disappointment was unreasonable. They hadn't spoken much since the kiss. Emily had asked after the business a couple of times, but Angela didn't go into it in much detail, and didn't dare ask for Emily's opinion on a few things she was struggling with. When Emily paid in full for her place, Angela was so excited, but she couldn't afford to let her feelings take control. She had been clear with Emily and there was no going back. However, there was a part of Angela that was looking forward to spending more time with Emily at the retreat. That couldn't hurt, right?

'Okay, team, are we ready to rock?' said Zoe.

Angela surveyed the belted-up passengers around her. 'All good back here, let's go!'

The group of women turned to look at Angela as she said this. There was a lovely sense of anticipation in the bus. The excitement had been building for weeks and now it was finally here.

'Woohoo!' cried Zoe, as she turned the engine on.

'How long until our first rest stop?' said Louise.

'Not long,' said Zoe, as she pulled away from the kerb. 'About an hour and a half?'

'That's all right,' said Louise, 'I only ask because I like to take lots of stops and enjoy the journey. You don't want to rush straight to a place. Miss out on too much along the way.'

Olivia sat forward and rested her hands on the sides of Louise's headrest. 'Have you been on many trips like this, Louise?'

'As a matter of fact, I have, my dear. When I was growing up our holidays were away to the seaside. That was before EasyJet and holidays to Spain became so cheap. That's how most people holidayed back then. Rothesay, Dunoon, Blackpool. Coaches would take dozens of families in them, all chaos and sing-songs on A-roads that are now motorways. So, coach holidays, yes, but not for yoga. Yoga didn't exist back then.'

Silently and unobserved, Angela raised a single eyebrow,

listening to Louise. Louise jumped in her seat as if Angela had tutted out loud. She turned around and looked over the top of the seats.

'Sorry, Angela. Before it came to Scotland, I mean. Thousands of years, was it? In India? I can never remember.'

Angela replied. 'Don't worry yourself, Louise, it has only been quite recent that yoga's got popular here.'

'Lovely, Angela. Always so kind, aren't you. I bet you were like this before you became a yoga teacher.'

Angela smiled a little.

'Sorry, love. I'll stop hassling you. It's your holiday as well,' said Louise, turning back around to face the front.

The van was noisy from the open windows and passing traffic. Zoe was doing a good job at handling the large vehicle. It was remarkably smooth as it navigated its way north west. The mood was upbeat and every other person on the bus was chatting, except Angela and Emily, who were sitting in silence.

As the chatter died down and they made their way along the motorway Emily closed her eyes and fell asleep. Angela became aware that Emily had fallen asleep by the gradual lowering of her chin to her chest followed by sudden lifts of her head, as if she was jolting awake, but continued to sleep. Angela sat beside her, quietly looking past her out of the window. It was peaceful sitting beside her. She was comforted by Emily's deep breathing. The longer they drove, and the longer Emily slept, Angela's eyes tentatively wandered to Emily's body safe in the knowledge that no one could see. She felt terrible about it but also unable not to look. Emily was wearing a V-neck T-shirt that clung to her body, and tight jeans. Angela followed the contours of her body upwards, taking in the shape of her thighs, towards her chest, rising and falling slowly. She imagined running her hand over Emily's breasts, caressing everywhere, then slowly letting her hand drift lower, going further than she'd allowed herself to go weeks before. The memory of it alone had been driving her wild since. Angela felt a throbbing between her legs. She bit her lip, looked away and took a deep breath.

What am I doing?

Emily's head rolled to her left and her ear dropped to her left shoulder, inches away from Angela's, until eventually it rested on Angela's shoulder. Angela could now see down her top to her breasts. Her body was screaming at her and her own breathing had deepened. The minibus went over a pothole and the vehicle lurched. Emily woke up with a start, raising her head from her shoulder. As if realising that she had fallen asleep, she abruptly straightened herself up.

'Sorry. Did I fall asleep on you?'

'It's no problem.'

'I always fall asleep when I'm travelling. It's the sound of the engine. Gets me every time.'

'Does it?' Angela looked forwards, hoping her face wasn't too flushed.

'Oh, that loch over there. Look.' Emily pointed out the window at a vast expanse of water, shimmering in the sunlight, below a mountain which looked so clear it was almost blue.

'We used to come here when I was young,' said Emily.

'Your family?'

'Yeah, and with two other families. My cousin and I used to play in the loch. There's a swing hanging off a tree over it. Sometimes we'd jump in. Freezing, but worth it. The swing's still there, I think.'

'It's beautiful here. You must have had lots of fun.'

Emily scanned the landscape, finding her bearings some more. 'See. That's it. Over there. That's where we stayed,' she said, pointing.

They both looked out the window and watched the holiday

park pass by. It had rows of chalets overlooking the loch, not far from the road.

'It looks smaller than I remember it.'

'That always happens. Things are never the same when you revisit them as a grown-up. I went back to Scotland's only theme park for my twenty-first birthday and it was totally different. Tiny. Tacky, almost. Or like when you watch a film you loved as a child and you realise that it's so, so wrong. Sexist, misogynistic, racist, homophobic. Things you don't really pick up on as a child.'

Emily stretched out her arms above her head and yawned. 'I know what you mean. You don't see any of that. It's that enchantment of being a kid and not knowing how horrible the world is. The wonder. The dreams. The fun.' Emily paused, looking sad. 'It's crap that we lose that.'

Reflecting on what Emily was saying, Angela stayed quiet. They watched the scenery pass by for a few minutes.

Emily spoke again. 'I do love coming up to the Highlands. I like proper rugged nature – you know? The retreat looks stunning by the way. I've clicked through the pictures on their website like a thousand times. The studio, the gardens, the greenhouse, the chickens. And that view out towards the Isle of Skye. It's going to be amazing.'

'Oh my God, it looks incredible, right? When Zoe and I found it online we called up immediately to book. They'd closed down for a few months to renovate over winter. I think they've only recently started back up again. That's why they were available in May at such short notice.' Angela took a deep breath and smiled. 'I already feel like I'm getting away from everything. The noise. The city. All distant memories.'

'I know. I feel the same. Turns out I need a holiday from being unemployed.'

Angela hoped the last month hadn't set Emily back. She had been making such good progress.

'I'm fine, no need to look so concerned.'

'No, I can understand that. A change of scenery is usually a good thing.'

'Do you think you'll get to relax, given that you're in charge of the group and stuff?'

'The family that owns the centre seem to have everything under control. I'm hoping that all I'll have to do is take the classes and make sure everyone's enjoying themselves. It's all been booked and paid for so I'm hoping there are no surprises. We've booked out the entire centre, you know. We're going to have the place to ourselves.'

Emily looked at her and smiled. 'I've been so looking forward to this. I can't wait to be served delicious homegrown organic food three times a day.'

Angela laughed. 'And the outdoor hot tub in the glass dome? That's going to be spectacular at night-time. It's crazy how close the Highlands are to us, we're so lucky to live where we do.'

'Would you ever move up here?'

Angela thought about it. 'Yes. I would. I can't imagine living in a city my whole life.'

'Me too. Shame about the midges though. Vicious wee things.'

Angela laughed. 'They shouldn't be too bad this time of year.'

Emily looked at her. 'Yeah, right. Wishful thinking.'

'I hope they're the only things that are vicious. I sometimes wonder if the small towns up here are a bit, you know, homophobic. At least, I worry that I would encounter more of those attitudes and end up censoring myself. Sometimes I think I'm a rubbish lesbian when I do that.'

'You don't want to be the only gay in the village?' said Emily.

'Exactly.'

'There's nothing that gives me more satisfaction in life than *flaunting* my sexuality, that is, being myself, and seeing this cause a reaction in some people. I *want* to be the only gay in the village. Change attitudes from the inside out. One public snog at a time.'

Angela laughed. 'We'd make the perfect couple.'

Emily looked away.

'Sorry. I wasn't thinking,' said Angela, instantly regretting that.

'No, it's fine.' Emily's face had hardened, and she was looking out of the window again at a new loch.

The bus zoomed around a corner and passed a lorry in the oncoming lane. Emily flinched back from the window. Angela scrambled around in her head for something to say. She wanted to say something to ease the tension but didn't want to address what was going on between them so close to the others. Angela settled back into the rhythm of the bus and her own thoughts. After a short while Emily turned to her again.

'How long have you been out?' She kept her voice low.

'What?'

'Are you actually out?'

'Yes.'

'Oh.' Emily was quiet again.

Angela lowered her voice. 'Why do you ask?'

'Have you heard of internalised homophobia?'

'I don't have that.' Angela replied, quickly.

Erin glanced around at them, as if noticing their conversation.

'What is it then?'

'What do you mean?'

This time, Emily lowered her voice almost to a whisper. 'What's making you so worried about what other people think of you?'

Angela felt cornered.

'Sorry. I don't mean to be rude. I'm just genuinely interested. In every other way you seem so confident, yet you'd let some small-town loony make you hide who you are. It doesn't make sense.'

Angela felt exposed, not used to being openly psychoanalysed. Yes, she had an ego. She was aware of it. She didn't think she was overly concerned about what other people thought of her. Her reasons for not getting involved with people who came to her studio were nothing to do with that. Were they?

Emily's voice was still just above a whisper. 'I've hit a nerve. I apologise.'

The minibus came to a stop at a junction and waited for a car to pass. The others in the group were talking about wanting to take a break.

Angela faced Emily. 'Don't. I care about what you think of me.'

Emily tilted her head back in her seat and swallowed. She dropped her head to the left and exhaled, ending up in a mischievous smile. 'My point exactly.'

Angela smiled back. They got lost in each other's eyes, neither seemingly wanting to be the first to break the connection.

'Angela,' called Zoe from the front. 'ANGELA.'

Angela flinched. 'Yes. What?'

'Okay to stop here, boss?'

All heads turned towards her, expectantly. Her mind had gone blank and she forgot for a second where she was and what they were doing. The sight of Zoe's expectant face in the rear-view mirror reminded her. She refocused on their mission.

'I think it's time for some air.'

Chapter 19

Spring was in full bloom in the Highlands. Emily admired the beautiful scenery as they drove past with her right elbow hanging out of the window. A light breeze came through, making the fine hairs on her arm dance. They passed by mountain after mountain, lochs of different shapes and sizes, and through huge glens. Little burns fed into rivers that the minibus followed. The rugged hills, lined with ancient dry-stone walls, were peppered with yellow gorse, golden bracken, and heather. She loved how the heather would transform into purple in the summer. Rows of closely planted immature spruce trees grew next to the remnants of their predecessors; beside them stood acres of tall spruce, some blown down, some leaning on their neighbours, the next victims of the timber industry. Single crofts popped up every now and again, next to the odd bigger farm. Cows and sheep dotted the hills, spread out over huge distances. Emily watched as the lambs played with each other while their mothers ate grass. Emily was in awe of the beauty of the land. Being in nature always made her feel happy.

As they neared the retreat, the minibus made its way downhill along a winding single track lane towards their destination. The only sounds came from the low hum of the engine and the tyres moving over the dirt track, squishing stones and soft mud. The van rocked heavily from side to side as it negotiated the uneven track and tried to dodge the many potholes along it. The vehicle ambled along for a while longer as the hills opened up and the retreat could be seen nestling beneath them. The sea could also be seen in the near distance. Emily closed the window and rearranged her clothes, pulling her top up as it had been riding down. She gathered her day bag from under her seat. She saw Angela smiling as the retreat came into full view out of the corner of her eye.

'Not long now,' called Zoe, from the driver's seat.

'It's just as well I know how to brace my spine, these bumps are something else,' said Louise.

'Look at it!' said Olivia.

'It's huge,' said Meghan.

Zoe parked the van adjacent to the reception, next to four other vehicles – a muddy Land Rover, an estate car, a small red Toyota, and an immaculate four-by-four. As the engine went off there was a collective sigh of relief as windows were shut and doors were opened. Emily put her bag on the seat left vacant beside her after Angela had sprung up.

'Oh, I need to get off this bus,' said Louise loudly.

When Emily stepped off the van onto the gravel with the rest of the group, she was struck by the beauty of the place. They were in the middle of nowhere, and it was quiet. The retreat was spread out over a large piece of land. Majestic Scots pine and silver birch trees flanked them, giving it a kind of enclosed feeling, but the undulating ground still allowed for excellent views out to sea. A main house made of stone with huge windows and steps leading up to an oversized front door, sat beside the car park. From what she could see, there were five or six different sized chalet-style buildings that made up the retreat and contrasted with but complemented the old house. Large pots with colourful flowers flanked the car park and the house, as did gorgeous planters with all sorts of thriving herbs. A little meadow sat off to the right of the house, next to a large well-maintained garden that included a children's playpark. Beards of lichen hung loosely from tree branches, confirming the freshness of the air. Zoe unloaded the bags from the back. Angela was talking to Karen, who had driven there in the red Toyota, her face serious as Angela explained things to her. Louise was admiring the view in Mountain Pose.

Emily helped Zoe with the remaining bags with one eye still on the group. She felt so at ease with everyone and realised that they had formed a little gang, a community of sorts, fixed into shape by pose after pose, week after week. Emily was fond of everyone who had come to the retreat. They each brought something different to the group, and there was a willingness to create a good atmosphere. They were all trying to improve their practice together, all at different rates, among a foundation of mental and emotional wellbeing and mutual support. Being an all-female group helped foster this nurturing safe space. It had become a big part of Emily's life in such a short amount of time, and she was grateful to be a part of it.

'Hello!'

Everyone turned around to see a woman coming towards them with open arms.

'You made it! Welcome.'

Angela stepped forward. 'Hi. I'm Angela Forbes.'

They shook hands, beaming at one another. 'I'm Zadie. Lovely to meet you.' Zadie then went around the entire group shaking hands and hugging people. A man, two little boys, and a dachshund appeared from the house.

'That's Wolfie, the dog. Oh sorry, and my two boys, Simon and Ryan, and Jack, my husband.'

The two boys were young, perhaps about five and seven. Jack smiled politely and wandered over to them.

'Welcome to our home. Here, I'll help you with the bags,' said Jack.

Zadie smiled broadly. 'Would you like to follow me into the workshop, and I'll get you all set up?'

'Fantastic,' said Angela.

The group followed Zadie past her family home, around a neatly designed path towards one of the recently renovated purpose-built buildings. Passing the impressive yoga studio with floor to ceiling windows looking out to sea generated lots of excited noises from the group. Other than that, it was so quiet, except for the odd sound of a pheasant in the distance and the quiet murmurs of the group taking in their new surroundings. One building had a living roof. Giving it a good look over as she walked, Emily already felt more relaxed. You didn't see grass and a wildflower meadow on the roof of a building every day. A white butterfly with orange-tipped wings fluttered past.

Arriving at one of the larger buildings in the centre of the land, the guests from Heart Yoga entered the workshop and chose their seats on comfortable chairs or long sofas. Angela stood at the front beside Zadie. The workshop had a lived in, quirky feel about it. Simon and Ryan came running past Emily, headed for some toys in the corner. Once everyone was settled, Zadie laid out room keys and picked up a bit of paper and a pen.

'We are so happy to have your presence with us and we hope you will have a beautiful time here. We want you to feel completely at home and experience the peace and tranquillity of our yoga centre and the surrounding area. You're going to be doing your own yoga, I believe?'

'Yes, that's right,' said Angela.

'We have lots of groups who come up here and do their own thing. Our resident yoga teacher is out of the country this month, so you've timed it nicely. We can do a proper tour of the place to get you acquainted, but first I think it's best if we get you all sorted into your rooms and let you freshen up.'

'Woman after my own heart,' said Louise.

Zadie laughed. 'You've come up from Edinburgh, is that

right?'

She was met with a round of nodding heads.

'Yes, we're from Heart Yoga, not AdventureScot Tours. The van is a bit misleading,' said Zoe.

Zadie laughed again. 'No, I like your style. Practical! Okay, rooms. So, all the rooms are down the path there to the left, with a full view out to sea. All are en suite and identical to each other, so it shouldn't matter who goes where. The ten keys are on—'

'Sorry, ten?' said Angela.

Zadie looked up at her, curious. 'Yes, ten guests, ten keys.'

'We're eleven. Or we will be when Jackie Hay gets here.'

'Oh!' Zadie's face fell in horror. 'Your booking says ten,' she snapped her head down to read the piece of paper again. 'Yes, ten,' she held it up for Angela to see.

Angela moved closer to her and read it. Wincing in recognition, she began to blush. 'It's my fault. I remember it now. See, this is what happens when you do things in a rush.'

'It's no problem, we still have space. We can put someone up in the house with us. We have a fold-up bed in the study. It's not somewhere we'd normally house guests, but at least we have an extra bed for you.'

'That's very kind. I thought there were more than ten cabins here though?'

'We have thirteen. You have booked ten of them, and there is a party of three that has already arrived.'

'A party of three? I thought we had the place to ourselves,' said Angela, looking confused.

This was awkward. The rest of the group began fidgeting and avoiding looking at Angela and Zadie. Some played with Wolfie. Others scanned the workshop or chatted. Emily watched on as the booking went from bad to worse. There was no denying it, Angela needed more help with the business.

'Yes, another yoga group – a group of teachers, I think.'

'Which teachers?' Angela's voice was hard. She shifted her weight on her feet.

Zadie picked up another sheet of paper and read it. 'The booking has been made under Cult Yoga.'

Barely stopping herself from getting involved, Emily clenched her fists.

Angela smiled thinly. 'They didn't tell me they were coming. Donna and I both trained to be teachers together with Jackie Hay. They're probably here to see her, even though I was the one who organised for her to come over. I don't even know how they knew she was going to be here.'

Zadie stayed quiet as a slow recognition crept across her face that this new information was not to Angela's liking. Angela stayed very still and barely blinked for a good ten seconds. It was shitty of Cult Yoga to turn up like this. Emily willed her to not let it get to her. She tried to catch Angela's eyes to show some support, but she didn't look her way. When a steely resolve came over Angela's face, Emily exhaled in relief. Zadie must have registered it as well.

'You could think of it as a reunion?' said Zadie hopefully.

'I might,' said Angela, glancing over at the group who were mostly occupied with other things in the quirky workshop now. 'Thank you for having us all at your beautiful retreat, I'm so pleased to finally get here.'

'So, who would like to stay in the house tonight?' asked Zadie.

'I'll join you. My students have paid for a sea view cabin, and that's what they'll get. Thank you so much for accommodating my mistake.'

Emily stepped forward. 'You can share my room if you want. You could put the fold-up bed in it. I'm sure there'll be space.'

Angela raised her eyebrows. 'No. No, thanks. I wouldn't

want to get in your way.'

'You wouldn't be getting in my way.'

'You might be more comfortable in the cabins,' said Zadie. 'We only have one bathroom in the house, would you believe it. We're installing another one in the summer. You're very welcome to stay in the house, of course, but I thought you should know. Each cabin has two main rooms: a sleeping area and a sitting area, and its own bathroom, of course. You probably don't want to miss out on that sea view.'

Angela considered her options. Zadie did not seem thrilled about her staying in their house.

'I really am sorry about the mix-up.' Zadie looked around uncomfortably and lowered her voice. 'We will need to discuss the extra payment for the last person. I can take off the cost of the room, but I'll still need to charge for the rest of the retreat.'

Angela's face fell. 'Of course. And it's me who hasn't paid. Oh my God, this is so embarrassing.'

'Please don't worry. These things happen,' said Zadie.

'I can pay you right now, if that's okay?'

'We'll see to it later, before supper perhaps.'

'Thanks.' Angela paused and looked at Emily. 'If you don't mind, I might take you up on that offer. Zoe snores.'

Emily did an internal squeal while keeping a completely straight face. 'Fine. No problem.'

Angela exhaled, puffing her cheeks out. They had gone slightly red, which Emily found highly endearing. 'Thank you.' Angela dropped her head forward so that she spoke to the floor. 'I couldn't have messed this up more if I'd tried.'

'Perfect. If that's all settled then, I'll get you all checked in,' said Zadie, visibly relieved. Zadie called out names, gave each person their key and ticked it off her list. Once everyone was completed, she addressed the group. 'Listen up, everyone, we're ready to take you over to your rooms, if you'd like to follow me. Your bags are over there already.'

Emily and the group stepped outside and took in the loveliness of it again, making excitable noises and pointing at this and that in wonder and approval. The main area exuded a hint of natural landscape gardening and signs of benefitting from a loving gardener. The space felt entirely natural, despite human-made paths crisscrossing between buildings. Wooden signposts directed the new guests to their cabins. A sign pointing to an underground sauna caught her attention. Mini-lights lined the paths suggesting a gorgeous atmosphere in the evenings. The city-dwellers trotted behind Zadie. When they turned the corner beside the cabins facing west people gasped. The view was incredible.

'Is this really where we're staying?' said Olivia.

'My days!' said Louise. 'This place is like heaven. Why have I never been here before?'

Jack was waiting beside the luggage now piled up in front of the cabins. As Jack directed people to their corresponding room number and helped with the luggage, Angela went back to the main house with Zadie.

Emily turned the key in the lock to her cabin. Walking in, she noticed it was roomier and more luxurious than she expected. The bedroom was on one side of the cabin, slightly sectioned off from a small sitting area on the other side. Thick tartan curtains hung down next to a large window facing right out to the water. An old telephone lay on the windowsill. There were two armchairs upholstered in the same tartan as the curtains. There was no television, and this she was very happy with. It would be a true retreat.

Emily put her bag down next to the bed and sat down. There was another window in the bedroom, and she could still see the sea from the bed. She let herself fall back onto the crisp clean covers and newness of the bed. It was huge, and the covers were so soft. It was the perfect place to relax and unwind in. She had been looking forward to a calm and peaceful cabin overlooking the sea all to herself. That was all she wanted from the weekend; that, and to absorb the healing vibes of the stunning retreat embedded in pure nature.

But sharing a room with the woman of her dreams, who had rejected her and thrown her off balance, threatened to dominate her experience entirely. She'd offered to share because she felt bad for Angela not having anywhere nice to sleep. But as she unzipped her suitcase, she wasn't sure if she was unhappy about sharing with Angela or excited about it. The fear and excitement felt about the same.

While putting her toiletries in the bathroom, she heard a knock on the door and found Angela outside looking sheepish with a pile of bags and a folding bed. 'I'm so sorry to be doing this to you. Sharing your room is probably the last thing you want to do this weekend.'

'I offered. Stop apologising.'

Angela came in and looked around. 'Wow. This is gorgeous. I can put my bed at the front here, by these two armchairs.' Angela got her bags in and Emily helped. Angela unfolded the bed.

'I need to wash my hands,' said Angela.

'It's right through there,' Emily pointed to the en suite beyond the bed. Emily read the welcome pack by the front window. When Angela came back, they stood in an awkward silence.

'How are you doing?' said Emily.

'I can't believe I fucked up the booking like that. This weekend was supposed to be relaxing and all I feel is stressed out.'

'You need more help.' Emily wanted to offer to help again but couldn't. Not after what happened between them. It wasn't good for her mental health.

Angela sat down on one of the chairs by the window. 'I'm

so glad you let me stay here with you. Thank you. I don't think I would have enjoyed staying in the house with the family very much.'

'I wouldn't have been happy knowing you were in the house with the family.' Emily smiled genuinely.

Emily stayed standing, quietly enjoying the sight of Angela by the window.

'Can you believe Cult Yoga have gate-crashed?' said Angela.

'No.'

'It's exactly the sort of thing Donna would do. I'm quite pissed off about it.'

Emily laughed. 'I thought you were meant to be all peace and love?'

Angela tied her hair up, roughly. 'Fuck that. I'm only human.'

Emily gasped teasingly. 'What would the others say?'

'Emily, just because I'm a yoga teacher doesn't mean I don't sometimes experience negative emotions or get insecure from time to time like everyone else. And it doesn't mean I shouldn't care about what other people think of me. It's how you self-regulate that matters. I can be civil to Donna, and I will be.'

'You'll be civil.'

'I know I'm not handling this perfectly, but I'm trying.'

The skin between Angela's eyebrows creased together in a V-shape and did its best to communicate how cross she was, but it only added more character to the many layers of her personality. She was so cute when she was ruffled. It wasn't a side of her Emily had ever seen before.

'What?' said Angela.

'Nothing.'

'No, what? You're making a weird face.'

'Cheers.'

Angela insisted with her eyes.

'Okay.' She paused. 'I was just thinking about how lovely you are.'

'Emily—'

'It's okay. I know where we stand. It's all good.'

'It's not that—'

Someone chapped the door, startling them both. Zoe called from outside. 'Are you in there, Angela?'

Angela opened the door and Zoe bounced in. 'How's it going in here?' She addressed Emily and gestured with her head towards Angela. 'Is there enough room for this one and her ego in here?'

Emily tried not to laugh. Angela didn't look impressed.

'Loads of space.' Emily replied.

'Nice one. I would have suggested you join me, but I remember you saying that you'd never share with me again after Greece. I guess I do snore a bit.'

Neither of them answered. Zoe looked between the two. 'So, Zadie's ready to give us the tour. A few of us are milling about out here.'

'I'm ready,' said Emily.

'Awesome,' said Zoe, smiling.

'I'll join you in a second,' said Angela.

Following Zoe out, Emily felt Angela's eyes watch her go. Fitting, she thought to herself.

Chapter 20

Zadie and Jack cleared the starters from the table as if they were working silver service. They danced around the long wooden table, in and around the basic wooden chairs. The sound of cutlery getting put on plates and plates stacking up clicked and clacked. The table comfortably held all the residents of the retreat at any one given time. Being in the middle of nowhere, the large purposely designed dining room made Emily feel like they were close to nature with its substantial array of windows and rustic earthy feel. They had a view of the surrounding garden and hills from the long dining table. A glowing wood-burner warmed the room and added to the peaceful ambience. The roomful of women generated a cheerful atmosphere of talking and laughter in contrast to the stillness outside. Emily imagined other groups enjoying the table on different occasions.

Tonight, the space hosted Heart Yoga, who took up the majority of the table, and three teachers from Cult Yoga. The character of the two studios was never more obviously different than by the stark contrast of the two ends of the table: one glamorous and the other completely down-to-earth. Donna, Andrea, and Clementine from Cult Yoga were dressed like they were going out on the town. Most of Heart Yoga were in fleeces or woolly jumpers. Angela and Donna sat at opposite ends, facing each other down the long table. Emily was sitting near the middle of the table and witnessed the exchange of looks between the two quite easily.

In one ear she had Louise talking about her bird feeder, and in the other ear she could hear Erin talking about the advantages of avocado on toast. Wolfie did the rounds of the table by going up to each and every person and asking for food. Zadie didn't seem to mind, and neither did the guests.

The plates were different shapes and sizes and the glasses were made from recycled glass. The starters were butternut squash and coconut soup or bruschetta, and the mains were wild mushroom risotto, salmon or three bean chilli. There was also a raw vegan option, but Emily didn't fancy it. For dessert it was vegan apple tart or an Isle of Arran cheeseboard. Prior to ordering, Zadie and Jack talked extensively about their food for the evening, including a description of its provenance and how it was made. Emily had enjoyed listening to them and appreciated that the food they were eating was both nourishing and made with love.

Olivia and Louise's voices were the loudest, right next to Emily. At the beginning of what sounded like a heated conversation, Emily tuned in.

'So why don't you eat meat?' said Louise to Olivia, directly across the table from her.

Sitting perfectly poised and relaxed, Olivia began to answer, as if she'd been expecting the question. 'I live a vegan lifestyle mostly due to a concern for the way animals are treated and consumed by humans, rather than being seen as individual beings in their own right. The food industry is also one of the most polluting industries on the planet. I find it perfectly fine to be vegan. I never feel like I'm missing out. I wouldn't be physically able to eat meat again; it's … yuck.'

'Don't you ever wonder how good it is for you to be that way? Our ancestors wouldn't have survived on salad alone. We all need protein, don't we?'

'That's one of the biggest myths there is. Our digestive systems are designed to digest a plant-based diet, with, at best, a tiny amount of meat in some form. Where do you think animals get their protein from?'

'Where? What do you mean?'

'From plants. We eat the animals who are all eating plants. Why not skip the slaughtering, the antibiotics, and just eat the plants?'

'In my day, if you were lucky enough to be able to afford meat, you were grateful. To turn your nose up at it, well, that's still something I can't get my head around. Honestly, the youth of today. You don't know how lucky you've got it.'

'I'd go one step further and say that consuming animals is akin to consuming the pain and suffering they were put through in order to get to your plate. It's death. I don't want that energy in my body. No thank you.'

Louise turned to Emily who by now was desperately trying to avoid the conversation. 'I have no words for this. Do you agree with her then? Are you a vegan too?'

'I'm not a vegan.'

'Oh good. Now, where's my fillet of fish.'

Angela got up from her seat. Emily watched her move by the table from the corner of her eye. She came to a stop beside Donna and her two friends from Cult Yoga. Emily listened in as best she could.

'Hi,' said Angela. 'I didn't expect to see you here.'

'And miss Jackie Hay? Unlikely,' said Donna.

Donna introduced the two other women and Angela shook their hands without much feeling in the gesture. Angela left them and headed towards the bathroom, gliding past the group and around the corner out of sight. Emily's eyes lingered on the area where she'd left, hopeful to see Angela walking back to the table. Reluctantly, she returned her attention to the conversation next to her. Taking a sip of red wine, she listened into Olivia and Louise, still locked in deep conversation.

'... None of the salmon up here is in good condition any more. The fish farms are all in the same area of water as the so-called wild salmon, it's just sectioned off with nets. The pesticides they feed to the fish simply leek out and infect the entire food chain. Most fish have enormous levels of mercury in them. That's toxic to humans, we're not meant to be consuming that, especially in these amounts,' said Olivia.

'Yes, but if it was that bad for us, why doesn't it say that on the back of the packet?' said Louise.

'You think if they advertised the fact that the ecosystem is ruined and all the meat is pumped full of chemicals on the back of it that they'd still sell?'

Louise looked at Olivia for a moment. 'They put those horrible images on cigarette packets and they still sell. So, yes. They probably would still sell. People probably know their food isn't good for them, but they still eat it, because they have no other choice.'

'Crap food is cheap and good food is expensive. That's true. But if you cut out all the unnecessary junk and you focus on buying quality nutritious food, I swear, in the end it's cheaper. You don't get sucked in. Being vegan actually takes out a lot of the temptation.'

Louise shook her head. 'I see what you're trying to suggest, but it sounds like you're overthinking it all. Life's too short. Plus, I just couldn't go without my cheese. Wine and cheese and lots of it. I couldn't do it, and I don't want to. So, I won't.'

'I was only stating how I live my life and how I see things. I wasn't trying to convert you.'

'Yes dear, but there are some things none of us wants to talk about at the dinner table.'

Olivia smiled politely, but her clenched teeth betrayed her obvious irritation.

Emily rested her head in her hand, elbow on the table, and wistfully gazed over at where Angela had gone. The retreat was supposed to be a fun escape from everyday life, not a full-blown critique of all the major issues in the world.

Sometimes Emily liked that type of conversation, but tonight, in such beautiful surroundings, she just wanted to relax and feel good.

When Angela appeared again, Emily watched her cross the room, quite unable to take her eyes off her. As a new topic of debate gathered pace between Louise and Olivia, the door opened, letting in a gust of cold air. Most of the diners stopped to look around. A woman stood in the doorway with a beaming smile and look of wonder. She had the wiry frame of someone who lived an active and clean life. Even from a distance, her eyes were a piercing blue and her smile was warm and genuine. Her slightly greying blonde hair was tied back at the base of her neck. Emily thought it strange that she was acting like a star coming onto a stage, waiting for the perfect second in which to enter. Angela and Donna both shot up to see her like dogs greeting their owner. Emily saw an elbow of Donna's quietly edge Angela out of the way.

The newcomer, no doubt Jackie Hay, immediately recognised the eager yoga teachers in front of her. 'My dears! *Quelle surprise!*'

Hugs were exchanged, and a few words Emily couldn't make out. Jackie carried herself in such a way that made you want to sit and watch her every move and mannerism. She was captivating. Emily could tell that Angela was highly respectful of her former teacher. She had only just arrived and Angela was standing that bit taller.

'Would you like more time before we serve the main course?' said Zadie.

'Goodness! I've interrupted your meal. How awful of me. Hello everyone,' she smiled again. 'Please forgive me for being so late. It's fabulous to be here.'

A round of hellos flooded Jackie's way and she nodded to receive the welcome.

'It's not an issue, seriously. You're the reason we're all

here,' said Donna.

'I look forward to getting to know you all over the weekend. But for now, let's eat!' said Jackie.

Jackie scanned the table and took one of the last remaining seats beside the three from Cult Yoga. Angela looked disappointed that she wouldn't be sitting with Jackie for the evening and went back to her chair reluctantly. Emily felt irritated by Cult Yoga. They hadn't been invited and were making no effort with anyone from Heart Yoga. Donna had an air of snobbery about her, as if she thought she was better than everyone else there. There had been no need for her to sit at the top of the table at the opposite end to Angela – that was a power play. It was a wellbeing and yoga retreat. Not a corporate boardroom. Emily did not approve.

Who does she think she is?

She wondered if anyone else had noticed their intrusion but didn't feel it was the right time or place to ask. Plus, Emily was wary about gossiping and did not want to put that energy out there.

Zadie and Jack appeared out of the swing doors from the kitchen, bursting into the room with plates in abundance. They stepped around the group handing out dishes with a homely elegance. Emily was having the risotto. Various shapes and sizes of freshly baked bread were passed around the table. Water and wine were poured amid laughter and rosy cheeks. Emily's cheeks were flushed from the heat from the fire and the excitement of the meal. Trying to be as discreet as she could manage, Emily repeatedly looked over at what Angela was doing, frustrated at being so close to Angela, yet not talking to her. Her previous resolve to keep her distance was fast fading. Then again, she wasn't in the mood for talking much, as a fire of emotions swirled within her.

Later that night when the meal was over, Emily left with

the first batch of people heading for bed. As she made her way across the grounds past the lanterns and the buddhas, she felt butterflies in her stomach at sleeping in the same room as Angela. The shadows from the lights and the silhouettes of the mountains which seemed so close in the night-time added to her sense of suspense. Each of the buildings was lit up in the evening giving the retreat an otherworldly feel. She tried to think about Angela's calming words during class in order to get a grip on her nerves.

The room was quiet when she went in. Its feel and smell still unfamiliar to her. Switching the lights on, she noticed Angela's things on the floor beside her. Realising she'd never actually seen Angela's personal possessions before, being beside them now without her, felt strange. One of her bags was slightly open. A yellow jumper lay folded near the top, beside a hairbrush. She had the urge to take the jumper out the bag and smell it, before realising that was too far. Way too far. Not expecting Angela back for some time, she shook her head at her own ridiculousness and got ready for bed. Angela was the person everyone wanted to talk to and spend time with. Her presence always lit up any room she was in.

Getting into bed, Emily felt self-conscious even though Angela was not even there yet. Leaving the lights on, she made herself comfortable on the bed and waited on her back with her arms clasped over her stomach. Wide awake, she didn't feel at all like sleeping, especially in a place she didn't know. After not very long, the handle moved and Angela came into the cabin, peering her head around the corner.

'I'm so sorry. Did I wake you? I hope I didn't wake you.'

'I wasn't sleeping.'

Angela excused herself and went into the bathroom, closing the door gently behind her. On the way back to her corner of the cabin, she paused beside Emily's bed, smiling softly at her. They found each other's eyes for a moment before Angela wished her a goodnight.

Emily listened as Angela got ready for bed. Emily couldn't see any of this, but her ears were on alert. After switching off the lights, the fold-up bed squeaked as Angela got on it, each spring gracing the room with its individual creak. Every time Angela moved an orchestra of springs played. It would be distracting at the best of times, but tonight, Emily was locked into every single sound of movement. Emily lay there completely awake. As time passed it was clear that Angela was still awake too.

When she was almost dropping off to sleep, she heard Angela get up and walk in her direction, and lightly walk past her into the bathroom again. Emily checked the clock on the bedside cabinet. It was after one in the morning. Angela came back out of the bathroom at a snail's pace, clearly trying not to wake Emily.

'Angela.'

The feet stopped. 'Emily? Are you awake?'

'Yes. I haven't slept.'

'Me neither.'

'Why don't you sleep in the bed with me? It's not fair you having to rough it out on that.'

Angela didn't reply.

'Or I'll take the fold-up bed. I'm not sleeping anyway.'

'Emily, please don't worry about me. You get some sleep, and I'll be fine. I'll be out like a light in no time.'

The squeaking of the springs on Angela's bed signalled that it was not up for discussion. Feeling embarrassed for offering that Angela sleep in the bed with her only to be met with another rejection, Emily sighed. The silence between them hung in the air and thoughts of what could be happening instead were like torture. Eventually, Emily got to sleep only to see Angela there in her dreams too.

***

Emily opened her eyes. Turning over, she lifted her neck up to see what was going on in the room. Feeling groggy, she sat up, yawned, got out of bed, stretched her arms overhead, and went over to see if Angela was up. The ground was cold underfoot. The fold-up bed was empty. Angela was asleep on her yoga mat. It was such an odd sight to see her there. Turning to leave, she heard Angela stir and turn over onto her back.

'Are you there?'

Angela must have sensed her presence. What was she doing checking on her anyway? 'Yup. I just got up. What are you doing on the floor?'

'The bed was unbearable, so I moved. It was a big improvement, actually.'

'That's dedication. You should tell everyone you are so in love with yoga you sleep on your mat.'

Angela rolled over and pushed herself up. She was so beautiful in the morning light streaming into the cabin. Emily could look at her forever. She brushed a strand of blonde hair from her face and looked up at Emily. 'I should. You're right. But then I don't want people to start suggesting I sleep elsewhere. I'm fine here. I'll keep it to myself. To us.' She looked hopeful at Emily. 'Would you mind? Not saying anything?'

That phrase from Angela jarred, but she was able to see past it. 'I don't mind.' She sat down on the fold-up bed and winced. 'Ow! That's awful. How could she have given you this to sleep on?'

'Maybe she's not used it in a while? She doesn't know how bad it is? She can't have known,' said Angela, shaking her head.

Emily didn't look convinced. 'First rule of having a guest

bed is to try the bed and see what it feels like. If you're uncomfortable, your guests will feel uncomfortable. It's a bit weird because the rest of the place is so comfy. Luxurious. That meal, the décor, all the buildings. This place is like heaven.'

Angela got to her feet a lot less gracefully than she normally did. Emily found it endearing that Angela was also human and not actually as considered about things as she continually portrayed in class. She immediately put a hand to her back and made a pained face. Arching it back and from side to side didn't seem to bring about the desired outcome.

It also wasn't lost on Emily that Angela was only wearing a T-shirt and the skimpiest of shorts. Fully aware of the inappropriateness of her thoughts the night before, she ached to rip the T-shirt right off and make love to her right there. Instead, she hid her feelings and was glad she wasn't blushing. 'Are you okay?'

'My back. It's sore. You'd think all this yoga would let me sleep on the floor for one night. My God, I don't want Jackie to find out. This is so embarrassing.'

'Hmm,' said Emily.

'Is this where you tell me "I told you so"?'

'I'm far too advanced for that, gorgeous.'

Emily gasped at herself. "Gorgeous" had slipped out without her permission.

Angela looked awkward at first but then regained her composure. 'You're on the fast track to enlightenment.'

'Can you do any yoga today if your back's sore?'

'I'm not sure. It might help it.' Angela twisted about some more and winced.

'Maybe you shouldn't move about so much. Let it rest,' said Emily.

'Yeah.'

Emily turned to go.

'You know what might help?'

'What?'

'A back massage?'

Emily was stunned and her mouth fell open.

'I can tell it's spasming and needs some tension eased out. Can you give me a back massage?' Angela looked at her with those penetrating grey-blue eyes.

Emily swallowed. 'Sure. I can do that.' She paused. 'Where do you want to do it?'

Angela looked around them. She folded her duvet in half and put it over her yoga mat. 'I could lie down here?' She lay down on her front, gingerly. Much more slowly than she normally moved about on a yoga mat. 'You could kneel beside me?'

'Angela are you flirting with me. This isn't allowed.'

Angela looked up at her. 'Emily. I'm not flirting with you, now get down here and rub me.'

Emily opened her mouth, slightly stunned, and got down on her knees.

'Good.'

Emily knelt down beside her. Angela's T-shirt had moved up, revealing her bare legs and shorts not quite covering each butt cheek. Her bum was perfect and round. Emily could feel herself getting turned on simply looking at her.

'Now you'll need to roll my T-shirt up a bit. It's my lower back that's sore. Both sides.'

Emily did as she was told, feeling the skin on skin contact as she moved up the T-shirt and enjoying the sight of Angela's slender and toned body in front of her. Emily hesitated, unsure where to begin.

'Emily, put your hands on me.'

Putting her hands onto Angela's back, Emily stared at the smooth skin beneath her, noticing the odd freckle and the bumps of Angela's spine. But she was awkward, leaning at

189

the side, reaching over her. Her own lower back was a bit strained from the leaning. She started to gently knead the area. It sent tingles all over her body and she felt Angela shiver as she massaged her.

Angela spoke, but it did nothing to relieve the tension of the situation. 'Thank you for doing this, I know I pretty much demanded it, but thank you. I need to be on form tod— ah!'

Emily lifted her hands. 'Sorry! Did that hurt?'

'Yes, but in a good way.'

'Where do you want me to touch you?' Emily's hands gently kneaded the muscles in her back, as she got her bearings on Angela's skin and muscles.

'Lower. Ah, yes, also there, but lower.'

She's got to be fucking kidding me.

'Lower?'

'Uh-huh.' Came Angela's response, deep and guttural, head down, resting on her forearms, with her elbows out wide. 'Move my shorts down a bit.'

'Is it okay if I sit on you?'

There was a pause. 'Yes.'

Emily could hardly breathe but she continued. Trembling inside, she sat up and swung one leg over and straddled Angela. Slowly lowering herself down, she let her body rest on the backs of Angela's legs. Moving Angela's shorts down an inch so she could get to her skin, Emily let her hands rest at the top of Angela's bum. Angela visibly shivered when she touched her. The skin on skin contact felt electrifying. Emily kneaded into her strong glutes as she felt herself burn for more than just a massage.

'Harder.'

Emily pressed harder and lengthened out her strokes, still in disbelief that they were doing this.

'That's perfect. This is really helping. You're a life saver.

Could you go back to my back please and do what you were doing before?'

Returning her hands to Angela's back, Emily pressed hard with her thumbs making slow, deep circles either side of her spine. Feeling Angela take a deep breath and fully exhale, Emily could also feel Angela's back muscles relax under her. As she let her hands glide over Angela's skin, she hoped that this wouldn't be the last time she got to be so close to her.

'I think that's enough now,' said Angela.

Reluctantly, Emily stopped. 'Glad I could help. Does it feel better?'

'It does. Cheers.'

Emily realised they were having a conversation with her still straddling her. Not wanting to move, she could feel how wet she was. Angela stayed exactly where she was too. Reaching out, she touched Angela's sides until it became a caress. Angela didn't stop her. She kept going, this time letting her hands move up her back, pushing up her T-shirt. Moving up, she sat on Angela's backside, their bodies pressing together separated only by thin fabric. Allowing her hands to roam down to the side of her breasts, she stroked the soft tissue under her arm. Angela let out a small moan. Having effectively mounted Angela, she stopped, wanting to go further, realising how far they'd already gone. Everything inside her screamed to lower her body and press directly against her but she didn't. Angela tensed up. Emily literally felt herself rise as Angela engaged her muscles. Emily moved off, disappointed. Angela sat up and rearranged her T-shirt. They stood up in unison.

'Thank you.'

'Hopefully, that's helped ease it off a bit.'

'You're good at giving massages. I like your energy; it's very gentle but also firm.'

Emily could think of something else it was, given the fire

within her she was feeling. 'How does it feel now?'

'A bit better,' said Angela. She smiled shyly at Emily and began gathering up the covers and putting away the fold-up bed.

'Let me,' said Emily, bending down to help her.

'No worries, thanks. I've got it.' Angela quickly folded the bed, put it to the side and lay the duvet over it. She spoke next avoiding her eyes. 'I'd better get ready.'

'Sure.'

Chapter 21

The whole group lined up in a row before Jackie, whose tiny figure belied her massive presence. Angela loved that Jackie had insisted on an equal distribution of the room's dimensions saying that it was necessary to face each student directly. That was how Jackie preferred to teach her classes. Their mats were especially close together given they were all in a row; but, despite this, the setting added a spaciousness to everyone's practice. The retreat's studio was outstanding and the view out to sea from the windows in front of them was spectacular. Angela noted that connecting everyone with the present moment seemed way easier to do in these gorgeous surroundings than in the bustling streets of Edinburgh.

Taking a class with her students at Heart Yoga felt strange, but good. Angela took a spot at one end of the row to let her students take the centre and get as much direct contact with Jackie as possible. Thankfully, Cult Yoga took the opposite end of the row and hadn't bullied their way into the centre. Listening to Jackie's voice as she described another of her advanced yoga poses, Angela kept an eye on her students along the row to see how they were getting on. Seeing that her students were on top form, she felt so proud of them. Plus, they were showing her in a good light to her mentor, but she knew that those feelings were all based in ego and that she shouldn't be operating on that energy level. While there was no pressure to be anything other than what you were around Jackie, Jackie also had a way of figuring out what you were thinking or holding back. Nothing got past Jackie and her sharp but kind eyes. Emanating smugness would be picked up on in a second.

Next to Angela was Emily. She watched Emily move through the poses with ease at pretty much the same pace as her own. They flowed together effortlessly, and it was enjoyable. Emily had learned yoga quickly and was now holding her own. Angela was very impressed by her improvement. More than that, Angela could feel the strength of Emily's practice and the fullness of her presence next to her. The difference in her was amazing. It was such a relief to see her coming through the bad patch she'd been in. But she did still worry about her sometimes, especially since they were no longer really talking.

From a lunge position with their arms out at either side in Warrior Pose, Jackie had them twist to the side, bring their hands together and let their elbows rest on their knees. Given their position in the row, Angela also couldn't get Emily out of her head. It was impossible not to look at her body being that she was, so close to her. A single bead of sweat dripped from Emily's arm and her muscles shook to keep her in position. All Angela could do was look at Emily so when it was her turn to twist the other way, she was pretty sure that Emily would be doing the same to her. The thought of it nearly knocked her off balance, which was not a particularly good look for a yoga teacher.

Taking a deep breath in, she put thoughts of undressing Emily out of her mind for about ten seconds. Angela continued in this vein for the duration of the class. Jackie took them through a painfully slow omming sequence, which Emily handled like a pro. Angela kind of missed the giggly Emily that had shown up to her class that first time. When Jackie brought them to the end, Angela lay face up on the mat, wrapped up in that same guilt and shame. As Donna prowled across the studio towards her, she felt uneasy.

'Manage that okay? Saw you struggling there a few times,' said Donna.

'I managed fine. How did you enjoy the class?'

'I aced the class, as ever, so yeah. I did.' Donna glanced over at her two friends. 'Right, so we have a bet that you can't do Crow Pose for more than a few seconds. Wanna prove me right?'

How rude. This was so like the sort of stunt Donna pulled at their training camp years ago. Clearly, she hadn't changed. Why did Donna not think she could do it? Emily shook her head in disapproval. Beside her, Olivia raised an eyebrow. Did Olivia think she couldn't do it? Of course she could.

'You want me to do *Bakasana*? That's too easy.'

'Probably not for you. But yeah, that's right. Let's see it.'

'Okay. You're on. But on one condition.'

'What?'

'You do it too.'

Donna scowled.

'It's only fair.'

'Right then.'

'Last woman standing wins?'

'Bring it.'

Angela got into position. She felt all eyes turn towards her and Donna. Donna took a spot beside her and smirked as she got set up. Together, they initiated the pose, starting in a squatting position, with knees flaring out. Angela concentrated on her body and away from everything else. Moving her weight forward onto her forearms, and using her core, she brought up her legs whilst shifting her centre of gravity. Angela did so with relative ease, completed the move and closed her eyes. With her lower body stacked above her, it was as if she was floating in the air. Feeling powerful and connected to her body, she had faith in herself under pressure. Listening to her breath she focused on the sensations in her arms and tightened her core hard. Pouring all her pent-up energy into it was working, and she could have stayed like that for hours.

Beside her, Donna fell onto her mat with a thud, breathing hard. She got up quickly and headed back to her friends. Angela held the pose for another minute to make her point. The students from Heart Yoga clapped politely when she softly came out of it. Like a victory in the boxing ring, Angela let the applause sink in and she stood up and smiled. Her students lauded her with praise. She looked around for Jackie but couldn't see her anywhere. She crossed the studio to shake Donna's hand, but Donna recoiled.

Angela had had enough.

Clenching her jaw, she spoke in a low tone into Donna's ear. 'If you ever pull a move like this again, wobbly, I will have you. You had no right turning up here uninvited and then the cheek to try and show me up in front of my students. What the fuck are you playing at?'

Donna, only inches from Angela's face, scowled and then left the building with her two colleagues in tow. Once they were gone, the energy in the room almost immediately lifted. Angela stood with her hands on her hips and watched them leave. But she was furious. Donna was giving yoga a bad name, behaving as she was. Angela made her way back to her yoga mat as the class filtered out of the airy studio to move onto the next activity. She lay back on her mat feeling drained. While she felt powerful from the win and took satisfaction from the look in Donna's eyes which said she wouldn't be messing with her or her students any more, the feeling of being so competitive and angry towards Donna didn't spark joy in her. Angela sighed, she'd fallen to Donna's level and she knew it.

Why did I have to prove her wrong? And why couldn't I just let it go?

Olivia and Meghan hung back for a minute, before declaring that they were going for a walk. When they disappeared out of the studio, Angela and Emily were left alone together. The early evening light cast soft rays of sunshine into the room. Emily was sitting at the window. Her hair was down, and she exuded a calm that was becoming more and more normal for her.

'How do you feel after beating your arch enemy?'

Angela grimaced. 'It does feel good to win, but I'm afraid I've done more harm than good with Jackie.'

'She was probably just giving you two some space to fight to be top dog. I'm sure she sees this sort of thing a lot.'

Angela laughed. 'I hope you're right. I just wanted to show her that I'm doing well and helping the world to be a better place. Not having a bend off with Donna. God only knows what she thinks of Donna.'

'Why does Donna have it in for you?'

'She was always a little funny with me when we were training. I really don't know what her problem is.'

'You don't think she ... you know ... *fancies* you or something.'

Angela laughed. 'Weird way of showing it if she does. No, I don't think so.'

Emily looked out towards the sea. The early evening sky was starting to cloud over, casting a brooding light over the grounds of the retreat and surrounding hills. She turned her head back to Angela. 'How's your back feeling?'

They locked eyes, and Angela got a flashback to the morning's massage, and to their first kiss over champagne. All Angela felt was her unfulfilled desires, the longing to let herself do the things she had been fantasising so much about doing, and the aching to get closer to the person who had had such an impact on her. Instead she projected the opposite and kept things low-key. 'It feels okay, thanks. Though that showdown with Donna might not have helped.'

'Well, if you need another massage let me know.'

The atmosphere between them was charged. Angela froze and looked out of the window to avoid Emily's gaze. Evading was both a relief and a sign of an obvious truth that was becoming more and more difficult to ignore. Emily continued quietly watching her. She could feel it.

'I should be okay, but thanks.'

Angela swallowed, and began clearing up the bits of kit that had been left out. Emily helped her with the task, silently going about the studio, picking up mats and yoga blocks off the gleaming wooden floors. They caught each other's eyes now and again. Sharing space again felt meaningful.

Angela went into the storeroom at the side of the studio floor to put the kit back in its place, attempting to stack the pile of yoga mats, which had been lumped together in one huge pile – something she wouldn't have tolerated in her own studio. Emily followed her in, closing the door slightly behind her, and lay down the two bolsters she was carrying. The look on her face was serious. Emily crossed the small room and stepped into her space. Angela's heart started beating fast. Angela knew what that look meant.

There were only centimetres between them. Emily tilted her head towards Angela's but didn't make contact. Feeling Emily's breath on her lips, Angela gave in, surrendering to the moment – no longer willing to resist the energy between them a second longer. With the smallest move of her head, Angela closed the gap. Their smooth lips connected as the world fell away behind them. Deliberately, Angela found Emily's tongue with her own and let her passion take over. Pressing their mouths and bodies closer to each other with each breath. The yoga mats wobbled behind them as they kissed deeper and deeper. It was as if it had been both an eternity since they'd last kissed and no time at all. Feeling as if she had been dying of thirst until this moment, she let her hands move around Emily's body, feeling every part of her figure. Angela didn't want their embrace to end as she was finally finding a way to communicate what she had been incapable of before.

Emily turned her head to the side to speak. 'I like kissing you,' and planted a slow, thoughtful, kiss on Angela's cheek.

Angela grinned. 'I can see that.'

They stood there beaming at each other, bodies still pressed together. What Emily did next surprised Angela, but in the sweetest way – she hugged her, fiercely. Emily wrapped her arms around her body and glued their bodies together so that they were finally immersed in each other. Angela felt the soft bulge of her breasts on hers, the quick pulse in her neck. She was struck by how strong Emily felt, yet also soft. Their bodies entwined, it felt so right. The hug was like home.

'I think you like kissing me too,' said Emily, over Angela's shoulder.

Angela planted a kiss on her neck. 'What gives you that impression.'

Emily leant back from their hug, not moving her lower body. 'Angela, I want to do that again. I know that you do too.'

A wave of pleasure shot right through her at that. Leaning in, she whispered into Emily's ear. 'I want you.'

Angela felt Emily tremble a little. A noise from the main studio disturbed them. They heard Olivia's voice grow louder.

'Fuck.' Angela whispered.

Emily put her hands to her head, looking slightly dazed.

Angela scrambled around in her head for a solution then tossed some yoga mats onto the floor. 'Pretend we were tidying up. I'll go out first.'

'Uh, okay.'

Olivia's voice sounded near. 'Are you still in here, Angela?'

'Yes,' called Angela. She left the cupboard with one last

look at Emily now kneeling on the floor among a pile of yoga mats. 'Emily and I were just sorting through the kit.'

Olivia walked barefoot across the studio. 'Always working on something, aren't you? Are you guys coming to meditation in the workshop before dinner? I think it's starting in ten minutes.'

'Yes, of course. I'll get changed and be right over.'

'Awesome!'

'Where did you go for a walk? You weren't long?'

'Right down to the water and along. We saw Wolfie chase a pheasant! Nearly caught it as well. I don't know *what* I would have done if he had. I haven't actually thought about how I'd cope in a sitch like that before. The moral dilemma of it is mind-boggling. It really got me thinking, you know, as a *vegan*.'

'Uh-huh, did it?'

'It did.'

Emily came out of the storeroom still visibly red faced and flustered. Angela took a little too much satisfaction in seeing the effect she'd had on her.

'Hey, Olivia. Hi, Meghan. Shall we go straight over to meditation and get good spots?' said Emily.

'Yes! Let's do that,' said Olivia. 'I want to be right up close to Jackie Hay. Angela, she's amazing.'

'She is.'

'You are too, don't get me wrong. But she's just so, you know, wise and stuff. Like she could shave her head and wear orange robes and she'd be perfect for it.'

'Shall we?' Emily had made her way to the door with Meghan and Olivia, who was still talking. She gave Angela a smouldering look as she left. This time it was Angela who trembled.

Chapter 22

Emily observed her surroundings in a blissed-out state. Compliments had to go to Zadie, who'd created the perfect rustic country lounge in the workshop with another huge wood-burning stove, and cosy sofas and chairs. There were tables made out of different items, such as trunks and chests. The group had eaten together, and Zadie had served another delicious evening meal. Now they were about to play games. Zoe was separating them all into four teams.

Taking a sip of red wine, Emily realised she was happy. Watching Angela from across the room, she saw a super cool, easy-going, and lovely woman talking to people and having fun. If Emily hadn't known otherwise, she would never have guessed the moment they'd so recently shared. When Angela looked up and they found each other across the room, Emily blushed a deep crimson. The look on Angela's face was meant for Emily only. It was so sexy.

'Which group are you in, Emily?' said Samantha.

'Group? Oh yeah. Two, I think. Wait. Maybe it was four.'

'You're in group four,' called Louise. 'We're over here.'

'Right.' Emily joined her team. They found their seats and settled into their respective tribes. Angela stood up in front of them all wearing navy-blue linen trousers turned up above the ankles and a yellow knitted jumper. Her clothes were casual, but she wore them with such style. Her hair was still a bit messy from earlier and her skin glowed next to the fire. Emily was spellbound.

'Ladies. Can I have your attention, please?' Angela spoke, authoritatively. 'Now that you're all in our groups, I can announce what the game is.'

'Please don't say twister. I've had enough of all that for one day,' said Louise.

'It's not twister, don't worry. It's,' she paused for effect, 'charades!'

'What's that?' said Olivia, scrunching up her face.

At once, all heads turned to face the young woman perched on an oversized cushion on the floor.

'You don't know charades?' asked Angela.

'Nope. Never heard of it. What is it?'

'That makes me feel old,' said Karen.

'You basically act out stuff instead of saying what it is. Like, the title of a book or a film. Or a song. Or a play,' said Emily.

'The more theatrical the better,' said Karen.

'Yeah, try to think abstractly and don't be afraid to put on a performance,' said Samantha.

'So, it's an acting game?' Olivia tentatively asked.

'Yeah, kind of, but the point is to make your team get what it is. You can choose to explain the words or paint the scene, so to speak,' said Angela.

Olivia didn't seem convinced. 'Can't we just stick on some music or something? Seems like a lot of effort.'

'It's called interacting with one another,' said Karen, with a sigh.

Olivia shrugged and slouched further into her cushion. 'Old school. Whatevs.'

'So, Jackie has kindly offered to be the judge for the evening,' said Angela, pointing in her direction as she spoke. Jackie was sitting in the only single seat. She smiled and waved like a monarch at a coronation. 'Okay. The rules. Each team nominates a player for each round who will pick out a strip of paper from each of your boxes. It will have the item on it that needs to be acted out. I'm assuming most of you know the gestures for book, film, TV show, number of words, and sounds like – and all the rest of it. It's easy to pick up, Olivia. Anyway, shall we go with three minutes to guess it correctly?'

People nodded and this seemed satisfactory to Angela.

'Three minutes. After all four groups have played four times we'll go into playoffs. Basically, we'll keep playing until the winning two groups play each other in a knockout. Sound good?'

The group cheered and made positive noises at Angela.

'Let's get on it, girls!' said Karen.

Angela smiled back at everyone clearly enjoying the good vibes. 'Enjoy!'

Jackie sat forward. 'How lovely. I'd also like to add that there's no talking when the other team is trying to guess. I've got the timer in my hand, and I'll be watching to make sure you all play by the rules.'

No one said anything for a few moments until Louise spoke up. 'Don't worry, Jackie, I've already had a sneak peek at the bits of paper.' She winked at Jackie suggestively and was met with a deadpan stare.

'Great! 'Who wants to go first?' said Angela.

'We'll go,' said Donna. Cult Yoga were in a group by themselves.

'And we're off. Good luck,' said Angela.

Donna got up in front of the group almost nudging Angela out of the way as she did so. Angela stumbled but took it in her stride and showed no signs of a negative reaction. Joining group four, she smiled warmly at Emily as she sat down. Emily's heart fluttered and she immediately held her breath, thrilled to be near her again.

Donna started off by winding an imaginary something close to her right ear.

'A film,' said Clementine.

She nodded promptly and held up two fingers as if she was

flipping someone off.

Jackie interrupted. 'I think that's the wrong way around, Donna.'

'Oh shit, sorry.' She rotated her wrist.

'Two words,' said Andrea.

Donna nodded. This time she held up one finger.

'First word,' said Clementine.

Donna nodded vigorously and then started to run on the spot like a sprinter, ending with a big swoosh of her arm. Her team looked confused.

'Cool Runnings.'

Donna shook her head.

'Running Man.'

Shaking her head again, she started the sequence all over, this time adding in a machine gun into the action. The other groups watched on in silence. Emily was glad to see Cult Yoga get involved and act nice for once. Although, the competition element was likely what they were most interested in.

'Forrest Gump!'

Donna snapped her head from side to side and let her hands fall in disgust, waving them wrong. She held up two fingers, again the wrong way around.

'Rude,' muttered Louise.

'Second word.'

Donna did a miming action of holding up one finger and then two, one finger and then two.

'You've got one minute left,' said Jackie.

Andrea and Clementine called out all sorts of things and the communication was totally breaking down. Donna acted out a machine gun. She did the running action again and then the swoosh. Then she did the two fingers in sequence, making a huge emphasis on the second finger.

'Running Fingers?'

'Star Wars?'

'Iron Man.'

'Thirty seconds,' said Jackie.

Desperate now, Donna took a few steps back, then slow motion sprinted and then jumped down onto the floor, holding out a straight arm and latching her hand onto a table when she landed.'

'And that's time.'

'Jesus Christ, guys! What happened to you? It was so obvious,' said Donna.

The pair exchanged guilty but blank looks.

'Would anyone else like to have a go?' said Jackie.

'Terminator 2?' said Emily.

Donna sighed and slumped forward. 'Yeah, that was it.' She took her seat not speaking to her friends.

'Hard luck, girls,' said Jackie. 'Who's up next? She looked around the room. How about someone from group four?'

Louise, Meghan, and Angela sat forward. Emily stayed where she was, perfectly comfortable with one eye on Angela and the other on the performance up front. 'Emily. Would you like to play for your team?' asked Jackie.

Emily took a moment to register that words had come in her direction. When she did, everyone was looking at her.

'Sure.' She got up hesitantly and padded to the front. It felt strange seeing everyone lined up before her, all in one place. She couldn't imagine doing this day in, day out like Angela did and it gave her a new appreciation of how challenging it must be. She picked, unfolded, and read a bit of paper: Groundhog Day.

Oh shit.

With the room staring at her, all she could do was start. Inhaling deeply bought her some more time to think. Vaguely, she remembered the film from years ago. It was about a day that kept repeating. She circled her wrist up by her ear and then held up two fingers, politely.

'Film,' said Angela quickly. 'Two words.'

Emily got to work. She held up one finger then tapped the inside of her arm with two fingers.

'First word. Two syllables,' said Angela.

Emily nodded as she tapped the inside of her arm with one finger.

'First syllable,' barked Louise.

Emily pointed to the floor, she walked around pointing at the floor.

'Floor, rug, down,' said Meghan and Louise.

Shaking her head, she tapped two fingers on her arm, then twiddled her earlobe.

'Second syllable. Sounds like,' said Angela.

Emily pointed at the logs for the fire.

'Logs,' said Angela.

Emily nodded her head and pointed. She held up two fingers again and twiddled her earlobe.

'Second word, sounds like,' said Louise.

'That's one minute left,' said Jackie.

Emily pointed at herself. Her team scrunched their faces up.

Meghan looked confused. 'Emily. The second word sounds like Emily?'

Emily shook her head and made sign language symbol for lesbian across her mouth. Her team said nothing.

'Thirty seconds.'

Emily toddled across the floor and then fell down dramatically as if she'd just been shot in a film. She did it again.

Angela called out. 'Groundhog Day.'

'Yes!' said Emily in relief.

'Well done,' said Jackie. 'I had no idea what you were doing there.'

'This game is hilarious,' said Olivia. 'Can I go next?'

Emily sat down next to Angela as Olivia and her team psyched themselves up. Most of the group were talking and laughing. Emily felt happy that Angela had been the one to get hers.

'Expertly done,' said Angela. 'I particularly enjoyed seeing you do this,' she did the lesbian sign.

'Took you long enough to get it, though,' replied Emily, her head spinning a little.

Angela leant over to Emily so that only she could hear. 'I got it at log.'

'Why'd you let me go on for so long then?'

Angela eyed her mischievously. 'I wanted to see you strut your stuff, didn't I?'

Emily felt that pull again. She looked down at Angela's lips and wanted to kiss her right there and then. Angela returned her attention to the group, leaving Emily stranded in her frustrated desires. Her thoughts strayed to later that night and them sharing a room. She didn't know if she was excited or terrified, or a bit of both.

Olivia was nearing the end of a stellar performance that her team were building and building on, having picked up all the hand signals perfectly.

'The Talented Mr Ripley!' shouted Zoe.

'That's it!' said Olivia.

'You're a natural,' said Angela.

'Go us. We worked for that,' said Zoe.

'Who put that one in? It's so obscure.' Olivia said.

'I had one of my grandkids pull them off Google and cut them up into wee pieces,' said Louise.

The teams played more rounds and got better with every go. There was competition but it was all good natured, even, in the end, from Cult Yoga. Emily was having fun but was finding it hard to relax fully. When her team crashed out in the semi-final, she considered excusing herself and going to bed. Or at least to calm down for a bit before they were both back in the room together. But everyone wanted to watch the final, so she decided to hang around a bit longer. Plus, seeing Cult Yoga lose to Karen's team was fun. Karen was standing up and waving her arms about like a raver. Olivia and Zoe were perched on the edge of their seats, earnestly trying to interpret the performance. They had to decipher a six-word book. They weren't doing well. The pressure was on.

'Is it a recent book?' said Olivia.

Karen considered this for a second and then ignored the question. She pointed at the wall of the workshop and then stayed there, waving her arm at it. Her team were so confused looking.

'Wall? Flat? Brick? Stone?' said Olivia.

Karen nodded and pointed vigorously at the last word Olivia had said.

'Stone.'

Ten seconds.

Karen was frantically waving and pointing her arms at the wall and anything else.

'Harry Potter and the Philosopher's Stone!' said Olivia.

'YES! That's it, that's it,' said Karen.

'I thought there wasn't supposed to be any talking,' said Donna.

'It's fine, they'd guessed correctly,' said Jackie. 'And the winners are group three!'

'I don't believe this. That was cheating,' said Donna.

'Donna, how can it be cheating when it was to guess the correct answer?' said Karen.

Donna rolled her eyes and sat back as if she was talking to a group of morons.

'Well done to group three,' said Angela, standing up. 'I hope you all had a bit of fun playing that.'

'It was great. I haven't stayed up like this in ages,' said Louise. 'I feel like I'm twenty-one again.'

It was late. They'd all stayed talking and chatting long after the meal. After the game was over, everyone drifted out of their assigned teams and set about making themselves more comfortable or turning in for the night. The wood continued to burn in the stove, giving a warm glow to the room, although it too had started to slow down. Emily saw Jackie excuse herself for the evening to Angela with a hug and a few words.

Heading for the cabin felt like a good idea. She'd had enough of being sociable for the day, and she wanted to think more about the kiss with Angela. And what a kiss it was. To be fair, it had been *all* she had thought about during the meditation immediately after it, but at the meal and over the game, it had sat patiently to one side as she talked and hung out with everyone. But now the exhilaration and anticipation came flooding back.

Yes, she needed to clear her head.

She finished the rest of her wine, put her glass on the table in front of her, and tucked her hair behind her ears. As she got up, she felt Angela's eyes on her. They locked eyes, and every nerve in Emily's body fired up as Angela seemed to peer right into her soul. The heat from the fire had made Angela's cheeks quite rosy. Her skin glowed and her grey-blue eyes spoke of things that Emily could tell were not for the others to know about. The woman looking back at her was the most beautiful woman she'd ever seen. Angela took a step in her direction; at the same time, Karen stood in her path and started talking to her. Angela gave an apologetic smile to Emily and began chatting with Karen.

Emily left through the side door into the cold fresh air. There was something comforting from the faint smell of smoke from the burning logs. She glanced in the window as she walked. The room inside looked so warm and cosy from the outside. Angela was in the thick of things talking to Karen and Meghan. Karen was still very animated, and Emily thought it was sweet how much satisfaction she'd taken from being in the winning team. Watching Angela as she talked, she bathed in how lovely and beautiful her whole aura was. Her tummy flipped again. They would be alone together again soon. And there was only one way that was going to go. So what if Angela wasn't looking for a relationship? Couldn't they just have fun tonight? Inhaling deeply, she then let out a short, shaky exhale. Moving away from the window, she took the path beautifully lit up by lanterns towards the cabins. It was a clear night, and there were so many stars visible. She probably could have seen where she was going even without the lanterns. She stopped when she was nearer to the cabin to really look up at the sky, the moon, and the expanse of where they were. Yes, this was definitely her happy place.

Chapter 23

'Emily, wait up,' Angela jogged the last few steps to catch up with Emily, whom she had seen standing at the end of the path with her head tilted back looking up at the sky. Emily turned around, with surprise on her face that quickly turned into delight. They were only a few metres away from their cabin.

'I thought you were still hanging out with everyone. It sounded like Olivia was about to crack open another bottle.'

Angela reached out and held Emily's hand discreetly. Their cabin was on the end, and she was pretty sure no one could see them. Emily looked down at their hands, then back up to Angela's eyes and held her gaze. She could almost still feel Emily's lips against hers from earlier. Her brain hadn't been able to stop processing the shape and curve of Emily's body. She'd watched Emily all evening and hadn't been able to not think about every which way she would like to undress her. Angela spoke honestly. 'I got away. I needed to see you.' She gave Emily's hand a gentle squeeze, to drive home the point.

Emily inhaled deeply and then a small smile formed at her mouth. 'About?' She raised an eyebrow slightly. Angela had never seen that expression on her before, but she loved it.

Angela was done talking. She led Emily along the last of the atmospherically lit path up to the porch of their cabin. Still holding her hand, she opened the door. Once inside, she shut the door gently. The room was quiet and lit only by the moonlight coming in the window. Emily looked almost shy as they stood in the cabin facing each other. Her full lips drew Angela's attention.

'About this.' Angela stepped into Emily's space, took her face in her hands, and let her forehead rest on Emily's. She inhaled Emily in as she let her nose gently nudge Emily's one way, and then the other. Their mouths, both slightly open, were so close that she could feel Emily's breath on her lips. Angela's heart pounded. Emily let out a little moan, a frustrated moan, which sent a wave of desire low down in Angela's body.

'Angela,' Emily whispered.

'Yes?'

'Kiss me.'

At that, Angela brushed her lips against hers before closing the gap between them completely. The kiss was slow, deliberate, and gently probing. Angela wanted to savour every second, as she knew where this kiss was heading. They both did. Angela kissed her deeper, and Emily let out another small moan, which again did things to Angela in a big way. She dropped her hands from Emily's face and let them roam up and down Emily's back, and lower, all over her glutes. Squeezing them, she pulled her closer so that their hips were touching. Emily ran her fingers through Angela's hair. Angela smiled through their kissing. 'That feels so nice,' said Angela.

Emily smiled through their kissing too. 'You feel like silk.' She kissed her again. 'And you taste delicious.'

Stepping over her yoga mat, Angela passionately kissed her again and walked her back to the wall. She felt Emily's tongue with her own and had to consciously force herself to remember to breathe. Emily squeezed her hands and looked into her eyes. Their fingers found each other and seemed to instinctively interlock. A moment went by, and then another. Their eye contact felt so intense. The look in Emily's eyes was more serious than Angela had ever seen, and full of desire. Silently, Emily led her into the bedroom.

'Wait here,' said Emily. She rounded the bed, shut the curtains, and switched on one of the bedside lamps. Angela watched her move and was sure she looked like a hungry animal. But she couldn't help it. Getting close to Emily had felt so urgent, so inevitable, so *necessary*.

'Angela,' said Emily, now back and facing her. Her voice was lower and almost husky. 'I think it's time you took your clothes off for me.'

Angela wasn't used to feeling like she wasn't in control during sex, but she liked it with Emily. She liked her assertiveness. It was not what she thought Emily might be like. She held Emily's gaze. 'Isn't it normally me who gives the instructions?'

'Not right now. I want to see you. All of you.'

Emily sat on the bed, leaned back with her arms out behind her, and pointed her head up towards Angela, waiting on her, watching her. Angela's insides almost melted. The look on her face was beyond sexy. Angela felt herself quiver. She couldn't remember feeling this turned on. With eyes locked on each other, Angela began to undress. She started with her shoes, then took off her jumper. It was a relief to get it off. She pulled off her T-shirt with both hands, lifting it above and over her head and then let it fall. Emily continued to just … watch. She slipped down her trousers, stepped out of them and stood there in her underwear. As Angela let her purple bra fall to the floor, she saw Emily's pupils dilate even further. Her brown eyes were dark and at the same time, soft and loving.

Emily spoke quietly. 'Oh my God. Angela, you're so beautiful.'

Angela slowly slid down her pants, keeping eye contact with Emily the entire time. She stepped out of them, leaving them on the floor by her feet. Emily's mouth opened as she continued staring at Angela. She could almost feel Emily's gaze as if she was physically touching her already. Emily moved forward, apparently wanting more than looking could give. In one move, she found Angela's hands, tugged her onto the bed and flipped her onto her back.

Emily straddled her. Angela used her core to lift herself up and tried to take off Emily's fleece. Emily was having none of it. Emily sat back and threw her fleece to the floor herself, before quickly removing her T-shirt and bra. There was a flicker of vulnerability on Emily's face, and Angela could tell she was trying hard not to show it. Unable to control herself, Angela reached out to touch her naked skin, but again Emily pulled back.

'Uh-uh. Not until I say.'

There was a mischievous grin on Emily's face as she tucked her dark hair behind her ears. Turning more serious, she bit down on her lower lip. She kissed her once, softly on the lips, and then planted kisses on her chest, on the space between her breasts, directly over her heart. It spoke to the connection between them that was beyond merely physical attraction. Angela felt herself surrender completely to Emily in that moment. Emily circled Angela's nipples and kissed and squeezed them with her mouth. She took her time and used her free hand to caress Angela's skin. Angela felt hot but noticed she had goose bumps at Emily's touch.

Emily looked up at her and they locked eyes for a moment before she trailed kisses down her tummy and repositioned herself between Angela's legs. Emily ran a hand along the fleshy part of her inner thigh and pushed her leg to open wider. She did the same on the other side so that Angela was completely exposed beneath her. She looked up into Angela's eyes again before planting little kisses everywhere around Angela's most sensitive spot. Angela couldn't help but lift her thighs slightly off the bed towards her.

'Please, Emily,' she whispered.

'Please what?' Emily whispered back. 'I want to hear you say it.'

Angela could take no more. Her heart was racing in anticipation. She swallowed, hard. 'Emily. Fuck me.'

Emily finally kissed her, slowly, and steadily. She used the tip of her tongue so lightly, and delicately licked her on her most sensitive spot. Angela could feel herself building already, and as she did so, Emily almost stopped until she drew back from the cliff edge. This continued for so long that Angela lost all sense of time, space, and what was going on. All she needed was for Emily to allow her to come, but she was teasing her. Drawing it out.

'Fuck, you're torturing me.'

They locked eyes. Emily's eyes were unbelievably naughty and sexy. She never wanted to stop seeing that look. But Angela threw her head back on the pillow. When Emily finally increased her pace and put two fingers inside her, she felt she would lose all control. Every muscle in her body tensed up, her heart was beating so fast, and her breathing was ragged. She made noises that she hadn't made in a long time, or perhaps ever. They started from somewhere deep within. Putting a hand over her mouth to stifle them, she lifted her hips off the bed as the pulses gripped her and sent her over the edge. Emily held onto her and expertly guided her through wave after wave of pleasure.

Breathless on the pillow, she let her hands fall away from her face, feeling more vulnerable in that moment than she had in a long time. Emily lifted her head and grinned. She fell into position beside Angela, and they faced each other. As they looked into each other's eyes, Angela became overwhelmed with emotion that seemed to bubble up to the surface. She fought to hold back tears from her eyes but was betrayed by one thick teardrop when she blinked.

What the fuck?

Emily gently wiped the trace of the tear. She clasped their hands together, interlocked their fingers and pulled Angela in closer. Angela smiled at her in a sort of relief. She couldn't help it. They found each other's lips once more and kissed deeply. It was soft, slow, and full of tenderness. Angela stroked Emily's face and neck as they kissed, drawing her closer and deeper into her. Emily had clearly given up on making her wait, much to Angela's delight. She wriggled out of her jeans and pants, hastily kicking them off onto the floor. Angela smiled at the sight of this out of the corner of her eye. Reaching out, she stroked Emily's breasts. Emily gasped at the touch. She pushed herself up onto her elbow so that she was leaning over Emily slightly and caressed the rest of Emily's naked body beside her, down to her belly, stopping at her naval, her fingers poised above the dark triangle of hair.

Emily bit down on her bottom lip and opened her legs.

'Is there something you're needing help with, Emily?'

Emily answered only with a look of pure hunger.

They held each other's eyes as Angela ran her fingers all around Emily's centre and Emily bucked in anticipation when she brushed past. When she touched her, Emily let out the sexiest moan Angela had ever heard. That, combined with the extreme wetness beneath her fingers, sent tingles through Angela's body once more.

She pressed down, exploring Emily, as she leant over and kissed her on the mouth. She slid her fingers deep inside her, feeling the warmth devour her fingers, circled, and came back out again. Emily closed her eyes briefly and moaned as Angela increased her intensity. Emily pushed her fingers inside her. Hard. Angela looked down at their entangled naked limbs in awe of how hot it both looked and felt. Emily's moans became quicker, as her body tensed up and her breathing became unsteady.

'I'm going to come.'

Emily came quietly looking into her eyes, covering her mouth with one had and still fucking her with the other. Her body shook and shook as she came hard. Angela kissed her lips and stroked her until she finally stopped. Emily's deep breathing was all that could be heard.

Once Emily's breathing calmed down, she removed her fingers from inside Angela and spoke quietly into her ear. 'So, is that all you wanted to see me about?'

Angela laughed softly. 'Well, I'd say we've only covered about a quarter of what I was wanting to see you about, but yes, that … I don't know what to say. Emily, that was—'

'Fucking amazing?'

Angela smiled from her soul. 'Yes. It was definitely that.'

Emily rested her head on her chest and nuzzled into her. Her skin was sticky against hers. Heat emanated from both of them. Silently, they held each other. Angela kissed her head through her hair and felt her own heart rate come down.

***

Emily woke to the feel of skin. Nothing but skin and softness and the smell of Angela. They had fallen asleep wrapped up in each other, with Emily's face in between Angela's breasts. She was a little surprised she had been able to breathe properly. Her left leg was wrapped around Angela's hips, and her left arm rested on Angela's waist. Angela lay on her side, with one arm underneath Emily's neck. The feeling of complete and utter peace washed over Emily. Last night had been incredible, and waking up next to Angela was a dream come true. Pulling back from the pillow of breasts, she looked into Angela's sleeping face.

Her face and jaw were completely relaxed. Even like this, she was stunningly beautiful. Memories of the night before washed over her, and she smiled. She licked her lips. They were a little bruised from all the kissing. She hadn't been with anyone in so long, and she was so happy that she had finally got close to Angela. That she'd finally been able to show her how much she had come to mean to her. It had been a wonderful night. A magical night.

Angela opened her eyes. 'Good morning,' she let out a small smile that spread to her eyes.

'Hey, you.' Emily stroked the side of Angela's face, gently brushing her thumb along Angela's cheekbone. She smiled gently as she looked into her eyes. 'How did you sleep?'

'The sleep that I got was good. I think it was almost daylight by the time we stopped.'

'Was it, I hadn't noticed.'

'And how did you sleep?' said Angela.

'Fantastic. I think I fell asleep in between your boobies.'

Angela laughed. 'That's right, you did.' She looked a little self-conscious in the light of day, which was uncommon for her and totally adorable. She liked that she had that effect on her. She liked being so close to Angela and seeing her react to things.

As they gazed into each other's eyes, Emily took her hand and interwove her fingers with Angela's, much like how she'd done the night before. She brought the back of Angela's hand up to her lips and kissed it lightly. Angela saw the duvet slip over Emily's nipple and let out a little gasp. Emily pulled the duvet back up.

'I caught you looking.'

Angela pretended to be innocent. 'Nope. Not me. Not once. Never.'

'Yeah, you did. I just saw you. Just like I did all those times before. Like *a lot*.'

'I wasn't that obvious, was I?'

'No, but after a while I began to notice certain patterns.

218

Like how you'd turn your head in my direction even though you should have been facing the other way. Then there was the moment we nearly fucked in my stairwell, that was a bit of a giveaway.'

Angela laughed from her belly. It was lovely to see. 'I don't know what came over me.'

'Um, I think I nearly did.'

Angela grimaced. 'Emily, I really was – am – sorry about how I behaved after we first kissed.'

'It's okay. Like I said, I understand. You had every right to say no.'

Angela had a faraway look in her eyes. 'What's wrong?' said Emily. Her tummy seemed to drop at the slightest flicker of doubt on Angela's face.

'Nothing.'

There was something slightly off. She glimpsed that same turmoil that Angela had been carrying. 'You don't regret what happened, do you?'

***

'No, not at all. I wanted it to happen. I really wanted it.' That was the truth. She *had* wanted it.

Emily took a deep breath and smiled at her shyly. Seeing the relief it caused in her made Angela's heart swell even more for her. Emily was such a sweetheart and a kind, beautiful soul. Angela stroked her cheek with her thumb and leant in towards her unconsciously. She kissed her on the lips very slowly and felt a gentle throbbing between her legs. There was no controlling how she felt about Emily. Physically or emotionally.

'That makes me so happy.' She paused. 'And if it makes you more comfortable, I won't tell anyone,' said Emily.

This jolted Angela's thoughts back to more serious

matters. Angela didn't know what to say. Emily didn't deserve to feel for a second that Angela might not be on the same page as she was. Because she so was. But for Angela, she had not expected this to happen, and she knew that she would need time to get her head around this. After a moment she replied. 'I think that might be best for now. I want you to know that I want to get over this thing about you being a student in my studio, I really do. I think I might just need a bit of time to get my head around it all.'

'I get it. Look, there's no pressure. We slept together; we didn't agree to get married.'

'It's not pressure. It's just ... if the word got out that I sleep with my students—'

'There'd be queues out the door?'

Angela laughed. 'That's not really the draw I'm hoping to achieve.'

Emily stroked Angela's fingers as she held her eyes. 'It's a secret. For as long as you want it to be,' she kissed the back of her hand again. 'Well, not too long, but you know what I mean.'

Something about the way Emily confirmed their illicit behaviour turned Angela on. But then, everything about Emily turned her on. Her dark brown eyes were even darker this morning. Images of their night came flooding back. Emily sitting back and making her strip; Emily in between her legs looking up at her. Never had she had such passion the first time she'd slept with someone. Never had she fit so well with someone straight away.

Emily moved herself back, so they were no longer talking almost nose to nose and found a spot on the other pillow. 'So, what do you want to do now?'

'Um, I hadn't really thought that far ahead.'

'Ooh,' Emily teased, 'problems thinking clearly; I must have made an impression.'

Angela spoke softly. 'You definitely made an impression.'

The skin between Emily's eyebrows creased. 'I can't believe you resisted me for so long.'

'Neither can I.'

A big smile crept onto Emily's lips and lit up her whole face.

'My God, you're so cute,' said Angela, leaning in to kiss her again.

'You are too,' said Emily, kissing her back briefly, once. 'Especially when you do exactly what I tell you. I like that a lot.'

Angela laughed. It was a pressure relieving laugh, and she felt better after it.

Emily propped herself up by her elbow. Holding Angela's eyes, she took the duvet off herself. Angela's mouth fell open as she took in Emily's gorgeous body beside her. Emily watched her as she took her time gazing upon every inch of Emily's body. The curve of Emily's hips and the dip at her waist were too much to bear. Her skin was flawless and so smooth. Seeing Emily in full view, right next to her while not touching her was highly erotic. Her nipples were dark and hard. Angela felt another flood of tingles down low in her body.

'That was the sexist thing I've ever seen. Emily, you're stunning.'

Her eyes rested on Emily's necklace. She paused there for a few moments and wondered what it meant to her and then lightly brushed her hand over her breasts making Emily gasp again.

There was a knock at the door. Emily looked up and froze. 'Who is that?' she whispered.

A huge dose of adrenaline coursed through her as she yanked the duvet up and over them. 'I don't know.'

'Angela, are you up yet?'

It was Jackie.

Angela's tummy lurched. 'Fuck. I'll go. Would you mind waiting here?'

'Of course not.'

Angela jumped out of bed, nearly falling over as she pulled up her trousers and put on her jumper as she walked.

'Angela?' called Jackie. 'Yoo-hoo.'

With one hand on the handle, she paused and took a deep breath. She opened the door, still flustered. 'Jackie. Good morning to you. I was just sleeping. Just woken up. What's up?'

Jackie assessed Angela's appearance and demeanour. She glanced down at the folded-up camp bed and unslept in duvet hanging over it. 'Sleep well?'

Angela cleared her throat. 'Yeah. I was really tired.'

Jackie eyed her closely and checked her over again. 'Great. Well, I'm going over for breakfast now. We were going to have a chat, remember?'

'Yes, of course. I'll be right there.'

'Where's … Emily? Aren't you two sharing?'

Angela hated lying. She hated lying with a passion, especially to her mentor. 'She's in the shower. I think.'

'Nice girl, Emily. I like her. Good aura. Sensitive.'

Angela felt her voice wavering. 'Yeah, she's great. I like her, too.'

'Okay, well, I'll see you when you're ready. I'll order some tea for us.'

'Thanks.'

Jackie turned and walked away. Angela watched her take the path around the corner behind the cabin before shutting the door and sighing with her back to it. All at once, a wall of tension hit her. Her heart wrenched at the situation. Her emotions were so conflicting – she was both elated at finally getting close to Emily, but she felt so guilty for crossing that line. It had been a close call, Jackie coming to their door *during*. With that dizzying thought, she didn't know if she and Emily had made any noise last night or this morning. They might have as it was so quiet at the retreat. A knot formed in the pit of her stomach.

What if she knows?

Chapter 24

Hugging Jackie goodbye by the minibus, Angela still prayed that she wasn't suspecting her of any misconduct. 'Thank you for coming. You were so great.'

Jackie smiled and shook her head, emanating that calm wisdom Angela had grown so attached to. 'You did a wonderful job at organising this. It really was special.'

'Thank you. Have an amazing time in Findhorn. I hope you get to take a back seat for a bit and relax.'

'I'm always relaxed, my dear. This weekend really was no difficulty on my part.'

'You've taken four classes over two days – that's a lot when you're retired.'

'I'm not that retired.'

'Yes, but when you're not in the habit of it.'

'Angela – it's good for me and it's energising, believe it or not. I haven't felt this good in months. And that's in part due to how fantastic a group you've built. They were a joy to work with.'

Angela smiled and glanced around. Everyone was milling around by the minibus and cars, hugging Zadie and her family, not quite wanting to leave the idyllic retreat. They had bonded and everyone knew it had been memorable.

Jackie continued. 'And well done for not letting Donna get to you,' she paused, 'but was humiliating her really necessary?'

Angela laughed nervously. 'She challenged me, what can I say.' Cult Yoga had already left and hadn't said goodbye. The last Angela had seen of Donna she was sniggering at her from across the breakfast table. Angela suspected something was up with her but didn't care to find out.

'I don't know what's going on between the two of you, but I can see that you are trying.'

'I don't do drama, Jackie.'

'Yes, I know that about you. And just as well, she's got a bee in her bonnet about something to do with you.'

'I have no beef with her. I'm just a mild-mannered yoga teacher.'

Jackie gave her a funny look and hugged her again. 'You were one of my best students,' she cleared her throat. 'Are. I don't believe we ever stop learning. Even me. I'm so proud of all that you've gone on to achieve. It's not easy going out on your own and you've done it so well. It took me years to take the jump you've made. And look at you. You're going from strength to strength.'

Angela gulped. It meant so much to her to hear that. 'Thank you.'

'It's the truth. Now go and get your people home.'

When they hugged warmly Angela felt a knot twist in her stomach. They parted as Zoe jumped out from nowhere and started herding people onto the minibus.

'That's it. Time to go. I hate to be the bearer of bad news, guys, but if we want to get home at a reasonable hour tonight, we need to get going,' said Zoe.

'Zoe's right,' said Angela to the group. 'Let's get the last of the bags on.' She watched as Emily hugged Jackie and they spoke a few words. Seeing Emily nod at something, she really wanted to know what they were saying to each other, but she was out of earshot.

People were taking their seats, sitting in the same places as on the journey up. Zadie and her family were standing beside the minibus, waiting to wave them off. Angela hugged and thanked them for a wonderful stay and was the last one to board the bus, again. Zadie's husband shut the door and Zoe reversed them out. Waves and smiles punctuated the end of their weekend retreat. As Zoe put them into first gear with a clunk of the gearbox, they took off along the dirt track. Jackie and the family faded into the distance still waving.

Angela smiled at Emily sitting next to her and took a deep breath as she contemplated the fact that they were heading back to the real world. To reality.

'Do you want to sit by the window this time?' asked Emily.

'No, it's okay. I don't mind.'

'Take the window. You get a better view.'

'I've got the best view right here,' whispered Angela grinning.

Emily spoke under her breath. 'I like it when you flirt. But take the seat.'

Angela smiled. 'Okay. Thanks.'

As Emily stood up and moved over so that Angela could take her seat, Angela got a flashback to the night before. Their night had been beyond sexy, and so intimate. Angela knew they had a special connection but last night had completely blown her away. Angela snapped her attention back to the present moment as Emily smiled at her in her new seat.

Louise stood up and turned around to face the rest of the bus with an arm on her headrest.

'I want to say another big thank-you to you, Angela.' Heads turned towards Angela as they all sat up straight to see each other. 'It has been a fantastic weekend and my mind and body feel completely refreshed.' The group agreed and cheered Louise on. She continued. 'But I will say this. I can't wait to get my hands on my phone again. Yes, I've realised I'm addicted. So, thank you for the "aha" on that as well, Angela. And Zoe, you've been absolutely brilliant too.'

Clapping filled the bus as chatter broke out and people echoed Louise's sentiments. Emily was smiling at Angela through all of this.

'You're beaming at me.' Angela said, under her breath.

'I'm happy. I'm happy for you. You've given us all such a wonderful weekend.'

'I'm so glad it's been a success.'

Emily held her eyes. 'In so many ways.'

Angela felt the tension rise between them again. Seeing Emily orgasm like that would never leave her mind. Ever. Angela just wanted to get her alone again.

'Who wants to take the scenic route?' said Zoe.

'Huh? The whole route is scenic,' said Olivia.

'Yes, but the world-class, take-your-breath-away scenic route is also an option. It'll only add about half an hour to our journey. Or, we can just go back the way we came.'

'I thought you were worried we wouldn't get home until late?' said Olivia.

'That was when you were all faffing around chatting.'

'I vote the scenic route,' said Emily. 'Glencoe is so romantic. I love it there.'

'Me too,' said Louise. 'Let's extend this magical weekend some more.' Nods and murmurs of agreement followed Louise.

'Scenic route it is!' said Zoe.

The indicators were put on and Zoe slowed down through the gears. The minibus came to a stop sign and turned left, ambling around the narrow single carriageway. Mountains and hills flanked them on both sides. The minibus fought ardently to get back up to cruising speed. Once there, the group settled down and got themselves comfortable for the long drive. Most continued to chat to the person next to them.

'Didn't know you were the romantic type,' said Angela quietly.

'There's a lot you need to learn about me.'

'True. I do.'

A quiet fell between them and through the rest of the group as the scenery unfolded dramatically through the windows. Angela felt peaceful as they passed through glen after glen. She was very familiar with the Highlands, from family trips and frequent visits for recreation and holidays as an adult. But it had been a long time since she was a passenger; she was usually the one driving. Taking the time to absorb the scenery was nice. The pressure of the weekend was over. The silence of the journey only seemed to intensify her memories of the night before with Emily and where they had got to this morning. Angela sighed and checked her watch. It was nearly four-thirty; they still had hours to go.

She couldn't deny it. Her feelings for Emily had grown, and now she had to face up to the fact that Emily meant a great deal to her. There was almost no way she could have resisted what was between her and Emily. She'd never experienced such a strong attraction, and never so quickly, with anyone else before. That was scary. She knew that if she and Emily were to find the space to keep seeing each other, she'd have to confront this issue. It was never going to go away. Even if Emily left the studio. She felt guilty for considering such things when she was lucky enough to have met someone as wonderful as Emily.

Emily cleared her throat, jarring Angela back to the present. Beside her, Emily leant forward, unzipped her blue fleece, and draped it over herself like a blanket, moving it over onto Angela without asking her so that they were both partially covered.

'Thanks,' said Angela, gesturing to the garment.

They turned onto the route which would take them down through Glencoe. The noise from the engine filled the minibus. Zoe also had some music on low in the front, but other than that, the minibus was quiet, with people either preoccupied with a book or with the views outside. Angela rested her elbow on the window with her head on her hand. She let her head drop to the side and enjoyed the increased warmth of the makeshift blanket. As she was zoning out, she felt Emily place her hand onto her leg, leaving it to rest there. It was like a bolt of lightning to Angela's senses and she shivered. Angela was wearing soft yoga pants and could feel Emily's hand on her leg quite easily through them. Angela's breathing turned shallow. No one could see where Emily's hand was, under the fleece, even if they turned around. Emily continued to look straight forward, giving no indication that she had her hand on Angela's thigh. Then she found Angela's hand, took it in hers and squeezed it. It was such a sweet, simple gesture, yet it had a monumental impact on Angela. It felt so right, so complete, so loving. What was happening between them was more than just sex. There was a real tenderness to their connection.

What is happening to me?

The iconic mountains were coming into view and the other occupants of the minibus started to stir and get excited about it. Emily leant over her to see, resting her other hand on her thigh, outside of the fleece. Emily faced her.

'Spectacular out there, isn't it?'

Angela was lost for words.

'Right. We're stopping,' said Zoe, loudly from the driver's seat.

Emily sat back and the group made positive noises about stopping to see the views. When the viewpoint was reached, the minibus pulled in and parked next to coaches and buses full of tourists. The car park was a concentration of human activity in one small area among the huge mountains. Droves of people meandered around the small car park and along towards the viewpoint, taking photos from different angles. Once out in the fresh air Angela took a deep breath and took in the view herself. They were in the grandest of glens, surrounded by mountains, with a steep cliff towering above the road behind them. There was hardly a cloud in the sky. Stopping by a knee-high dry-stone wall, she closed her eyes, listening to the wind and a little stream trickling down the hill. Taking in a few slow deep breaths helped to ground herself from the high of Emily. Opening her eyes, she felt pretty good and rejoined the group, who were standing in a circle. Emily watched her as she moved back to the group, sending a flutter of butterflies through Angela.

'Hey,' said Emily, holding her gaze.

'Hi,' Angela returned the eye contact, feeling herself close to blushing.

'It's really beautiful here,' said Emily to Angela from across the group. 'Breathtaking.'

'Not too bad for a few hours' drive from home, eh?' said Louise.

'I've never been here before. What's it called again?' said Olivia.

'Child. What *have* you been up to all your life?' said Louise.

'What? We holidayed abroad in my family. My mum's a sunseeker.'

Louise held her hands out to her side to indicate the sunny day. 'No sun here.'

'That's what they always say though, right. It's always raining and miserable in Scotland,' said Olivia.

'And that's exactly what we want everyone to think,' said Louise, winking at the others.

After the minibus rejoined the road, Emily's fleece came off again, was draped over them, and they held hands, secretly, for the rest of the journey home.

***

'Oh my God, I can't believe I went three days without my phone,' said Olivia, gripping it tightly.

'Glad to see the retreat's made some lasting impacts,' said Angela.

They were standing beside the minibus. Dusk was starting to set in as it was well after nine in the evening. The door to Heart Yoga was open and the main light was on. Angela had come out with the box of phones. The desperate mass of hands coming towards her had been a bit zombie apocalyptic and more than a little unnerving. The goodbyes were more muted than before; people seemed more interested in being reunited with their devices than anything else.

Zoe didn't hang around. She sped off, having offered to drop people off who lived further away from the studio. Angela said goodbye to Erin and Faye, who were walking home together, as they thanked her for a wonderful weekend. Emily hung back. When they were alone, they went through the brightly lit door of Heart Yoga and Angela closed it behind them. Her heart was racing and her legs felt like jelly. Being back in reality after everything that had happened was terrifying.

'Home sweet home,' said Angela.

'I love that this place is like home to you.'

'Add a bedroom and it would be.' Angela paused. 'Do you have to rush off or can you stay for a—'

'I can stay.'

Angela locked the door to the studio. 'Good.' Angela found herself going to the office for privacy even though they were there alone. Emily walked after her. She'd never quite checked what you could and could not see from the street when it was dark outside and light inside. She suspected you could probably see quite a lot. In the safety of her office, they stood in front of each other. Emily put her hands lightly on Angela's waist. Angela felt an overwhelming sense of affection. She wanted to both rip her clothes off and hug her tenderly. Emily stepped in and wrapped her arms around Angela's body and rested her head on her shoulder.

Angela got lost in the hug.

'This is good,' said Emily, squeezing her tighter. Emily lifted her head and gently kissed Angela on the lips. Angela felt so familiar with her cues now, her soft skin and her taste. The kiss got heated quickly. She broke away, flustered. 'Would you like to come over tonight?'

'Yes,' said Emily, eyes twinkling and smiling. 'I'd love that.'

Angela inhaled deeply and grinned. 'That's wonderful.'

'I'm ready to go whenever you are. Actually, hold that thought. I just need to jump to the loo. Then I'm yours.'

'Jump away,' said Angela, instantly wondering why she had said that, and then realising she was actually a little nervous still. It had been amazing with Emily, but she hadn't fully processed what she was doing yet. Deep down she knew she had crossed a line; she felt guilt rise up in her before pushing it back down. She didn't want to stop and think. She'd been in a daze since they'd kissed in the storeroom. All she knew was that she felt very strongly for Emily and she wasn't able to fight it, not tonight. Tonight, she would enjoy her company again and try not to think about what it all meant.

She picked up her phone and switched it on. The start-up sound was quite loud, so she switched on the mute button and found herself absent-mindedly looking at the home screen. Angela heard Emily using the eco hand dryer. Holding her phone again felt good. It had been a challenge to detach from it for a few days. Numerous notifications on her social media accounts for Heart Yoga lit up her home screen.

That's odd.

Tapping onto her Twitter account, she tried to remember if Zoe said she'd put some pictures on it but nothing sprang to mind. Zoe wouldn't have had time as she'd only just got her phone back and was driving. When the app opened, she froze. There was a picture staring back at her that she had no idea had been taken. An image of her and Emily kissing glared up at her.

Angela stopped breathing. She read the comment:

Yoga teacher pounces on vulnerable student at retreat. I know this so-called yoga teacher, who's also a lesbian, and have suspected her of creeping on students for a long time. But this is a new low. Shame on you @angelaforbes of @heartyoga. Just awful. Wonder what Jackie Hay will have to say about this.

Angela felt sick. Her stomach twisted into a painful knot of tension. Eyeing it closer, it appeared that someone had taken a picture of them in the storeroom through a crack in the door. The zoomed in snap showed clearly hands where they shouldn't have been and tongues searching. Somehow, both of their faces were recognisable. It was posted the day before, not long after the kiss happened. There was no escaping it. Tapping quickly onto Facebook she saw even more notifications. The same post had been plastered all over every other social media platform and tagged far and wide in the yoga world. Angela's heart was beating fast and she felt the blood drain from her face.

Donna.

Chapter 25

Emily dried her hands under the hand dryer and did a little happy dance as the hot air feebly did its job. It was an eco-dryer and took twice as long. This did nothing to dampen Emily's spirits, though, as she was so looking forward to getting back out to see Angela and where the night might lead. Normally she would've been tired from a weekend away, but tonight she felt energised. Ecstatic, even. She burst through the door when she was freed from the warmish-air and let it swing shut behind her. Angela was at the front door on her phone with all her bags around her ready to go. Emily smiled at this, but quickly registered that something wasn't right. Coming to a stop beside Angela, the smile was gone from her face.

'What's wrong?' said Emily.

Angela was engrossed in her phone and didn't answer straight away. Emily waited.

'Angela.'

'Someone took a photo of us kissing and has put it all over the internet.'

'What? Who? When? I don't understand. Let me see it.'

Angela's face was deadly serious. It sent a cold shiver through Emily. 'Here.' Angela showed her the picture of the two of them in the storeroom.

'Who took it? We were in there by ourselves.'

'Donna. We must not have heard her come back.'

Emily felt confused. 'And she's posted it online? What for?'

'To ruin me. I knew she had a mean streak, but this is horrific.'

Emily felt like she'd been punched in the stomach. 'Ruin you? Horrific? Is that what you think this is?'

'She was clearly upset at losing that silly little contest, and this is how she retaliates. No, it's more than that. She can't stand that I've gone out on my own, that I'm making a success of myself. She's trying to pull me down.'

'So, you do think it is?'

'Of course it is.'

'Being with me is horrific?'

'What? No! That's not what I meant.'

'Why are you so upset?'

'Emily, this is my livelihood. My business. She's tarnished me to the whole community. There's no coming back from this. I've read some of the comments and they're not very forgiving. Some of them are brutal.'

'So what? You know the truth. Why are you so concerned about what other people think? I keep asking you. I'm beginning to think it's got nothing to do with your reputation. Honestly, why should what anyone else thinks matter?'

'Because it *does* matter, in this business reputation means everything. And she's probably right.'

'What do you mean?'

'I shouldn't have let anything happen between us. You came to my studio in a bad place. You were vulnerable and I let myself get too close to you.'

Emily felt her breathing come in short, shallow draws. She couldn't believe what she was hearing.

'I thought you said you didn't regret it. That you wanted it to happen. You said that just this morning. And just now in the office, you said you wanted to get to know me better. Which is it then?'

Angela didn't answer – which was enough of an answer for Emily.

'If that's how you feel then I can't help you. And if you're so concerned with your reputation then you're a lot less spiritual than you make yourself out to be. You're only human, you get to have feelings too.'

'It's not as simple as that. I took an oath.'

'I think you know that we're more than just a sex thing. We could be, anyway.'

'Yes, but that's not the point. Other people won't see it like that.'

'Of course they will.'

Angela stepped away from Emily. 'What are you not getting? I told you this was a real concern for me. Can't you understand?'

'I do understand. I said we'd keep it quiet.'

'And now it's the opposite of quiet.' Angela spoke quickly, her voice finishing not far off a shout. She looked agitated and gripped with fear. 'It's just all happening too quickly. I need some time to process how I feel about all of this.'

Emily looked at the ground for a good ten seconds and then back up at Angela. There was resentment in Angela's eyes. 'Why are you doing this? Why are you pushing me away? It's like you're relying on how others see you because you don't feel good enough on some level. But you are. Can't you see?' She paused, realising that wasn't all. 'You're afraid of getting too close to me.'

'I'm not sure what you're talking about. I just feel like this is going to damage my business. It's got nothing to do with how I feel about you.' Angela paused, and put her hands to her head. 'I'm sorry. I can't do this right now. It's just too much.'

Emily snapped her head around to look for her bag and picked it up roughly. 'Fine. Forget it. I don't need to be told to fuck off more than twice to get the message.'

'Emily.'

'What?'

'Can't you just let me deal with this first and then we can see how things are after that? I really like you, and I want to see where this goes. But I need to manage the fallout from this.'

'You're unbelievable.' Emily unlocked the door and threw it open. 'And you are *all* ego.' She didn't look back as she slammed it behind her.

***

Angela flinched as the door slammed shut in her face. The past few minutes had been a blur. Her worst nightmare had come true. She couldn't get the image of the picture on social media out of her head or Emily's hurt face before she left. Feeling awful, she couldn't think straight. It was all happening so fast. Her phone vibrated in her hand and she looked down to see Zoe calling. Having missed five calls from her already, she slid a finger over the screen to answer it and shakily held the phone to her ear.

'Have you seen it?' said Zoe.

'Yes.'

'Don't worry, it's not as bad as it looks. Well, it is pretty graphic, you have a whole hand over her boob, but nothing that we can't fix. Good for you by the way, getting some action, finally. Kept that one quiet didn't you. Dark horse.'

'How can we fix this?'

'First, I honestly don't think you've done anything wrong.'

'Thanks.' Angela put Zoe on loudspeaker and sat down at one of the café tables letting her back slouch and her shoulders stoop in defeat. 'And second?'

Zoe continued. 'There's nothing to worry about. I know it's something we're forbidden to do but come on, this stuff happens, and I think it happens a lot more than people think.

As long as you're both consenting adults it's fine. I once had a crush on a student of mine; oh my God, he was so hot. We fucked, once. I never thought twice about it. The only reason you're getting all this shit is because of Donna. She's spinning it into something it's not. Emily isn't vulnerable. She's a consenting adult who was clearly enjoying your … your attention. Two women kissed, big deal. You're not her doctor or her therapist. We may have ethical principles and the last three thousand years of yoga wisdom—'

'Five thousand. Sorry. Carry on.'

Zoe ignored the interruption. 'But there are no statutory rules against it. You're fine. It's just a load of nonsense created by that Donna and it will blow over. And by the way, I'm never freelancing at Cult Yoga again after this. I've been unhappy there for ages. This performance of hers is the final straw.'

Angela felt a little better but still wasn't convinced it wouldn't sink her business or hadn't also now caused her to jeopardise things with Emily.

'What do the comments say?'

Zoe didn't reply immediately. 'I think Donna is writing them all herself or has recruited some meanies down at Cult to troll you. I can't imagine anyone genuine giving this much of a shit.'

Angela still felt sick. She'd heard social media could be brutal but had never experienced it until now. 'Tell me what they say. I can't look.'

'Why? Are you sure about that? If I were you, I'd ignore them.'

'Tell me.'

'Okay.' Zoe paused and Angela assumed she was scrolling for a comment that wasn't too damning, serving to confirm in Angela's mind that it really was a reputational disaster.

'Here's one,' said Zoe. '*So what, she got it on with a student. It's not as if she killed someone. It's bad enough with men giving women a hard time on the internet without women slaughtering other women. Give it a break, ya fannies.'*

'That was a good one? Fucking hell. I'm ruined.'

'Angela, chill. She was defending you.'

'I'm being compared with a murderer. Sure. We need to respond. Tell them it was a kiss and no more.'

Zoe sighed loudly down the phone, catching Angela off-guard. 'Jesus Christ, Angela. Will you stop freaking out about this. How is Emily? Does she know?'

It was Angela's turn to go quiet.

'She knows, doesn't she. Did you take it out on her?'

'Where are you? Are you finished dropping people off?'

'Changing the subject again, nicely switched. Yeah, I finished my taxi duties. Olivia was the last one to drop off, she talked the entire time. Bless. I wish I was twenty-four again. Don't you, sometimes?'

'I'm not really in that headspace right now, Zoe, but yes – I guess I do.'

'So, Emily knows, and you've had an argument about it?'

'Uh-huh.'

'So, saying you said publicly that you "only kissed and nothing more", how do you think Emily would take that?'

Angela realised that was not a good idea. 'Badly. I get your point. I wouldn't do that to her. And it's also not true. Last night we had an incredible time together. God, I can't believe I even considered denying it. I'm a shitty human being.'

'Harsh on yourself much? Jeezo. You're probably the most decent person I know, Ange.'

'Thanks. I need to hear that right now.'

'You don't know it about yourself? Angela, you don't need me to tell you that sort of stuff, and I say that as your best friend.'

'I thought you were my minion?'

'I make you think that, I can tell you like to be the boss.'

Angela laughed, surprising herself.

'See, that's what I like to hear. This will blow over, I promise.'

'I hope so.'

'So, are you two a thing?'

'Zoe, do you mind if I don't talk about it? I'm still trying to process.'

'No worries. Sorry I probed.'

'Cheers.'

'Are you going to see how she is?'

'I will. I really hope I've not hurt her feelings, but I think I have. I'm an idiot.'

'It's understandable you freaked out, pal. But don't let it ruin what you two have. Even if it was just getting frisky in the storeroom. If you have something between you, I'd try to keep that going.'

'It's more than that. I really like her.'

Zoe was silent. 'I knew it. Then best not leave it too long, before she really gets upset with you.'

'I think she already is.'

'Hmm.'

'You really don't think I should comment or engage with this?'

'I strongly recommend that you don't. Anything you say will make you look guilty. Not unless you say you're getting married. You could save things with a good old-fashioned romance. Keep your integrity and seem like less of a threat.'

'Fuck. You think I seem like a threat and have lost my integrity?'

'No.'

'Zoe, that's what you just said.'

'I mean, yes, that's how Donna is trying to make this look. But it's not what I think. I know you. You care about your students and you're definitely not a perv. Well, I've caught you checking out my ass once but that's because I have a great ass. I don't blame you for that.'

Angela laughed. 'Zoe, I've never checked out your ass.'

'I know! See. You haven't even checked out my pert little bum. You're an angel.'

Angela felt a little better. Her head was starting to clear. She took a deep breath and looked around at her studio, her business, and all that she'd poured her heart and soul into.

'And if something has happened between you and Emily, I'm sure it's very special. You know, I could tell that there was something between you two. You've clearly tried to keep things professional. What's that now, three or four months? You should be commended, if anything. Donna is so out of order. I'm going to sort her out.'

Angela laughed again and felt so grateful for having Zoe in her life. 'When shit hits the fan we're all peace and love, aren't we?' said Angela.

Zoe laughed loudly. 'Ha! The irony. Fuck, though, she was such a destabilising influence all weekend and now to have done this and still be sitting in her flat trolling you is the lowest of the low. I've half a mind to go around there right now and kick her door in or something.'

'Zoe. Now it's you who needs to chill. Going radge on her would end this place. Thank you, and all, that's so sweet of you. But no, I think that would most definitely make things worse. She'd probably film it and post it for the world to see. She threatened to do that with me recently when I asked her to leave. It would go viral.'

'Fuck it. I'd do that for you right now. I've never heard you this upset before, and you so don't deserve this.'

'Zoe. I do feel guilty for crossing that line though. It's been plaguing me for weeks now.'

'Weeks? Is that how long something's been going in? Dark.

Horse. I love it.'

'What will Jackie think? What will the rest of the studio think?'

'That shouldn't matter. They'll be fine with it. As long as you're not giving the sultry eyes to everyone, they'll be cool with you being happy. If you have feelings for Emily that's really important. What if she's the one for you? Would you risk not exploring that?'

Zoe's words hit her right in the chest. 'You're so right. You're completely right.'

'I am right. That's unusual to hear, but, on this occasion, I think I am.'

'I've fucked it up with Emily, and my business is in tatters. I'm a mess.'

Zoe was quiet. 'Propose to her. That's my advice.'

Angela wasn't in the frame of mind to laugh right now. She let the comment pass.

Zoe continued. 'I think you should let Donna's shitshow fizzle out. She'll get bored if you don't react.'

'What about the damage to Heart Yoga's reputation? I won't get the chance to be dignified about it now. It's all out there.'

'Let it pass.'

Angela exhaled sharply. 'Right. Okay, I will. It's not like I've got any clue how to fix any of this now, and you're saying I shouldn't do the one thing I want to do and that's to get right on every platform and start defending myself and this studio.'

'Angela – real talk – that will make you look like an actual weirdo. Don't do it. Wait. Be patient.'

Angela took a long slow deep breath, feeling herself relax. 'Okay. Thank you.'

'I think you should go and see if Emily is okay and call Jackie for a chat if it's really playing on your nerves.'

'I can't do either of those. I'm feeling too raw.'

'Stop feeling guilty and ashamed. You've done nothing wrong. How many times have I got to tell you? If Jackie Hay's going to give you a hard time about it then she needs to understand who's she talking to i.e. you, and that it's not like you've not tried to ignore your feelings and keep things *profesh*. I've seen you around her. It was kind of sad. Yes, we can't go around using our classes like Tinder, but that doesn't mean that when love does come a-knocking we ignore it either.'

'Didn't you say that you slept with a student?'

'I'm not perfect, what can I say. He was,' Zoe paused, 'extremely hot.' Anyway, there is one thing we've not said here.'

'What's that?'

'That the fact that you two are both lesbians makes it much less bad than some rapey guru abusing his power.'

'Ew. Don't even make that comparison.'

'I know. Sorry. It's gross, but your situation is so not like that.'

'She was in a bad place when she came here.'

'And you gave her a new lease of life. You two bonded and she helped you with the business. I say you two are perfect for each other. And from the looks of that picture you're compatible in other ways, too.'

'That's what I mean. A picture says a thousand words. This is going to haunt me.'

'That's it. No more of that defeatist shit. It's really not that bad. Now go see if Emily's okay. Check if Jackie's chill or don't. And know that you're a good person regardless of any of this.'

'Why do I need her approval so much?'

'Because she's Jackie friggin Hay! We all love her, and she makes a big deal about no sexing with students. It probably means she's had it on with a few too many, and this is her way of keeping her conscience clear. I see a dominatrix in her, you know; beneath all that gentleness and peace, she's a tough cookie. Who survives growing up in care and becomes like her? She's an inspiration, but she's not perfect either.'

'Zoe you're sounding so wise tonight.'

'I know. I think it's from spending three days with Jackie. She has that effect on you.'

'She does. Right. You're right. I'm going to deal with this, and it will be fine. It's all an illusion anyway, right?'

'Exactly.'

'Thanks for your support, Zoe. You're amazing.'

'I am amazing and you're welcome.'

'And thanks for everything this weekend. I couldn't have done it without you.'

'Ah, I'm sure you could have but that's okay. You're welcome.'

'Bye for now. Speak tomorrow.'

'No posting, remember? Don't get involved. Let Donna hang herself with this. She's the one who looks like the real arsehole here.'

'Thanks, Zo.'

'Laters,' said Zoe.

Angela hit the red button on the phone on the table in front of her feeling like a different person to the one who answered the phone call. Stretching her arms out in front of her, she rested her forehead on the table and closed her eyes. Emily had left so upset. All she could see was the hurt on her face. Texting her to apologise was the right thing to do, but she couldn't bring herself to hit send.

Chapter 26

Emily stared up at the ceiling. It badly needed a fresh coat of paint, but she knew the letting agency wouldn't be interested in doing it. She could do it herself, but she'd have to ask for permission. Anyway, it was the last thing she felt like doing. Her bedroom was her cocoon, and it was the only place she could manage at the moment. Emily had barely moved in over three hours. After lying awake for most of the night, tossing and turning, she'd slept late, knowing she had nothing to get out of bed for. For this reason, she was still lying in bed with no further intention of getting up. Hunger had passed, leaving an empty hollowness in her physical body to match her soul. The motivation to do anything had completely gone. There was nothing coming up in her life that she was looking forward to. Time had slowed down, stretching out behind and in front of her. There was no telling how long this feeling, or lack of feeling, was going to last. The numbness was familiar to Emily by now, and in some way it comforted her. In many respects, the past couple of months were out of the ordinary, and this was her getting back to normal.

It was cold in the flat as she'd left a window open all night and hadn't got up to close it. The cold air served to remind her that there was a world outside. But the thought of the outside world was too much, and every time these thoughts came in she felt a pit in the bottom of her stomach. Yet, she still couldn't make herself swing her legs out of bed, walk the two metres to the window and close it. Sighing, she turned over into the foetal position and drew the covers completely over her head so that she was submerged. And so it began again. Unwanted thoughts of all the things that had gone wrong in her life plagued her mind. There was no escape. The most recent debacle, fresh in her mind. The rejection from Angela had left her feeling empty inside, as if she was worthless and no good. The most insulting thing was the fact that Angela had rejected her not once, but twice.

What sort of a person goes back for more like that?

The self-hatred was growing stronger by the minute. The only thing giving her a hint of hope was the prospect of starting her own business, if she was able to find the energy and enthusiasm to do it, which was feeling highly unlikely. Peeking her head out of the covers, she lazily reached for her phone. It was Monday afternoon and there was nowhere she needed to be. Not having a job was hard as so much of her previous identity had been derived from it. Her phone was on silent but there were no missed calls or texts from Angela. Only some concerned messages from Anna but she didn't have the heart to reply. She didn't dare look at social media or even WhatsApp. Disappointed and angry, she threw the phone across the room. It bounced off the overflowing laundry basket and hit the floor with a thud. Her head flopped back onto her pillow and she snatched the covers over her head and buried herself underneath them again.

Before long, the fuggy humidity of her breath forced her to pull the covers down over her shoulder. She turned so she was lying flat on her back again. After a few moments of completely spacing out, the back door to the stair opened and she heard someone moving around the garden. It was unusual to hear anyone use the back green, so she turned her attention towards the window. A stream of sunlight was tentatively making its way into the room. No more sound came, and she wondered if the person had gone back inside. A guitar string pierced the air. A few chords were played about with, then a pause, then a coherent tune began to take shape. Emily's whole body felt glued to the sound. The guitar was played softly, as if for the ears of the player only, but the notes effortlessly made their way up to Emily's room. The song was folk-like and very Scottish. All that was needed was the gentle lilt of a Scotswoman singing and it would be perfect. A tear fell from her eye. Emily lay listening as song after song fell out of the guitar player's hands.

***

Later that day, Anna had come around because she had been worried after Emily hadn't replied to her calls or messages. She would be missing putting Russell to bed, and for that Emily knew she must be worried. Coming through with cups of tea, she sat down on the sofa next to Emily. It was nearly six in the evening.

'Seeing you like this, Emily, I'm worried about you. You know you can talk to me, right?'

'I do.' Emily's eyes glazed over and her face went red. 'You're amazing. Thank you for coming around.' A few tears fell from her face. She cried, feeling grateful that she had such a loving, supportive friend. The one thing she had going in her life.

'You poor thing,' said Anna, placing a hand on Emily's shoulder.

Emily cried harder.

'Has she contacted you yet?'

'No,' said Emily, between sobs.

Anna did an audible gasp. 'That shit's cold,' said Anna. 'You'd think she'd want to know if you were okay or not.'

Emily frowned and sat in silence. 'Sorry Anna, I'm really not in a good place today. I appreciate you coming over, but I have nothing to say. Maybe it's all too soon. I feel wounded.'

Anna put down her cup of tea on Emily's coffee table, sat back and turned herself around so she was directly facing Emily on the sofa. Emily felt better for having her friend near. It was like having an attentive angel on her shoulder.

'When I first saw the post, I thought it was great. Not the flak Angela was getting, mind, or the mention of you being vulnerable, but I thought you'd be happy at finally getting your girl. Then you dinghied all my DMs, and now I find you like this, honey. What the fuck happened?'

'This time yesterday I was ecstatic. What we shared over the weekend felt very special. And then we held hands all the way home on the bus. I really felt like this was going somewhere.'

'That's sweet,' said Anna.

'... but then she found the picture online and freaked out. She called the picture horrific. She said she wasn't sure if she could *do* this, that it was all moving too fast, that it was a mistake we'd slept together, and that it was going to ruin her – whatever the hell that means. Her whole demeanour changed towards me, or maybe I saw her attitude towards me for what it really is for the first time. Clearly this was just a casual thing to her. You wouldn't do that to someone you cared about. It's not as if she didn't tell me before that she wasn't looking for a relationship. Funny way of showing it, though. Och, I don't know what to think, but I do know how I feel, and she's made me feel ... not good.'

Anna sighed heavily. 'That sucks. She didn't have to do that. You've also just been through a really rough time with your redundancy. That's maybe why you're more sensitive to this situation.'

'I'm a mess.'

'No, you're a badass going through a rough patch. It's not your fault she's done this. The stuff online is a joke if you ask me. It really puts that Cult Yoga person in a bad light. Trying to publicly shame people is so fucked up,' said Anna.

'Well I feel really ashamed, so she's achieved something.'

'You've nothing to be ashamed of. That's some internalised homophobia right there, misses.'

Emily shrugged.

'I'm pissed off about the way Angela's been treating you. I say you get her tae fuck and move on. She's not good for you.'

'I know, but I really like – liked – this woman. But if she could do this to me so early, who knows what she's capable of,' said Emily. 'How could I ever trust her again?'

'It's a tough one. Trust is essential for a relationship to have legs.'

'I think that's just it. We were never in a relationship. I shouldn't be surprised.'

'Yeah but it's okay if it still hurts. She really pulled the rug out from under you.' Anna frowned.

'I know. That's what's making it so bad. Literally one second we were on cloud nine, and the next she was dumping me. In that moment I saw that she's got some serious issues to work out. Which is weird because she seems like she's so sorted. I mean, why is she so worried about what people think of her.'

'Isn't that a thing? That stereotype of the super spiritual hippy who's got a massive ego,' said Anna.

'I hate to admit it, but I think so. It's so obvious now I think about it. I thought she was the best person I'd ever met. Apart from you, of course. But, you know, the best person I'd ever had a crush on. She got me out of my funk, got me into yoga and meditation, and I was starting my new business and all that. Now look at me. A mess. Probably worse than I was before I met her.'

'What are you going to do?'

Emily paused. 'I'm not sure.'

'Take your time, honey.'

'I don't know. What if I'm running out of time, Anna? I can't sit here unemployed and miserable for much longer.'

'Will you keep doing your yoga?'

'I'm never going back to that studio, that's for sure. But yes, I think I will at some point. I have really fallen for it. Keeps my mood balanced.'

'Good,' said Anna.

Emily threw her head back on the sofa in frustration. 'She's tossed me to the kerb so many times. It's embarrassing.'

'You've nothing to be embarrassed about. You chased your girl. It was brave.'

'Have you seen any more comments about it today?' said Emily.

'I've read most of them. I don't recommend you do. It won't help you move on.'

'Has she commented?' said Emily.

'No.'

'Why the radio silence?'

'Maybe she's having a pyjama day as well?'

'I just wish she'd have been more level-headed about it. Why couldn't we have dealt with this together? She didn't have to push me away.'

'No, she didn't. She fucked up. What if she's regretting it?' said Anna. 'She might be.'

'It's so confusing. All I know is that I feel pretty low and she's the cause.'

'You're so strong. You've been through worse. You'll be back on your feet in no time.'

'I *have* been through worse. Much worse.'

Anna took a sip of tea. 'I do this thing when I'm worked up about something: I ask myself whether this will matter in a week? A month? A year? Ten years from now? Most of the time, it won't. It's just the small, utterly painful lessons life throws your way to help you grow.'

'When did the life coach arrive?'

Anna repositioned the cushions behind her on the sofa. 'That'll be a hundred quid, please. So, are you going to see her again?'

'No. I'm not going to seek her out any more. She's messed me about too much.'

'I think that sounds like the right thing to do. At least for now. It's such a shame she couldn't have been cooler about the photo. There was no need to treat you like that over it. All she had to do was ignore it,' said Anna. 'But what's done is done. You have to move forward.'

Emily felt tears running down her cheek again, independently spilling her emotions without her consent. With nowhere to turn, Emily closed her eyes and dropped her chin to her chest.

'Shit, sorry, I didn't mean to make you cry.'

'It's not your fault. It's my life. It's a total mess. I'm sorry, I can't help it. I don't,' Emily sobbed, 'know where it's coming from.' Emily's tears got worse. Unable to control them she let herself sob and struggled to get a grip of her breathing. Her life had fallen apart again after she'd tried to rebuild. Just when she felt like she was turning the corner she was back to square one. The weight of her failure pressed down on her making her feel even shorter of breath.

'Let it out, honey. Let it out,' said Anna.

'I'm such a loser.'

'The fuck you are,' said Anna. 'Hey, hey,' Anna took hold of Emily's chin and turned her head towards her. 'You've achieved so much when nothing was ever expected of you. You've overcome the hand life dealt you and grown into this wonderful person: kind, clever, funny, charming, and loving. Most people in your shoes would have crumbled. But you didn't. You got out. You've made something of yourself.'

'What have I made? Look at me. Unemployed, single.'

'It's not your fault. You're being tested again, that's all. You can handle this. You know you can. You've dealt with much worse. But there comes a point, Emily, when you need to know how strong you are. It kills me that you can't see it sometimes.'

'I'm sorry.'

'Don't apologise!' said Anna. 'You have nothing to be sorry for.'

'I don't want to upset you.'

'Don't worry about me. This is what friends are for.'

Emily wiped the last tears from her face and smiled. 'Thanks.'

'You don't need to thank me. You've been there for me so many times, right? This is a two-way street.'

Emily laughed.

'There it is. Want to see you laughing and smiling again, honey.'

'I do too. I don't want to feel this way. I need some time to lick my wounds and get back on my feet.'

Anna handed Emily a tissue from her pocket.

'I'm not clinically depressed, mate, you don't need to worry.'

'You don't need to be clinically depressed to warrant some empathy,' said Anna. I'll stay over tonight. I said to Jason I might before I came around.'

'Honestly, you don't need to do that. I can see the light at the end of the tunnel. I can see myself getting through this. I'll wallow for a bit and then I'm going to get my life back on track. Yeah, it's been a disappointment with Angela, but I think these past few months have given me enough of a start to keep going. I'm not going to harm myself or anything, if that's what you're worried about.'

'I'm not worryied about that. I'd like to stay though,' said Anna.

'Don't be silly. You've got to get back to Russell.'

Anna put her feet up on Emily's coffee table and got her phone out. She wrote something quickly and then put it down. 'Done. I'm all yours tonight – but not in a gay way. I wish it was, but alas, I just love you as a friend.'

This was a well-practised routine for Emily and Anna. Emily would then proclaim her undying love for her but this time she broke with convention. 'You have strange wishes.'

'I wish for my pal to feel good about herself again. That's what I wish.'

Emily crossed her arms and sighed. 'I wish for that too.'

Chapter 27

Angela lifted her head from her yoga mat and invited the class to come out of Child's Pose. Hiding her head on the floor offered a momentary respite. A day off would have been good to get her head around things, but she had classes to take and things to do at the studio. Closing would have felt like defeat, so she dragged herself out of bed and got on with it. The day had been one long string of horrible realisations about what a huge mistake she had made by hurting Emily. How crushed Emily looked as she walked away last night haunted her. How could she have been so stupid? Yet, she couldn't find the courage to call her or even formulate a message. Every time she went to do it something stopped her. It could have been the confusion or the guilt, she wasn't sure. Everything had happened so quickly, and she needed time to process.

Angela felt in over her head and a little lost. That – coupled with the instant exposure of her romantic involvement with Emily to the world – had left her a little shell-shocked. She knew that she wanted to fix it with Emily but didn't know where to start. The time they'd spent together over the weekend was magical. She was falling for Emily and it completely terrified her.

The studio felt stuffy despite the windows having been open all day. The day had been a hot one by Edinburgh standards. Angela still had no desire to fit air-conditioning in the studio. It didn't fit with her principle of keeping everything as sustainable and as friendly to the planet as possible. People weren't just coming to a class, they were coming to a vision of life that she could offer, even if just for an hour a week. The class tonight was packed, and she'd had to turn away two newcomers who hadn't booked online. It showed that either they hadn't seen the picture or hadn't cared. It had been a relief to see people at the studio, even if the first class of the day was with Susie.

After taking the group through a much-needed lie down and meditation at the end, she closed the class. Bodies became infused with movement as limbs were made use of again. Angela watched as students tripped over each other at the end of class. Something would need to be done about that. They needed more space.

'Great class, Angela. Thank you,' said Louise, who didn't normally come to classes on Mondays.

Angela tucked some hair behind her ears and avoided eye contact. 'Thanks.'

'What's the matter?' said Louise. 'It's not that nonsense online, is it?'

Angela nodded once.

'Oh, for goodness sake. What a nonsense. I saw it on Facebook last night when I was reading in bed. I had a brilliant time, but you young ones really tired me out, you know.'

'Do you think I'm awful?'

'Of course not! Donna's got some cheek trying to get at you like that. But don't you let it affect you.'

Angela smiled in relief and hugged Louise before she could stop herself. 'Thank you so much, I've been a nervous wreck all day.' Angela lowered her voice, 'I'm convinced that everyone thinks I'm a perv or something.'

'Don't you be so silly, young woman. Have you seen how people love coming here? Look at tonight, that was people showing you their support and not needing to ask you about it. People don't care or they are happy for you. Or, they are disgusted at that Donna and her vitriolic ranting. Take no notice, my dear. You are, as they say, above that shit.'

Angela laughed from her belly. It felt so good to release some of the tension she'd been holding in a way that wasn't controlled and predictable like her classes. 'Thanks, Louise.'

'You keep your head up, hen.'

Angela smiled for the first time that day. She was very fond of Louise and grateful for her support. They said their goodbyes and Louise made her way out. Angela watched her as she left.

A group of girls was talking in the middle of the café area. Some she didn't recognise. To think she had got new students in today of all days was a mystery to her. When she neared, they beckoned her over.

Olivia spoke for the group. 'We want you to know that we're one hundred percent behind you. What Donna did was super low, and we support you. I've been fighting the trolls for you. Very classy, by the way, not commenting. Makes Donna look like an even bigger twat.'

Angela felt another weight lift off her shoulders. 'Cheers for sticking up for me, guys, I really appreciate it.'

The group made their way out, already talking about something else. Angela smiled again, feeling lighter with each passing moment. The door closed behind them and Angela sighed in relief at the day being over. As Angela turned her back to the door and went inside the studio, she heard the front door open once again.

Spinning around she found Jackie Hay standing there. Jackie had never been to her studio before and her larger than life presence seemed oddly out of place in Angela's small inner-city studio. Jackie scanned the studio before finding Angela and smiling with her eyes. Gliding towards her, as if her feet were lovingly caressing the ground beneath, she took Angela's face in her hands and gave her a big hug. Jackie squeezed that bit harder, before stepping back to look at her.

'My sweet Angela. I'm so sorry I've never visited your delightful studio before. It's stunning. Let me see the rest of it.'

Angela gave her the tour and a commentary on what she was aiming to achieve with it. Jackie followed her and took it all in.

'It's absolutely beautiful. I'm so proud of what you've done here.'

'Well, thanks. What are you doing here?' Why aren't you in Findhorn?'

Jackie paused. 'I wanted to see how you were doing.'

Angela's heart slammed faster and her face blushed. 'Really, why?'

'Angela, I wanted to know that you're doing okay. I saw the picture.'

Angela felt the room swallow her up. Her mouth felt dry and her palms sweaty. 'You did?'

Jackie nodded. 'You might imagine how surprised I was. I must admit, I was shocked at first. I went to such great lengths to outline the ethics and values of being a yoga teacher to you all.'

'You did, I'm so—'

'Before you start apologising, I want you to know that I'm not happy with Donna doing this to you and bringing down the reputation of our industry. I've had a word with her, and she's taken down the picture and deleted the whole shambles from the internet. I've asked her to apologise to you. Although, it may take a while for her to see the error in her ways.'

Angela's mouth dropped open as she shook her head in disbelief.

Jackie continued. 'I'm so sorry you have had that thrown at you. Donna's behaviour this weekend was absolutely dreadful. She's not in touch with the divine energy, I'm afraid. She's clearly operating from a dark, fear-based place. I can only apologise if I've had anything to do with this unfortunate turn in Donna. Donna has a lot of issues she needs to work through. She's a good girl, really.'

'You're apologising to me?'

'I don't condone relations between yoga teachers and their students, as you know. We must uphold our principles and we must make sure we offer a safe space for our students.'

'Right,' Angela nodded.

'I've known you a long time, Angela. I know that you will have taken great care over your conduct. You are the most respectful, kind, gentle, ethical student – and teacher – I've ever known. If you are pursuing something with this woman then I trust that she must be very special to you.'

'You're saying it's okay to bend the rules for me because I'm a nice person?'

'Angela. I saw you and Emily together this weekend. You light each other up. Don't let me or anyone else stand in the way of love.'

Angela swallowed. 'I tried to ignore it. I really didn't want it to happen. I know I have a duty of care and that I broke it. But that's something I wanted to talk to you about, actually. I want to see where this goes with Emily. I've decided that I'm going to pursue the relationship. That is, if I haven't already ruined it.'

Jackie held up a hand, silently signalling that Angela shouldn't go any further. She sat down at a table and gestured with her eyes for Angela to join her. After a few moments, Jackie continued. 'Thirty-five years ago, when I was learning yoga, I had an affair with my yoga teacher.'

Angela's eyes widened. 'What? You?'

'Yes, me. I was a naïve and vulnerable young woman. I thought I was in love. I thought he was my soulmate,' she threw her head back and laughed. 'I couldn't have been more wrong …'

Angela leaned forward over the table, listening intently.

Jackie took a deep breath. 'He was married. He knew exactly what he was doing. In the end, I was heartbroken by it.'

Angela found it hard to believe Jackie could ever have been in such a situation.

'I recovered, of course. Although, I carried the hurt of the experience for a long time. So, the potential for teachers to take advantage of students was always something I wanted to stamp out of yoga if I could. That's why I focused on it so much with my teacher training. I can see why now.'

'You did focus on it quite a lot.'

'I think I probably put too much emphasis on it, and it might have caused you to deny your feelings towards Emily. I've come to believe that people come into our lives for a reason and to help us learn and grow. If you feel a strong connection with Emily, and she feels the same, you shouldn't ignore it.'

Angela was having a hard time following her mentor. 'You're saying it's okay for me to date a student now?'

'I'm saying that you have my permission – not that you need it. And I'm glad you have already decided to pursue a relationship with this lovely woman. Angela, you don't need other people to validate you. Other people's judgements about you have nothing to do with you. It's almost none of your business. You need to make your own mind up about who you are and whether you're doing the right thing or not. I want you to be strong as you move forward with this. Love is so precious. I'm sorry if that sounds harsh. I say it with love.'

Angela was silent. Something that Jackie said had struck a chord with her. Sitting across from her mentor, she saw that she was far too concerned with what other people thought about her. She had to be perfect. She had to be nice to everyone. She had to put her needs last. Especially with her parents. She felt terrified of people's disapproval and now she might have ruined things with Emily over it.

'How is Emily?' said Jackie.

'I don't know. I let her go. I shouldn't have. What have I done? What do I do?'

'I can't answer that for you.'

Angela closed her eyes. She saw Emily standing before her, smiling. Deep within her, she knew that what had happened between them was something real, something good, and something worth fighting for.

Flopping forward and resting her head on her forearms beneath her, Angela spoke into the table. 'I've made a huge mistake. I should never have pushed her away. I think I might have really hurt her, again.'

'You've hurt her before?'

Angela lifted her head to look at Jackie. 'Yes, after the first time something happened. She was very depressed when she joined Heart Yoga. I was afraid.'

'Oh, Angela.'

Angela stood up. 'I have to see if she's okay. I have to apologise right now. I have to tell her how I feel.'

'Angela, come on, sit down. Breathe. Get inside your body, anchor yourself in this moment. Get grounded.'

With military obedience, Angela did as she was told with the tools she so readily taught to other people. Starting with her toes, she did a mindfulness meditation, moving upwards through her feet, and her legs and upwards through her body. She concentrated on the sight of her mentor in front of her and the familiarity of her beloved studio. It helped a bit, but she still had an overwhelming desire to fix the situation right there and then.

'Feel any better?'

'To be honest, not really. I need to talk to her, like, right now.'

'Well, if that's how you feel. Do you know where she is?'

'At home? I think. I don't know.'

'Could you call her?'

'Yes, I'll do that,' Angela dashed into her office and found her phone without any messages on it. Walking, looking at the phone in her hand, she bumped into a table. 'Ow. You've no idea how many times I do that.'

Jackie acknowledged Angela but never commented. Angela wondered if Jackie would be thinking that she needs to be more present. Pausing for a second, she considered what to do next.

'Would you like me to stay with you while you make the call, or would you like me to give you some space?'

'Could you stay?'

'Of course.'

Angela filled her lungs with air and prayed that Emily would still talk to her. Tapping Emily's name on her phone, she listened as it started ringing. The phone felt cold in her hands next to her ear. It kept ringing until the standard voicemail operator asked her to leave a message. She hung up quickly.

'It went to voicemail. She's ignoring me.'

'You don't know that.'

'I feel it. I'm going to go around to her house. Now.'

'Are you sure?'

She looked at her mentor with certainty in her heart. 'I've never been surer of anything in my life.'

***

Angela pressed the buzzer to Emily's flat and waited. She

looked at her phone and the lack of reply from Emily. She'd texted Emily six times in the last thirty minutes and called ten times. The desperation of her behaviour was not lost on her, but she couldn't stop. It was nearly ten at night, but she couldn't wait any longer. Her heart knew that she was doing the right thing and that she couldn't afford to endanger what she had with Emily for another second. After all, she'd effectively dumped her the day before. It felt as if her life depended on getting her back, and she was operating from a new level of clarity – one where her physical body and her emotions were in complete alignment.

After pressing the buzzer several times to no answer, she moved back out onto the pavement and looked up towards Emily's flat. There were no lights on. It started to rain. A fire of certainty burned in her chest and she was not deterred. She took a lungful of air and called up towards Emily's windows.

'Emily.'

Silence.

'Emily.'

A young man walked past and looked at her like she was mad. The rain got heavier.

'EMILY.'

A neighbour's window flew open and a gust of air brought half a curtain out with it. A woman appeared and shoved her head out of the window down to Angela's direction.

'What the actual fuck! What's wrong with you! Every time you buzz up the whole close can hear it. She's obviously not in, so will you stop annoying this whole fucking building.'

'I'm sorry to bother you, but I know she's in. Can you let me in? I'm not going anywhere until she speaks to me.'

'NUTCASE!' shouted the woman, before slamming the window and yanking her curtains shut.

Angela considered her options. She couldn't stand outside

Emily's flat all night. Plus, she wasn't keen on disturbing Emily's neighbours. As she looked at her phone droplets of rain landed on the screen. Wiping them off with her sleeve, she tapped on Emily's number again. Pressing the phone to her ear she looked up at her window as it started to ring. Her hope of talking to her that evening was diminishing with each ring. Emily's voicemail played again. After the beep Angela started speaking.

'Emily. Please pick up. I've made a huge mistake. I need to talk to you. I'm sorry. I'm so sorry. I hope you are okay, and I want you to know that I'm ready now. I'm here. If you could answer the phone or let me in, I can explain everything. I know what it was all about now. I know why I was so afraid, but I'm not any more. I really like you, Emily. I should never have called things off like I did, I was just scared.'

Hanging up again, she continued to stand on the street staring up at Emily's window.

Out of the stillness of the night, Emily's window opened. However, the person who peered over the ledge was not Emily. Angela didn't recognise the woman. Panic rose within her.

Who is she? Where is Emily?

'Hi Angela. Look, Emily doesn't want to talk to you. Please stop trying to contact her. You better go home. It's raining.' The woman went to shut the window.

'Wait! She's there? Can you tell her I'm so sorry and that I … need to speak to her?'

'I've told you already, she doesn't want to speak to you. You hurt her pretty bad, Angela.' The woman looked behind her, into the room, obviously speaking to Emily. She turned back. 'And you're still upsetting her. You need to leave. Now. Christ, or that neighbour might lynch you if you keep shouting in the street like that.'

'Can you tell her I've realised my mistakes and I want to

start again.'

'It's not all about you, Namaste. Can't you see that? You can't treat people like shit over and over again and expect them to just forget it.' The window shut with a thud.

Angela closed her eyes. A searing pain shot through her head behind her temples. Her whole body felt drained and depleted. Stone-cold judgement from strangers had knocked her. She stumbled down the road back towards her own flat. Stepping in a puddle and getting her foot covered in water barely registered with her. Crossing the road, she stood in the middle of the street and took one last look back at Emily's two windows and saw that the lights had been put back on.

***

Emily rolled over in bed onto her other side. It was well after midnight. Anna was sleeping in the spare room and seemed to be perfectly comfortable in there when they'd said goodnight. Emily was not so comfortable. Her mind was plagued with thoughts of Angela and everything that had happened between them. Feeling tired yet wired, she couldn't sleep. Agitated, she turned back over onto her other side, and landed with a thud on her pillow. Rain tapped at her window, providing a strange sort of comfort. The room was dark. Her phone lit up with another message, and she reached over for it immediately. It was Angela again. Her breath caught in her throat. The words I'm sorry were visible before the message was opened.

I'm sorry, Emily. I'm so so sorry. I know you don't want to talk to me right now, but I had to let you know that I'm here and that I'm thinking about you and I hope you are okay. I don't know what I was thinking yesterday. I do want to get to know you better. This weekend was magical. I don't care about the photo. Please can we just put this behind us? With all my heart, Angela xxxx

Emily put the phone back on her bedside cabinet. Her first reaction was hopeful. On the surface, it was exactly what she wanted Angela to say. And Emily desperately wanted to believe that what Angela was saying was true. The pain of rejection was still stinging from yesterday. The pattern of behaviour in Angela was clear. She would keep saying one thing and doing another. Or would she? Angela's text did seem genuine. Maybe she could believe her? But the fact that the photo had been taken down also made her doubtful. Would Angela still be saying those things if the picture was still online?

Sighing, Emily shut her eyes and tried to feel what she was feeling inside. To make sense of the thoughts swirling around her mind, and to get a handle on what she felt. She sat with her pain for a while, which was excruciating. The urge to numb the feeling was powerful. Slowly, she began to recognise the pain inside her. Her body felt hollow. Empty. Her breathing was rigid. She felt so rejected. She'd felt like this before, when her father had so cruelly abandoned her as a child. Nonetheless, Angela's face was still all she could see in her head. Her beautiful, kind, and loving face. Or so she had thought. How could she have hurt her like this? She picked up her phone again and spent a few minutes composing a text, her fingers frantically tapping in words and editing them to perfection. A sentence materialised that she was semi-happy with:

Why is this so difficult? I can't take being tossed aside by you at the slightest thing. I don't know if I can trust you. I don't know if you're good for me.

The words on the screen captured exactly how she felt. Her finger hovered over the send button. But a conversation was too much right now, so she deleted the text, switched off her phone and put it down. Love shouldn't be this hard so soon. Maybe years down the line but not this early. Exhausted, she closed her eyes, and vowed to go no contact with Angela. She would allow this experience to be as it was, she would learn from it, and move forward knowing that only she had the power to make herself feel better. She didn't need to chase people. Her body and mind relaxed a little. Her face and jaw loosened, and some of the tension dissipated. Taking control felt good. Protecting herself felt long overdue. She would start to be a source of energy to herself, and no longer attract people into her life who would hurt her. Instead of yoga, she would look for a therapist. Instead of fixing Angela's business, she would start her own. Instead of thinking about relationships, she would focus on healing her inner wounds, getting her life back on track, and being the most positive, happy version of herself she could be. And with those affirmations, she drifted off to sleep.

Chapter 28

Emily glanced at herself in the full-length mirror in the café toilets. Her business-casual look had been out of action for months, but now, having the clothes on, she was feeling much more positive about things. Her royal blue blazer always made her feel good. Powerful. She finished drying her hands and made her way back into the café where she was meeting a new client. Her first client. People in suits crowded the sparse, minimalist décor. The baristas were suitably cool, and you got to choose which temperature you wanted your flat white. Emily chose this place as she knew it would give a good impression to her would-be client. She ordered at the counter and found the last free table in the corner next to the white brick wall. A man at the table next to her sat typing away on his laptop, engrossed. There was a near constant background noise of the coffee machine.

Emily was slightly early. Watching for him to come through the main door, Emily realised she was a bit nervous. The enquiry was perfect for her. She knew she could help him. But it had been ages since she'd really been in work mode. Taking out her notepad and pen, she put them on the table. In the notepad was the application form that Ben, owner of the struggling craft beer company, had sent her. Her coffee arrived and she thanked the waiter. She took a sip immediately and didn't burn her tongue – it was, indeed, the perfect temperature.

The door opened and a man came in, looking about him. He was dressed smartly in a fashionable grey tweed jacket and dark blue jeans. Emily waved and he spotted her. Ben strode over, holding eye contact with Emily the entire time.

Emily got to her feet, noticing how polished he looked. Emily stood tall, with her best professional face on. They shook hands firmly.

'Emily?' said Ben.

'Yes. Pleased to meet you, Ben.'

'Likewise.'

'Take a seat,' Emily gestured to the seat across from her. 'What would you like?' She stepped around and moved towards the counter.

'A flat white, please.' Ben smiled.

Emily went back to the counter and ordered again, before coming back to the table in seconds. Ben leaned back in his chair and smiled again when she sat back down.

'Thank you for agreeing to meet with me,' he said.

'You're welcome. So, how can I help? You're in the craft beer business?'

'Yes. And we've been operating for about eighteen months. There are three of us: I'm full-time, my employees are both part-time. I got a business start-up loan, and I remortgaged my house. I've put everything into this. But we're failing. I'm at my wits' end; if I don't turn things around soon, we'll be bust within three months.' Ben sat back, defeated. 'I don't know what to do. I came across your website and thought you might be able to help.'

Emily sat forward and clasped her hands. 'Don't worry. It won't come to that. I know I can help.'

Ben's coffee arrived. He glanced up at the waiter, clocked his impressive beard, and thanked him.

Emily continued. 'Now, tell me everything.'

***

Emily got back to her flat still buzzing from her successful first client meeting. It went so well, Ben had already agreed to work with her for the next month, paying her a handsome rate at that. There was no doubt that Emily could help turn Ben's business around. She'd done it many times before, albeit for bigger companies, but the principles were still the same. But this time, the businesses would be worthy of her help, and there would be no middleman taking all of her credit.

In the weeks since she'd stopped seeing Angela, Emily hadn't stopped. She'd worked constantly to get her business up and running. She felt strongly about offering affordable advice to businesses who needed it most, and that passion flowed into everything she did on the business, even the stuff she wasn't so fond of. There was also a good chance she would get funding from the bank, as she'd had encouraging initial feedback about her applications.

Still in her business casual clothes, because she wasn't quite ready to take them off and return to jogging bottoms, she walked about her flat seeing new possibilities. Tomorrow evening would be her first session with a therapist. She would go to the gym first thing in the morning and come back to start preparing for going into Ben's business in the afternoon.

The buzzer went, which was odd. She wasn't expecting anyone or anything. She buzzed the person in, not bothering to ask who it was, assuming it was a delivery for a neighbour. When her doorbell went, she promptly opened the door to a delivery of flowers. As she took the flowers from the young woman in a baseball cap, she was handed the note which they came with. The flowers were a gorgeous arrangement of different coloured roses. After putting the flowers gently down on her coffee table, she opened the note. They were from Angela.

Dearest Emily, I understand you don't want to talk to me any more and I respect that. I will give you all the space you need. I am so sorry for how I behaved towards you. Please know that I am always thinking of you and I hope one day you can forgive me. With love, Angela xxx

Emily put the note down on the coffee table next to the flowers and sat back on the sofa. Rays of sunshine streamed into her flat, warming her up. She took in a deep breath, held it, and let it out slowly. This was something. It was the first time Angela had contacted her since the night she had stood outside in the street below calling out Emily's name. The flowers *were* beautiful, and she did appreciate the thoughtful gesture. Beautiful memories of their night up in the Highlands, that she'd been trying not to think about, came flooding back, as did the pain of Angela telling her that they'd made a mistake. She knew in her heart that Angela hadn't meant to hurt her. But she had. If Angela was genuine, she sympathised with her, but she couldn't go back there again. At least not until she'd spoken to a therapist. The whole thing had been so intense. She was still trying to make sense of it all.

Seeing the flowers lying on the table didn't feel right, so she took them through to the kitchen, washed a dusty vase and arranged them as best she could in the water-filled vase. Carrying them back to the living room, she caught their scent and smiled before putting them on the table by the window. Closing her eyes, she put her nose to one of the white roses and inhaled deeply.

Chapter 29

Emily peered out from behind her stall at Edinburgh's annual gala in one of its biggest parks in the heart of the city – the Meadows Festival. Music from the main stage reverberated around the park, bouncing off the trees. Thousands of people filled the park on a gloriously sunny day in June. The next chapter of her life was taking shape. She'd thrown herself into her new business and it was all coming together. Her business was on track for opening new premises the following month and she had been busy promoting the grand opening. She'd been at the festival getting set up since seven in the morning and had already spoken to dozens of people. The reaction from people was overwhelmingly positive and she was growing increasingly confident about the interest she was generating for when she opened. The location of the stall near the pavilion in the centre of the Meadows was excellent and was helping with visibility and encouraging lots of people to approach. But as it was nearing late afternoon, fewer people were coming up to her as party time at the festival was kicking in.

All sorts of businesses flanked Emily's, all selling their products or getting people to sign up for their charitable organisations. The stall to her left was an organic soap business. Every time Emily looked over there were people there turning over bars of soap or picking them up to smell them. To the back of the tent, she could hear boxes being opened, more soap being unpacked and put out to help meet the demand. Further along, stood the car-boot-sale-style stalls, with old trinkets and unwanted junk on display.

Emily's stall was more like a tall tent with an area to walk in. It trapped in the heat from the sun, despite standing directly under a cherry tree. Emily was wearing a turquoise jersey belted beach dress, but she was still a little hot. Many people had staked claim to the grass for their own little picnic party areas. Smells from the food stalls wafted over intermittently. Anna was there helping her, but she had mostly been marching to and from the funfair with Russell, her little one, rather than helping. They were there to promote Emily's new business, but she also wanted to see something of the festival too. After a quiet spell, Emily decided to take a break.

'Do you mind covering the stall for half an hour while I take a wee break?'

'Course not. You've been on it all day. Go, have fun. I wouldn't go near the fair, though. We've seen at least two children being sick on the Waltzers.'

Emily laughed. 'I'll avoid it in that case, cheers.'

'What am I saying again?'

'You tell them what the business is, give them a free workbook, and get them to sign up to our newsletter and social media pages.'

'Right.' Anna read from the script Emily had prepared for her to say when a customer approached. Russell waddled out of the tent, arms flapping but determined. 'Russell! No!' Anna darted off to pick him up and returned, putting him back on his seat. The tiny face didn't look impressed.

'I won't be long.'

'I'll try not to ruin your business.'

'You'll be fine.' Waving Anna away, Emily left her in the tent and stepped out into the thoroughfare of people. The sunshine blazed down on her head and shoulders, and she had to squint to see anything. Unused to such exposure, she put on her sunglasses, which offered instant relief. She wandered past the funfair full of children and families. There was a loud clank from a ride about to start. Children screamed in delight as parents watched on, not matching the delight but doing their best to seem interested. Thankfully, she couldn't see anyone being sick.

Next, she strolled past the local dog and cat home's area. They had taken up a large patch of grass; the main attraction was the agility course. This was one of the best attended stands, with a large crowd that encompassed the course. The people looking on seemed amused by something. Emily followed their eyes to see a golden retriever trotting around the course with a pole from one of the jumps in his mouth. A professional-looking photographer stood clicking away with a smile on her face while the dog's human tried to rescue the jump. The human replaced the pole, jumped it himself and took a bow as the crowd cheered him on. The retriever darted around the jump and licked his human in the face.

She passed by some food stalls, mostly run by local cafés and restaurants. The smells were delicious, and the queues were long. She headed for some shade. Finding a tree without many people around, she leant against it and observed the crowds of people enjoying the festival atmosphere. She smiled. She had been feeling much better over the past few weeks, in so many healthy, productive ways. After a very low spell after Angela, she slowly began to pick herself up and through concentrating on her new business, had lifted her spirits and energy. While she no longer felt depressed, one thing still ate away at her soul.

Angela.

Mostly, she wondered how Angela was doing and how she was coping after the negative exposure – as Angela had perceived it – to her business. Emily had been so scarred by the way that Angela had discarded her that she hadn't had the nerve or the strength to look online to see for herself how bad things had got for Angela. Not since the first and only time she'd looked at the picture. The picture, in Emily's mind, was *lovely*. It captured the moment so perfectly. If it hadn't been for Angela's reaction to it, Emily might have liked to have had it framed. They were on such different wavelengths about the situation. Angela had stood outside her door in the rain begging for forgiveness, but Emily no longer trusted her. Despite this, Emily still hoped she was okay even if she couldn't face speaking to her again for fear of further rejection. After that night and the flowers, it wasn't as if Angela had tried that hard to get her back, so Emily assumed she had given up and moved on. Which is what Emily was doing too.

As her tummy growled at her, she pushed herself away from the tree and the shade and followed her nose to the array of food stalls. Coming to a stop outside a Mexican food truck, she eyed the menu. It all looked good. She ordered a vegetarian burrito. Picking up some napkins, she made her way over to where people were sitting down and found a spot with a nice view of the main stage. The main stage could be seen from most angles in the conflation of all the quadrants and paths near the top of Middle Meadow Walk, but it was nice being so close to it. Sitting cross-legged on the sun-scorched grass with her back to the sun as she ate her burrito, a new band started playing. It was an all-female band and they were amazing. Engrossed in the band, she opened a can of beer from her bag and smiled gently. Life felt pretty good. After a good but short set, the band finished, and filler music started playing at a lower level. Soon after, there was another band lining up to play and unpacking their equipment, most likely also taking the opportunity to get their name out there at the free city-wide event.

With that, Emily realised she'd forgotten all about her own stall and Anna there on her own speaking to potential clients. As she was packing up her now finished can of beer and wrapping, she overheard a woman talking to someone behind her.

'Want to go to Yoga in the Park next?' said the woman.

Emily heard a male voice laugh in reply. 'Nah. You go if you want. I'm staying here with the beers.'

'Suit yourself,' said the woman. 'I've never done yoga pissed before, so this should be interesting.'

Emily smiled to herself and watched as the woman staggered her way through the crowd towards one of the quieter quadrants of the park. Emily hadn't done any yoga since the retreat. It felt like doing a Downward Dog would be like forgiving Angela. Everything about yoga reminded her of Angela too much. She had noticed the difference as there was a tightness in her body and chest. Her body missed yoga as much as her heart missed Angela.

As she walked back to her stall, she contemplated whether or not she should go over and check out the yoga. Maybe she was now ready to let go of the past and finally move on.

'Did you have fun?' asked Anna as Emily neared the stall.

'I had something to eat and saw this great band, actually. Sorry if I was ages.'

'Don't be silly. Jason came by to pick Russell up, by the way. He was getting restless. I think the funfair really took it out of him.'

'Aw, wee sweetheart.'

'So, I'm as free as a bird. Do you have any of those beers left?'

'They're in the cool box.' Emily got two out and passed one to Anna before sitting down on a fold-up chair behind the table. 'Did many come over?'

'Yep. Two more people have signed up. They seemed really keen.'

'Great. Cheers to that.' They clinked cans. 'We've got another hour left on the stall. Would you mind if I quickly went to see this other thing and came back?'

'No problem. What other thing?'

Emily hesitated. 'It's a yoga event. Looks like a stage over there. Seems quite interesting.'

'Emily.' Anna's voice was stern. 'You're not looking for a certain someone, are you?'

'No. I'd like to see what's going on. I might take it up again soon – but this time in my living room.'

'Be careful, mate. Be careful.'

Emily stood up and took a few gulps of beer. 'It's just some random event. There's no need to worry.'

'Yeah but you've been doing so well since you stopped yoga. Stopped seeing *her*.'

Emily made her way out of the sweltering stall and looked back in at Anna sitting in a deck chair looking like she was worried Emily was about to score a bag of heroin after ten years clean.

'I won't be long.'

Anna frowned.

Emily left her friend and made her way towards where the yoga was taking place. Anna was a lovely, caring friend but had a tendency of being a bit overprotective sometimes. As Emily walked over a path and past the trees that lined it, she noticed that the crowd was a little thinner in this part of the park than in the main sections of the Meadows. The sun had moved around through the afternoon as it neared four o'clock, but it was still hot. Some families hovered at the side in the shade. She couldn't believe how busy it was. Free yoga was a big draw. People were getting themselves set up, as if waiting for a regular class to begin. There was a small stage facing the crowd, in front of the university library. It was also playing some music. You could only hear it the closer you got. It was very relaxing yoga music with gongs and gently struck bongos. It reminded her of the tunes Angela used to play. The vibe in this quadrant was fairly chilled out with a mix of students, hippies, and fit women in their thirties. Emily felt like she was coming home. It was her vibe tribe. A few groups were still drinking alcohol and having their picnics like nothing was going on around them. Emily wondered how the drunk woman was getting on.

Spotting Zoe and Samantha near the front with the Heart Yoga regulars – Louise, Karen, Olivia, Erin, and Meghan – she tensed up. Her heart rate picked up at the possibility of Angela being there. Despite feeling happy to see her yoga friends, she couldn't face going over to speak with them, so she moved towards the back of the crowd. She saw Donna and her friends from Cult Yoga sitting in a circle, not taking part but eyeing up the main stage. It looked as if the entire Edinburgh yoga community was there. Standing at the back of the crowd, beside other onlookers not participating in the mass yoga class, she searched through the crowds, scanning for Angela's face. Not finding her, a dull ache filled her heart. An overwhelming sense of loss took grip of her. They could have been there together, enjoying life together. Enjoying each other. Never had she felt so strongly for someone. Never had she felt so heartbroken. Being surrounded by people on yoga mats was only filling her with pain. She'd had enough and turned to go. As she did so, a voice came through the loudspeakers from the stage, thanking everyone for coming to Yoga in the Park.

It was Angela.

Her head whipped around to find Angela's strong and slender frame standing in the middle of the stage. She had on a white vest top and purple capri leggings. Emily watched on, spellbound, as Angela took hundreds of people through a yoga class with ease. For over fifteen minutes, Emily stood rooted to the spot, not joining in, with her eyes fixed straight ahead at the presence that was filling the stage and filling the

Meadows. The person that had filled her heart and soul with so much warmth. The person who had brought her back to life. Seeing Angela again, for the first time since that night, was a little overwhelming. The emotions she had been trying to contain over the last few weeks threatened to dismantle her. And yet, Emily found herself moving forwards through the crowd. She found a spot and started to join in.

'Let your head fall to your heart centre and breathe,' said Angela.

Moving in time with the crowd to Angela's voice made her feel so connected to her again. She missed her so much. The way in which Angela lifted the spirits of the crowd, got them moving and got them all doing yoga had a strange effect on Emily. The peace emanating from Angela onto the crowd was palpable. Seeing her happy, and in her element made Emily wonder if she ever thought of her any more. Or if their feelings for each other had meant nothing to her. Feeling invisible and unworthy, a swell of emotion started bubbling up and her eyes started to water. She felt physically weak. Unable to take it any more she headed for the safety of her own tent, gently pushing past some people in the crowd, averting her eyes downwards.

As she made her way out of the crowd, she glanced back at the Heart Yoga gang near the front, following Angela. Louise was paying more attention to a group of children playing on picnic blankets, probably her grandchildren. Karen wasn't looking at the children, she was doing the class. Olivia and Meghan had clearly brought some friends and were enjoying showing off their popular yoga teacher. Erin was there kitted out in the best fitness clothes, making it look easy. Even the girl from the street with the baby Angela had spoken to was there. With a heaviness in her heart, Emily kept on walking. She missed everyone. Angela's words flowed out mellifluously. Emily stopped and looked up at the woman who'd got into her heart up on stage, magnificent and glowing.

The woman she thought she'd fallen in love with.

'That brings Yoga in the Park to a close. Thank you, dear ones, for being here today and sharing this space with me and with each other. My mission is to make yoga more accessible and to get more and more people taking it up. This is by far the largest class I've ever taken and possibly a record for Edinburgh?'

Angela was answered by a polite round of applause from the crowd.

'So, I'm so proud to stand in front of you today. And for those of you who have never done yoga before, well, now you have.' The crowd applauded. 'And to those of you with the beers in your hands while doing Warrior Two, you guys knocked it out of the park.'

The crowd roared in approval this time.

Emily let out a small smile.

'If you enjoyed this today and are interested in finding out more, make sure to come by to Heart Yoga's wee stall at the back, we'd love to talk to you. You can also find us online and on all the social media platforms.' Angela paused. 'And before I go,' her voice shook a little, 'I wanted to take the opportunity to share something with you all, if you don't mind.'

Emily had followed her heart to the front again. Curious. The front area was lined with what looked like university students enjoying a free yoga class. Not wanting Angela to see her, she stayed off to one side next to the others standing. So close to the stage, Emily saw concentration on Angela's face. And also strain. Not so much that anyone else would notice, but Emily did. There was a heaviness in Angela that Emily hadn't seen before.

Chapter 30

Looking out at the crowd of strangers, peers, and potential new clients, not as a yoga teacher, but for a second, as simply Angela, was terrifying. The huge crowd had been so unexpected. The festival organisers said it would be a fringe event, on the edges of the main festival, nice and quiet for a gentle afternoon of yoga. The opposite had turned out to be the case.

Angela had most of the crew from Heart Yoga there supporting her and the studio, which she was eternally grateful for. Since Emily had gone, she'd come to rely on Zoe and Samantha more. It was obvious that she would have to employ an assistant and consider moving to a bigger studio. The classes were fully booked for the next month, and she was at her utmost limit for engagement. If they took on more students after today, she'd have to start turning people away.

Knowing what she was about to do next, Angela searched the faces in front of her for Emily's. For the past few weeks, walking through the streets, she had been doing the same. And at the start of every class. Waiting for Emily to come back. To see her smile again. But she always came up short. Emily had left a huge gap in Angela's life. Angela centred herself before continuing, taking a full deep breath and directing her attention to the feel of her feet on her mat.

'Too often in yoga we get so caught up in this type of practice or in that type of practice, in being *perfect* at yoga, in the identity of yoga, in the *ego* of it all, that we forget the most important part: to be at one with yourself. To *connect* mind, body, and soul, and to stand in the truth and total acceptance of who you are. Whatever that may be. Full disclosure: I felt I needed to be the perfect yoga teacher. And I valued other people's opinions of me before my own. So, when I met a woman who came to my class and lit up my world, I wasn't in a place where I could easily accept that I was falling for her. And I did. Fall for her.' Angela paused, feeling shaky. Someone in the crowd did a wolf-whistle. Glancing briefly down at the front row, there were phones out filming her. 'But then I messed it all up. I believed the perfect yoga teacher would see any relationship with a student as completely unethical. Without, rather ironically, any flexibility in that rule. I lost her and I've never felt so devastated. I know that some of you in the yoga community openly criticised me for being with a student, but I won't take that on, because I realise that you can't control who you fall in love with. Emily … if you're out there, I hope that you can see how sorry I am for caring what people would think about us, and that I've realised how crushingly stupid I was. I was completely wrong to hurt you and push you away the way I did. I still live in hope that you will one day forgive me, and I hope with all of my heart that you are happy and thriving. I don't expect you to give me another chance, but if you did,' she could feel her voice breaking, on the verge of tears, 'know that I would never hurt you again. If you were to give this another chance, it would mean everything to me.'

The crowd was silent. Angela felt like she was naked. All she wanted was for Emily to be back in her life, to see the beautiful light of Emily's soul once again. She pulled herself together, putting on her best professional face.

'So, yoga is about union. Union with the self. Pure and simple. Teachers are guides. But we're also just people. And all people have needs and flaws and stuff to work through. So if you do find your way to Heart Yoga one of these days, I can promise you that you will be welcomed, and I'll do my best to create the space for you to make the connection with yourself.'

Angela brought the palms of her hands together in front of her and bowed her head. 'Namaste. Which in yoga translates to something quite beautiful: the light in me honours the light in you.' She took another deep breath, consciously aware of the hundreds of people before her and the loving atmosphere they had created together this sunny afternoon. 'Namaste.' She looked up. 'Thanks for taking part. Thanks for listening. Thanks for sharing this experience with me today. Enjoy the festival and the rest of your day.' A massive round of applause began and gathered momentum. Angela could not believe the wall of support and praise and emotion being sent her way. Angela stood there the whole time just smiling, and letting it sink in. This went on for another few moments until it died down. It was funny because she knew that she no longer needed it. But it was nice. Once it was finally over, she closed it out.

'Wow. Thank you for that support. Take care of yourselves. Bye!' Angela took her earpiece off, feeling completely spent.

And then she saw her.

Emily. Staring back at her, only a few metres away off to the side near the stage. Angela trembled. Her heart skipped a beat. Emily's expression was neutral and gave nothing away. There was almost a visible wall up around Emily, and a coldness in her eyes she'd never seen in them before. Emily looked down at the ground, then back up at her, gave a sad smile, and then moved away. Angela watched as Emily turned and walked away from her, into the dispersing crowds, and then she lost her. Her insides felt hollow and the pain of watching her go was like a punch in the stomach. A tear welled up in the corner of her eye. She shook her head, wiped it, and left the stage, taking care down the three steps to the grass as her legs felt shaky. The urge was there to chase after her, but she saw that look in Emily's eyes. It sent shivers down her spine and rooted her to the spot. There was even less hope now of Emily ever changing her mind. The loss of Emily felt devastating. How had it come to this? Why had she let her shallow fears get in the way of something so special?

Zoe appeared in front of her with her vape. She blew out as she got closer, sending a cloud of strawberry right past Angela. 'That was great up there. Didn't know you were going to get all spiritual on us in the Meadows, though. Nice touch.' Zoe grimaced. 'I'm sorry you're still cut up about Emily.' Angela didn't respond. 'By the way, I've been meaning to tell you something.' Zoe was looking at the ground as she spoke. 'I, I'm going to India. I'm going to go live in an Ashram for a few months, and travel around India for a bit – maybe until the end of the year.' Zoe finished and looked up at Angela, registering the look on Angela's face. 'What's the matter? Are you mad at me for leaving? I know that I should have told you earlier. I know that I've got a job to do at Heart but—'

'It's not that.' Angela shook her head, struggling to cope with two blows at the same time.

'Do you not think the class went well? Because it did. It was really lovely. Your speech was genuinely moving. Even the dogs were getting into it.'

Angela stepped back to allow two small children to pass through them. As the mother walked past, she smiled and thanked Angela. 'You're welcome.' Angela replied. When they'd left, Angela's shoulders slumped again.

'What, what is it?'

'Go – to India. Live your best life. The studio and I will be fine.' Angela attempted her best smile in the moment.

'Why do I not feel that you mean that?'

'I am … I mean I *do* mean it. I'm happy for you. But I've

283

just seen Emily.'

'What! No. Where?' Zoe stuck her neck up, aiming for more height than her small frame allowed.

'She's gone now.'

'Are you okay?'

Angela felt ill. 'No. I don't think I am.'

'Did you speak to her?'

'She looked me right in the eyes and just turned and walked away.'

'Oh God, and I've just announced I'm abandoning you too.'

Angela covered her eyes with her hands. She knew it was dramatic but the tears welling up in her needed to be shielded. Blocking the sun from her eyes was also a relief.

Zoe touched her arm. 'Angela. Shall we go? Let's get you out of here. I'll come back and get the stuff.'

They made their way back up towards the road running through the Meadows. Some people looked over at her as she passed. Were they judging her for her outburst of honest emotion on stage? No, she reminded herself of the huge round of applause. She was just being insecure. They were probably just looking at her because she was on stage a few minutes ago. Her fledgling understanding of caring less about what others thought about her compelled her to hold onto what she thought about herself. What did she think about herself? She was a good person, wasn't she? This was something she'd need to think more about. They reached the pavement at Melville Drive.

'Zoe. I think I'm going to go for a walk. Myself. Would you mind?'

Zoe smiled gently. 'Course not. I'll go get the stuff and take down the stall.'

'Cheers. I just can't be here any more. I'll see you later.' Angela turned to leave.

'Look after yourself, yeah?'
'I will.'

Chapter 31

Emily kept her head down and walked briskly back to the tent. Her heart was pounding. Seeing Angela had floored her. Hearing her speech had sent her head into a spin. And as for looking into those soulful grey-blue eyes, of course she had frozen. Taking flight felt like running for safety, yet turning away from Angela in that moment, after the things she had heard her say, also felt wrong. Her heart told her to run into Angela's arms, but her mind had won out. The hurt in Angela's eyes as she did the very thing that Angela had done to her was too sad.

Emily found Anna sitting in the fold-up chair, forearms resting on the sides facing the sun like she was on a beach in Spain. Two empty beer cans lay underneath the chair, squeezed in the middle. Anna wore large sunglasses, but Emily could tell that her eyes were closed. Her yellow vest top sharply contrasted with the developing pink of her chest, arms, and shoulders. A stack of sign-up sheets sat beside her on the stall table underneath a penguin paperweight. Only a few passers-by were left, as most people were in picnic groups or watching the main stage where a man was singing or possibly howling. Still, the music added something to the normally quaint Meadows.

Emily put her canvas bag on the stall table and Anna flinched awake, sat forward, and looked around her.

'Fuck sake. I nodded off.'

'You must have needed it. Might want to cover up your arms there, cooked lobsters would be jealous of that "tan".'

Anna looked down at her chest and felt her arms. 'Oh. See, this is what happens when you learn to sleep sitting upright.'

She took her sunglasses off and regarded Emily. 'You okay? You seem a bit peaky.'

Emily was tongue-tied.

'What is it? Did something happen?'

'She said she's fallen for me.'

'Who?'

'Angela.'

'Oh.'

'She was on stage taking a yoga class to a massive crowd over there,' Emily waved an arm to her left. 'Everyone was there. I stayed and watched. At the end she went off on this big speech about yoga and about how fucked up it is and about how she's fallen for me.'

'How's yoga fucked up?'

'Dunno. She was saying that there's a lot of perfectionism in it, teachers being all holier-than-thou. At least that's what I think she meant.'

'How did she then go on to proclaim her feelings for you? That's big coming from her, no? In front of all those people.'

'Exactly. She said she realised how wrong she was to give a shit about what others thought, and that she's devastated she lost me. She basically gave the finger to all her yoga peeps and said she loves me.'

Anna sat back in her chair. 'Fuck me.'

Emily took a big deep breath. 'I know.'

'She still has feelings for you, Emily. Clearly.'

Emily stayed standing. Adrenaline still pumping through her. 'And then at the end, she saw me. I just couldn't. I didn't know what to say to all that. I came straight back here.'

Anna got out another beer from the cool box next to her. She looked over at Emily. 'Do you want one?'

'Yes.' Emily puffed out her cheeks and took a seat on the ground in the shade next to Anna. She crossed her legs like she was in yoga class.

Anna handed Emily a small can of IPA. Their cans clicked and skooshed open satisfyingly. Anna took a few big gulps and set her drink in the cup holder. 'You lesbians and your drama. How did I not see this coming?'

'Anna, I think she's changed. She seemed so genuine. Part of me believes her. I do, believe her.'

'Do you think she's earned your trust back?'

'Maybe. Yes. She was so brave to do that. But is it enough? Och, I don't know.'

Anna was quiet for a while as Emily studied the writing on her can.

'What are you going to do now? Is she still over there?'

'I think so. I don't know.' Emily looked up at Anna. 'I still think about her. I still have feelings for her. I miss her.' She took a massive drink of her can. 'I feel a bit calmer now.'

'God bless alcohol,' said Anna, looking up at the sky.

'That's it. I'm going to go over there. I'm gonna talk to her and see how I feel.' Emily stood up.

Anna stood up too. 'I know I should be saying that you're making a big mistake but … if there is a chance for you two then maybe you should take it. Everyone deserves another chance, right?'

Emily hugged her friend and took another deep breath. 'Thank you for that.'

The more she neared talking to Angela the clearer things were becoming. She had to do it. It felt right. After she'd downed her beer and gathered herself for a moment, she made her way across to the yoga park all the while scanning the crowd for Angela.

The party vibe in the Meadows was in full swing with a few groups playing the bongos, BBQs getting started, the distinctive smell of the weed in the air, and skinny topless young men balancing along straps tied between trees, arms out to the side, as young women sat beside them passively watching. The small stage Angela had been on was now empty, and parts of it were in the process of being dismantled by men in identical blue polo-shirts. A few stalls came into view and Heart Yoga stood in the middle. There was still no sight of Angela even from a distance. Making a beeline for it, Emily felt a nervous excitement flow through her, and the cautious side of her brain shouted at her to turn back. Ignoring them both, she neared the stall and found Zoe packing up. One of Angela's many Buddha statues sat majestically at the entrance to their stall. The tent was draped with oversized fabrics that looked both Indian and Celtic. Boxes with leaflets in them were nearly empty. Emily hovered, feeling disappointed not to have found Angela.

Zoe glanced up and saw her. She stumbled briefly then steadier herself. 'Hey, Emily.'

'Hi. Is Angela here?'

'I'm sorry, she's not.'

'Oh.' Emily felt so awkward.

'She's gone for a walk. She left straight after … um, her class.'

Emily nodded in slow recognition. Angela must have been upset. 'Do you know where or which direction?'

Zoe smiled softly and pointed east along the road. 'She went that way; I don't know where. I could phone her?'

Emily followed the point and nodded. 'No, it's okay. I know where she is.'

'Emily?' said Zoe.

'Yeah?'

'She knows how much she messed up. She really does care about you.'

Emily inhaled, and looked away, then back at Zoe.

Zoe continued. 'She's not been gone long. Maybe fifteen or twenty minutes?'

Emily nodded. 'Cheers, thanks, Zoe.' Emily dashed away,

feeling grateful for Zoe's kindness, determined to find Angela. She didn't want to call or text, she wanted to see her in person, and there was only one place Angela could be.

The walk through the streets went past in a blur as she marched over the roads whenever a gap in traffic allowed. The landmark of Arthur's Seat neared, and the streets thinned out. Emily pressed on until she reached the grass park underneath and made the long straight walk to the foot of the hill. The path was scorched and dusty from the current heatwave and heavy footfall. On her way up, the sun beat down on her back as she zigzagged her way upwards towards the top. Taking the most direct route, which was also the steepest, she climbed the relentless steps, quads burning. Her pulse was high from the climb and the nerves of potentially finding Angela at the top. There was so much she wanted to say, and so much she needed to hear. Emily was in a better place now, but despite the excitement of seeing Angela today and all that it represented, there was a part of her that was still cautious. Despite the niggling reservations, she bounded up the hill, growing lighter underfoot with each step.

When she reached the top, the view opened out onto more hills behind the rocky peak, Emily frantically looked around for Angela and followed the trail around to where she couldn't see. She climbed a little higher onto the rock, stopping once to let some walkers pass her, then looped around to the other side. There she was, sitting facing out to the city with her back to her. She looked smaller somehow, and vulnerable, unaware she was being watched, and deep in thought.

Chapter 32

Angela sat with her knees to her chest on Arthur's Seat in her favourite spot. She wasn't quite at the top, she left that for the tourists. Her spot lay off to the side, still high enough to call it the top, short of a few metres of jagged rock. She hadn't been there long. The walk over was a slow one as she lacked her usual energy. Emily didn't want to know her any more. And she couldn't blame her. Looking out over the city offered a small relief from the pain. The city's historic buildings and panorama reminded Angela of the impermanence of life, of the people long dead who had lived here long ago. Only the hill that she sat on was permanent. And even that was known to be an extinct volcano. It had lived an explosive life before fizzling out, dying, and becoming extinct. It too would be subject to time one day. Erosion would get it.

'Angela.'

Snapping her head around, she found Emily standing behind her, smiling softly. Angela's breath caught in her throat. She stayed in that rotated position for a few moments, stunned. Emily was luminous, and not just from the sun shining on her. There was something different about her and certainly different from under an hour ago. Her heart filled with hope and emotion. 'Emily, I'm so happy to see you. How did you find me?' Angela turned around to get up, but Emily stopped her and sat down next to her but kept a good, polite distance on the rock.

'I remember you saying that you come up here.'

Angela stared into Emily's eyes. The coldness was no longer there, but she was still holding back a little. 'I've missed you, Emily. I've thought about you every single moment since we got back from the Highlands. You've no idea how much I've wanted to talk to you since then. To apologise in person.' Angela took a breath and swallowed. 'I should never have reacted like that. I should never have cared about that bloody pict—'

'It's okay,' said Emily. She looked out towards the view and then back at Angela. 'I heard you on stage.'

Angela blushed. Even now, Emily had that effect on her. She felt completely emotionally exposed and vulnerable at her declaration of love and desperately hoped Emily felt the same.

'You were like a rock star up there.'

Angela laughed, nervously. 'I was only approached for the event at the last minute. I thought there might have been about twenty people there and then I turned up and they'd put up an entire stage for us. Then all those people turned up. It was crazy.'

Emily smiled. 'That's so like you.'

A short silence fell between them.

Angela tensed up at the importance of their conversation, not knowing how it was going to go. 'How have you been?'

'Um, well, I've got my business going and I'm getting back to my old self again. Actually, I'm feeling better than I have in a long time.'

Angela could feel the change in Emily. There was a lightness to her that she had only seen glimpses of and a distance that wasn't there before. Their time apart had clearly had a good impact on her.

'I'm so pleased for you. Really, I am. I'm so happy you're here and that you're okay.'

'I was in a pretty bad way after you dumped me. Dumped me before we'd even said we would date each other. For the second time.'

Angela winced.

'And, to be honest, I'm in a much better place now.'

Angela gulped in fear of what was to come.

'But you told the world about us. Did you really mean what you said up there?'

Angela replied straight away, speaking quickly. 'I meant every single word.'

'How can I be sure that you'll never hurt me like that again.'

'I won't. I will never hurt you again. And I know that I hurt you and I want you to know that I value trust very much. I want to make it up to you and to show you, if you'll let me, just how much I care about you. I've grown.' She reached out and took Emily's hand. A small tear crept from Angela's eye. Her voice was shaking. 'I want you. Only you.' Angela took a long pause trying to gather the right words. 'I can't stop thinking about you. I think about what you're thinking, about what you're doing … I want to know all of you, your hopes and dreams, your sorrows, your past. Your stories. You're a beautiful person inside and out, and I would be so happy, so grateful, to have you in my life again. Mostly, I want you to know that I just want you to be happy and I want to be the person who makes you happy if you'll let me. I'd give up my studio if it means I can be with you.'

Emily inhaled. 'I'd never ask you to do that.'

'I know but I would.'

Feeling the tear run down her face, she saw Emily watch as it dropped off her jawline and onto the warm rock beneath them. The sun's strength was starting to fade, and a cool breeze began to pick up. Reaching over, Emily gently brushed away the tear about to follow it.

'I'm sorry I pushed you to be with me. You told me you weren't comfortable getting involved with a student and I never listened. I know that you were in an awkward position.'

'I could have handled it better. I could have been kinder and more honest with you.' Angela's heart was pounding. Sitting beside Emily, she could feel that warm loving energy that she had always felt with her. She missed it. A lot. 'I've missed you so much.'

'I've missed you too.'

There was a sincerity in Emily's eyes. She could see that she meant it. That she had been hurt by her but that she was open to letting her in again. The relief in Angela was instantaneous. Taking Emily's hand, she stroked it with her thumb. Emily interlocked her fingers with Angela's and moved closer to her. Angela guided Emily's hand to her lips and kissed it gently. Finding Emily's eyes, she saw the pain begin to disappear. Not wanting to waste another second, Angela put her cards on the table.

'The truth is, Emily, I love you. I'm in love with you.' Angela gazed into Emily's eyes, desperate for an answer, for some confirmation that she felt the same.

A slow smile crept onto Emily's lips, with Angela's words still hanging in the air. After a few moments, Emily finally spoke. 'You see, I'm a big believer in fate. Almost everything that's happened between us has felt so right. Even now, looking back on the upset of the last few weeks. You needed to get that out of your system for us to ever be together. I needed to get back on my feet on my own. There was a reason we were both at this festival today, a reason I found myself in your audience at the right time. Fate. Destiny. The universe. You have no idea how much being around you has helped me get back on my feet. And it's not because you were my yoga teacher. It's you. You had that effect on me. I've been literally in fucking awe of you since I first came to your class. I've never felt so strongly for someone in every way. And I do have feelings for you still.' Emily dropped her gaze to Angela's mouth and then back up to her eyes. 'Very intense feelings. Angela, I love you too.'

Angela leant in and wrapped her arms around Emily's neck, hugging her closely as Emily squeezed her back. The space between them disappeared as they found each other's mouths and kissed tenderly, not letting each other go, oblivious to their surroundings and position above the city. Angela felt her whole body and soul completely merge with Emily's in that moment. She didn't want the kiss to ever end, she wanted to live within this moment forever.

Emily tilted her chin down, breaking the kiss, and put her forehead onto Angela's. 'So, what now?'

Angela put a hand on Emily's chest and looked deeply into Emily's eyes. 'That's up to you. But I want to say this. I want to take you out on a proper date. To start again, *properly* this time.'

Emily gave her the most beautiful smile at that. 'As long as you don't freak out about stuff any more, I think we might have a chance.'

'No more freaking out.'

'God, and all this before the first date?'

'Well, in lesbian years, we have known each other for an eternity.'

Emily laughed. 'True. But I'm not moving in with you until *next* week.'

'Of course.' Angela kissed her hand again. 'I need to earn my place in your life.'

Emily looked out over the city, gently touching her necklace and thinking about something.

Angela touched the necklace on Emily's chest. 'I always meant to ask you – what does this mean to you?'

Emily regarded her quite seriously. 'Rebirth.'

Angela nodded her head. 'I see. That's beautiful.'

'I got it not long after I first met you.'

Angela smiled and stroked Emily's forearm.

'I love that you noticed.' Emily was glowing.

'I want to know everything about you. I'm fascinated by you.'

Emily's eyes darkened. 'I know you are. And attentive. Yep, I know that you are attentive.'

'And giving?'

'Yes, very giving. A good trait, one might say.'

'Are you free tonight? Please say you will come back to mine for dinner. I can't wait to get you home.'

'I'd love to. I've never seen your place.'

'I'll cook, I'll look after you. We'll talk more.'

'Not too much talking. I have plans for you. I've been doing *a lot* of thinking.'

Angela grinned. 'I'm so happy.'

Emily stroked her cheek, the same way she had in the bar before their first kiss, but didn't say anything.

Angela smiled gently. 'There is one more thing that I forgot to tell you.' Angela paused. 'I'm opening up another studio. Can I be one of your new clients?'

'Wow, that's amazing!'

'I know. Will you help me? Will you take it on? I'll pay, whatever it costs—'

'Of course I'll help you. You can be my prized client.'

'Oh, how the tables have turned. I want to be your star student now.'

Emily laughed. 'I was never your star student. I could barely move when I first started.'

'And look at you now.'

Emily smiled broadly, her eyes lighting up her face. Freckles had appeared since the last time she saw her.

'I am more supple; I'll give you that. Despite the fact I've not done any yoga for weeks.'

Angela frowned. 'I'm sorry to hear that.'

Emily looked out at the view for a moment and then back

at her. 'It doesn't matter. Let's just put it behind us and see where this goes.'

'That's all I want. More than anything.'

A comfortable silence opened up between them. It felt peaceful and full of possibilities.

'So, what do you say we do some yoga together later? Some *naughty* yoga?' said Emily.

Angela laughed, having not expected her to say that. 'You're on.' She stared into Emily's eyes. 'You know, you seem lighter in yourself. Happier. It's lovely.'

Emily took a moment to reply as the sun shone onto her face. 'You're right. I think I am.'

Thank you for reading *The Light in You*. If you enjoyed this book, and you have a moment, please leave a review and make the author's day!

ABOUT THE AUTHOR

Lisa Elliot is a Scottish author. She loves writing stories about lesbian characters and lesbian romance. When she's not writing, she works as a research manager for a sustainable transport charity. Her other passions are coffee, crossfit and yoga. She lives in Edinburgh with her wife and their dog. *The Light in You* is her second novel.

Find her at www.lisaelliotauthor.com

Instagram: lisa_elliot_author

Twitter: lisa_elliot

Facebook: lisaelliotauthor

Email: lisaelliotauthor@gmail.com

Goodreads: Lisa.Elliot

Also by Lisa Elliot, *Dancing It Out*.

Kate has moved to London and is embarking on a new life. She has become an independent, high-achieving young lawyer, who still hasn't figured out who she really is yet. But when she moves into a house-share in north London and meets Lorraine, an enigmatic filmmaker, whose room is next to hers, an intense bond quickly develops. After an epic night-out clubbing, Kate's crush on Lorraine leads Kate to question and discover her true sexuality. A slow-burn romance about awakening desire and finding the courage to follow your heart.

Printed in Great Britain
by Amazon